C⊕DA

A NOVEL

Maryann B. Murray

CSan Communications
Ocean Park, ME

Published by
CSan Communications
Ocean Park, ME 04063-7213
www.CSanComm.com

Printed in the United States of America

Author photo by Molly Haley (mollyhaley.com)
Book design by Clarity Designworks (claritydesignworks.com)

ISBN paperback: 979-8-9874632-0-8
ISBN e-book: 979-8-9874632-1-5

First Edition

Disclaimer
Coda is a work of fiction. Names, characters, places, and incidents are the products of the author's imagination or are used fictitiously. Any resemblance to actual events, locales, or persons, living or dead, is entirely coincidental.

To Rose

"Just as a girl practicing the piano, when I thought I'd reached the end of the sonata, there was a coda, sending me back to the beginning to start again. I was too impatient, of course, to appreciate it heralded the breathtaking, dramatic, finish…"

—Elizabeth Devereaux

Chapter One

Even as Elizabeth Devereaux crumpled the telegram in her fist, she knew her life was over.

Lowering herself unsteadily into the armchair by her beloved piano, her hand reached out instinctively toward the grand instrument—the one certainty in her life she could always rely upon. How to proceed now, as the life she had struggled to build here in France with her husband crumbled? How to salvage her very existence from the debris? Music might be a comfort, but it had no answers.

Unaware of the sinking afternoon sun, or the cool breeze that billowed the muslin panels from the windowpanes, Elizabeth didn't notice that the boy who'd just delivered the final, devastating blow was still outside, treating his horse to a handful of oats, or hear the stones of the front path crunch as the young man climbed up into the saddle and trotted off toward the road. Her fingers clawed at her high lace collar as if to free her throat to take in more air, her stunned mind consumed in a futile attempt to reconcile the events of the previous evening—the hopes so cautiously raised—with the news she'd just received.

All had become quiet, finally. All the angry words were shouted, the tears shed. Then, nothing. They just sat and looked across the room at each other, across the cavernous distance they'd created over the years together, the silence roaring between them. The grandfather clock in the corner ticked away the seconds. The minutes. At long last, she spoke.

"I simply cannot continue, Philippe," Elizabeth said to her husband in a near whisper. She gestured aimlessly around the room, the home they had shared for the past five years: her honeymoon cottage in Montpellier, France. What hopes she'd had when she left home in America to start her life here with him, what important work they had planned to accomplish. Years of broken promises—and vows—had dashed those hopes and crushed her soul. "There is nothing for me here, nothing but your lies and betrayals…and the confrontations with your paramours, like today, on my very own doorstep! I can only hope to extricate myself from this nightmare with what little self-respect I have left. When you return from Paris, it will be to an empty house."

Jean-Philippe Devereaux, among the most influential earth and life scientists of the waning 19th century and inaugural chairman of the Department of Botany at the University of Montpellier, folded like a rag doll in his chair, head in hands. "I cannot be without you," he murmured. "You know this. You know you are my life. You know that I am the one who simply cannot continue. Not without you by my side."

"Such beautiful words, Philippe," said Elizabeth as she rose from her own chair and dropped to the floor to collect the remains of the vase she'd hurled across the room only moments before. "My heart breaks this evening as, finally, I hear them as simply words. I have become hardened, closed against them. I need my heart to be open, to be joyful and proud of who I am and what I do. But here, with you, I feel nothing. I am nothing."

"I have failed you. Utterly." Philippe dragged himself from the chair and got to his knees on the floor beside his wife. Gently taking the shattered pieces of pottery from her hands, he raised her fingers to his lips and held them there in a soft, silent kiss.

"I don't deserve a second chance, don't deserve to have you in my life. But please…please find it in your heart to allow me to make it all right. To finally prove how much I love you. Need you." He dropped her hands and reached to pull her to him.

Elizabeth summoned her resolve and turned away from him with a sigh. This time, she must find the strength to stand her ground, to resist her husband's dynamic charisma, his ability to stir in her the hope that anything was possible.

"Yes, Philippe, you have failed me. On this *point we agree. You don't deserve another chance."* She gathered her voluminous skirts into one hand so she could bring herself to standing, to distance herself from him and the grief she knew her departure would cause him. Tonight, she could not be caught up in his pain; her own had gone on too long. Over at the dinner table, she began to collect the remnants of the evening meal this latest altercation had kept them from sharing. Yvette would clear the sideboard before heading to bed, she reminded herself; no need to fuss further. *"I might find it in my heart if it were indeed a second chance, or even merely the tenth time we've found ourselves battling the terms and provisions of our life together. How can I believe the outcome will be any different tonight?"*

"You can *believe! You most certainly will see a different outcome,"* Philippe said as he scrambled to his feet, rushing over to his wife. *"In fact, life itself will be very different for us in just one week's time!"*

"Yes, Philippe. Life will be different: You will be here, back from Paris, alone. I will be on my way home to Chicago, where I will try to reclaim my position with the orchestra. At 35, I am not a young woman and I've lost precious years here, attempting to make sense of the chaos you leave in your wake, to help you in your work." And then, with narrowed eyes and razor-sharp voice, *"And to compete with the village trollops you keep always at your side."*

"Elizabeth, my love!" the Professeur took his wife in his arms and buried his face in her chestnut hair. "You are everything to me!" He heaved an exasperated sigh and looked at the ceiling. "I am a weak man…I beg your forgiveness!"

With this latest apology delivered, he guided her to the sofa, sat her down, and took her hands in his. "I leave in the morning for Paris, but when I return, all will be clear. All will be well! And we shall embark on an intriguing project together. It's what we've been waiting for, what we had planned. In fact, you will marvel at the mission before us—and at its import!"

Elizabeth looked into her husband's ice-blue eyes and pushed a lock of thick black hair from his forehead. Such a boy, she thought, such an enchanting, jubilant, thoughtlessly cruel boy. She offered a smile, one more sardonic and sad than sincere. And yet, the dimmest glimmer of hope fought stubbornly to flicker within her.

"Your compassion for the people you help made me want to be with you, to work with you," Elizabeth said softly. "And made me fall in love with you." She held up her hand as her husband tried to speak. "You say you love me, Philippe. I need you to also respect me…as a person, as a partner. Such a maddeningly elusive desire, it seems, to expect the men in my life to hold me in esteem…"

Philippe sighed and fell against the back of the sofa, seemingly exhausted. "I have no one but myself to credit for your loss of faith in me, Elizabeth," he said. "And no defense. I have no rationale to offer you to trust me once again. I have only this project…"

"Ah. This project," Elizabeth repeated. "Are we to revisit the vineyards to complete the grafting against the phylloxera? Or to conduct the research to support your thesis on the tainted drinking water? Perhaps your attention returns to the cholera outbreak in Germany…"

"No, no, no!" Philippe cried, leaping from the sofa and pacing the parlor in excitement, energized once again. "All important work, of course. But those valiant missions were for us to begin and for others to take forward with the chores of implementation. Now, our gifts are required on a much more critical project which will have an enormous impact on a wider scale—a global scale!"

"All I see is your latest haphazard abandonment of import-ant work," Elizabeth responded. "Cholera has, and will again, threaten the globe. You visit Germany for data, to plan our approach to stop the spread to France, while I work to gather the academics for the symposiums. Yet upon your return, the effort is cast aside without explanation. Your passions last moments, Philippe! And you leave me at a loss, unable to proceed, to feel a sense of completion. I long, for once, to have participated in a success—any success!" Her eyes narrowed in anger once again.

"Cholera is contained in Germany…we've no need to fear it in France," he replied. "Much more intriguing innovations are taking seed there—and, unlike disease, they must *be spread. And we, my love, are in a position to do so. We will work to expedite a critical global collaboration that will change the world!"*

"You have dangled such prospects before me for years, Philippe," said Elizabeth, watching him pace and struggling in vain to resist the lure, once again, to surrender to his enthusi-asm. "And I've trotted behind, trying to make sense of it all. No longer. I must take steps for myself—toward something, some-place, where there may be some hope for me."

"And so you shall!" Philippe cried, throwing his hands in the air and smiling broadly. "And so you shall! I will return from Paris with authorizations to embark on a scientific, dip-lomatic undertaking to benefit the world. You, with your clev-erness, your diplomacy, your well-placed connections…you, my

love, will be instrumental in bringing it to its fruition...in the United States of America! I shall bring you home!"

Philippe's words had taken her breath away—as had his soft lips on hers, gently kissing away her questions. Gone, too, was Elizabeth's fragile resolve once her husband's arms tenderly gathered her to him and he guided her up the stairs to her bedroom.

Today, too, her breath failed her—but in pain and regret rather than in passion and hope. Now, the pull on her heart to have faith and to believe was gone. She felt as though her very soul itself was gone, leaving nothing but a yawning, fathomless nothingness.

After some time, jolted back to the parlor and the awareness that the sun was nearly set, Elizabeth got up to pull the windows shut against the chill. As she stepped across the room, the telegram crinkled under her leather boot. She picked it up and read it again:

P, my love. Yes, to Paris! I am yours. M.

Apparently a waylaid message from a woman accepting Philippe's invitation to join him in Paris, the telegram had extinguished the last flicker of hope she had been able to muster. For the best, perhaps. Elizabeth took an uneasy breath as she felt her husband's spell seeming to loosen its grip. With sudden clarity, she recognized her dream of doing meaningful work with him as merely that: a dream; knew her last chance to offer something more than an unfulfilling music career in America was gone. Her only choice now was to return to her benefactors who fancied themselves champions of the arts and hope to wring from them a living wage. Such a mortifying defeat.

Elizabeth looked around once again at the home she'd lovingly created. Stepping back to the grand piano that commanded the parlor, she bent down and ran her fingers along the keyboard, placed her palm on the smooth, rich mahogany and slid her hand along its cool, sleek surface. Like a living being, it shared its energy with her through the wood, even as it stood majestically silent.

Music gave her peace, taking the lead in her most joyous, thrilling experiences, providing an anchor during her most violent storms. Accolades for her performances and her own compositions stoked her vanity; her fame and notoriety gave her access to the greatest minds and talents in society. She took what she needed from her music. It nurtured and sustained her. She would turn to it now, of course.

And yet, as much as it supported her, Elizabeth could never see music as her purpose in life. She longed for a meaningful way to give, not to take. Performing to raise political and financial support for a fledgling symphony wasn't a calling. Hers were not skills that could change minds or save lives. She saw her existence in America as superficial, trivial even. What a gift she thought she'd found in Jean-Philippe Devereaux, his causes and his efforts to help his countrymen. It was a frivolous career she had left behind in the hopes of making a true difference here with him in France.

Today, her self-confidence and self-esteem in shambles, Elizabeth knew she had to look elsewhere. Again. With no other prospects to support herself, she would reluctantly accept the position as pianist her patrons held for her in the newly introduced Chicago Orchestra. She barely had time to get herself there before the spring season began. Should she be grateful for the telegram that finally forced her to truly commit to the decision?

Her eyes scanned the room with all its familiar reminders of her hopes for life in France: a sculpture purchased on a trip to the Pyrenees; the sumptuous Persian carpet from their dear friends Luc and Marie Masset; even the piano itself, a gift from her new husband. Uncertainty crept into her heart once again. So much to leave behind.

Then, her gaze fell on the portrait of her husband that hung over the fireplace, an oil painting she'd commissioned for his 40th birthday. How striking he looked, seated in his leather chair, looking pensively toward the study's window into the sunlight, his ruggedly handsome features aglow. Elizabeth tried to recall presenting him with the painting. Had they even celebrated the occasion together? Or was that evening one of the many she was left alone, with only remorse and tearful apologies days later? Her uncertainty turned to fury.

In three long strides Elizabeth reached the fireplace and wrestled the poker from its stand. She hurled it at the portrait. The wrought iron hook caught the canvas satisfyingly close to Philippe's head; its weight dragged it down, slashing the painting as it progressed, cutting its subject in two. She pulled the poker from the frame and swung it at the sculpture, knocking it from its pedestal. Then, back over to the piano, iron rod at the ready.

"Madame!" Yvette, the young, petite Devereaux housemaid, burst into the room and rushed to her mistress's side. She reached up and somehow took hold of the poker, gently easing it from Elizabeth's grasp. "No, Madame. You do not want this!"

"I do want this—and worse," Elizabeth replied. She grabbed the poker from Yvette and flung it upward at the crystal chandelier. Shattered begets rained down on them, the fixture rocked precariously. Yvette quickly retook possession of the fire poker as her mistress stormed toward the staircase and up the stairs.

"I'll see them both rot in hell…if I must arrange it myself!" she cried before slamming her bedroom door.

Chapter Two

The carriage pitched and swayed behind its horses as they sped toward Montpellier. Inside, Jean-Philippe Devereaux clung to the head rail to steady himself; his companion clung to him.

"Must he drive the horses so unmercifully?" the woman called over the noise of the rolling wheels. "I, for one, am not so anxious to end our jaunt just yet."

Devereaux glanced at her briefly, regretting—yet again—her presence on this trip. Five days prior, her unexpected appearance on the train platform as he began his journey was decidedly unwelcome, yet he was too distracted to argue at length against her joining him. As the trip progressed, however, his dismay only magnified. There had been much to do in Paris, and he was beholden to others' schedules. With no time to entertain the woman, he was forced to suffer her sulkiness and ill temper.

"The *Comité Académique* will not wait if I am overdue, Monique," he murmured absently as he peered through the swinging curtains. The French countryside, bathed in red twilight as evening approached, rushed by him unseen. Yet again, his thoughts returned to his prepared remarks as his stomach twinged with anticipation. "While not my most outlandish proposal, it's sure to stir up controversy. Being late for the presentation will not improve my chances for acceptance."

He smoothed back his dark hair as best he could, knowing that appearing before his university colleagues looking like a street urchin would also fail to contribute to his cause. Dropping his head onto the back of the tufted leather seat, he glared at the ceiling. Damn the railway for becoming disabled at Lyons! Had it been thirty, even twenty years ago, he might understand. But in 1894, the very dawn of the 20th century, one would expect modern means of transport to be marginally functional. Not so for the railways of southern France! Hiring a carriage was the only chance of getting to the school on time, uncomfortable a decision though it was. Even a strong, healthy body begins to feel its years after forty of them, and his could stand little more of the coach's jostling.

"Your ability to create controversy is among your most endearing qualities, Professeur," Monique said with a sidelong glance. The raven-haired young woman grasped his hand from the rail; her green eyes narrowed as they locked onto his. "Do let's confront Elizabeth. What more delicious controversy than to reveal our passionate love for one another?"

Devereaux glanced again toward his unsought companion with a wrinkled brow; he wondered what other delusions fermented inside her empty head. With little interest in exploring her thoughts, he returned to the window and ignored her suggestion as well. It was merely his cowardly aversion to conflict that had led him to succumb to her pleading and bring her to Paris, he admitted to himself, nothing more. Dare he hope her ever-wandering husband might return to take control of the woman? A brood of chicks would certainly keep her from underfoot. Pulling back the curtain a bit more, Philippe feigned interest in the white-capped women finishing up their work in the fields.

Suddenly, he longed to be in his own home, before the fire with a glass of Cognac at his elbow. Dinner would be served late tonight, he thought, imagining his wife whipping together her household in preparation for his arrival. His lips tightened as he leaned closer to the window, away from the woman next to him. Hell would be a welcome refuge from Elizabeth's fury if she learned Monique was with him at this moment. Memories of their heated exchange prior to his departure for Paris flooded his thoughts. The twinge he felt this time was one of dread. Why ever had he given in to this vixen? Why hadn't he sent her home where she belonged? Merely to avoid an unpleasant confrontation, of course. He shook his head dispiritedly, dreading the horrific confrontation he might very well encounter soon at his own home.

Devereaux stretched his legs and rubbed his face with both hands, so weary to be yet again battling himself and his choices.

Why Monique and her ilk? Opportunity, availability; ego, perhaps. Would it be better if there were more to it? If the women who made themselves so available to him offered more than what he had with Elizabeth? He knew his wanderings had little to do with the willing mademoiselles who flocked around him, had nothing to do with anything he lacked at home.

"Why does she suffer me?" Elizabeth deserved better.

"Because I love you, my dear Philippe," Monique answered him.

Devereaux was startled to realize he had spoken aloud.

"Silly, silly girl," he replied with a smile, pecking her cheek. Yes, he relished the Moniques in his life. Mere dalliances! If only his wife could see them as such.

Again, he longed for his armchair. And his wife. Elizabeth was so much more than an evening of pleasure and distraction. She was his touchstone. He thought back to his days in America. Frustrating, lonely days lecturing at the University of Chicago. None of his initiatives had blossomed, none of his ideas had inspired support. Only the phylloxera! He had been thoroughly sick of the effort. His protocols for rehabilitating the diseased vines in France were completed and published, yet the Americans' fascination for his processes were limitless. Frustrated beyond bearing, he had abandoned all hope of moving on to something new.

Until Elizabeth.

How delighted he was to learn that the pianist he and several students saw perform at the newly completed Orchestra Hall—a woman, shockingly—was sister to one of their party. John Wellington, a third-year, arranged for the group to meet her backstage after the concert.

If not as moved as the rest by her performance at the keyboard, Devereaux was mesmerized by the musician herself. Her simple, wholesome beauty and her curiosity in him and his research; her almost intuitive understanding of how to summarize his initiatives into coherent, compelling prose. When she organized a salon for him to introduce his thoughts on forest preservation, she brought together some of the greatest minds in environmental conservation. From engineer Octave Chanute representing the railroads, to journalist John Muir, to landscape architect Charles Eliot… Anyone who might have had an interest or an influence in the field answered her call. What progress was made that night! He owed so much of it to Elizabeth and her ability to reach people and bring them together for a greater purpose.

While his reputation flourished and opportunities abounded, his heart was no longer his own. He would not rest until Elizabeth agreed to return with him to France. No matter she would only do so as his wife. He would do and say whatever necessary to have this woman in his life. And she had been all that he had imagined—providing not only a warm home life for him, but when confidence in his research lagged and his doubts seemed insurmountable, she was there, offering hope. In turn, he had proved a disappointment, of course.

Philippe scowled. He was merely a child given free rein in a sweet shop, he thought to himself as he put his arm absently around Monique and caressed her shoulder. Nothing more harmful. Why must Elizabeth see it all with such different eyes? He sighed heavily. No matter. The price to pay this time would be dear if word of his companion reached his wife. No need to fear a confrontation, in that case; he'd surely find her gone upon his return. He removed his arm from around Monique.

In a few short months, spring will have done her worst, Devereaux thought. A trip up into the mountains would soothe Elizabeth's wounded soul. It always did. On this next visit, they would discuss the details of their new project that would be finally approved and authorized for implementation tonight—and lay out his plans to accomplish it. No, it couldn't wait! She was expecting to hear about it all when he returned from Paris. It would be the ideal peace offering to strengthen her still-fragile confidence in him. He knew she would be amazed and intrigued by this undertaking, and proud that it was from her own work with him in the U.S.—connections she helped make for him—from which the initiative grew.

This undertaking. He must focus on his presentation—which simply had to be convincing enough to gain university support in Montpellier. With the University of Paris, the government, and Chanute now behind him, he would spend no more time in this quagmire. The global consortium could now be established, funded, and move forward!

It was then that his eye caught sight of another carriage close beside them. Too close.

"Claude!" called Devereaux, banging his stick on the roof of the carriage. "Mind the coach on your left!"

Just as the words left his lips, violent contact was made.

Devereaux and Monique were flung to the floor as the passing carriage hit the left side of theirs. Broken glass spewed about the compartment as the vehicle was forced off the road. With their passengers crying for help from within, the horses dragged the coach along the rocky side path before finding their way back onto the thoroughfare at last.

As the world righted itself, Devereaux picked his way over a whimpering Monique, briefly irritated by her clambering among his papers which now littered the floor. Finally reaching the undamaged door on the right, he put his head outside and saw the recklessly driven carriage immediately ahead of them.

"Claude!" he yelled, but the wind forced the words back down his throat. Craning his neck in search of his valet-turned-coachman, Devereaux's heart froze in his chest as he realized that Claude had been tossed from the carriage. They were driver-less! Unrestrained, the horses steadily picked up speed as they headed onto the Arneau Bridge crossing high over the raging River Lez. The Professeur caught his breath as he watched the vehicle in front of them seem to purposely maneuver itself into the path of his frightened horses. Another collision was imminent.

"Stop this carriage!" shrieked Monique.

For an agonizing moment, Devereaux remained paralyzed, clinging to the pitching carriage. No one was there to help, he scolded himself; his life was in his own hands. Reluctantly stripping down to his leather waistcoat, his heart pounding, he opened the door, leaned out again, and stretched for the driver's seat railing.

"No!" came more howling from within.

The railing was too far. Philippe hesitated, looking hopefully toward the carriage before them. Surely the driver would veer off, he reasoned. Why maintain this collision course? As he watched the carriages inch ever closer, realization washed over him in a sickening wave. *They were trying to kill him.* At last, anger edged out the fear as Devereaux determined he had no choice: The horses must be brought under control, and he must be the one to do it.

Easing his way around the swinging door, the stiff wind stinging his eyes, Devereaux stretched again toward the driver's bench. After two attempts, almost losing his footing, he managed to grasp the bar and pull himself unsteadily forward. Gaining confidence as he reached the bench, he lodged his boot into the seat's grating and started climbing into the driver's perch. Just as he moved to take the seat, the driver ahead pulled up his team. Devereaux scrambled for the reins as his horses veered to the right and swung the carriage around, crashing it into the bridge's rail.

Jolted loose by the violence of the impact, Devereaux found himself hanging in midair with nothing but the river's rocky shore below him. He clawed at the emptiness, trying to grab the carriage, the rail, whatever would support him. He reached out toward the splintered railing and caught it with one hand.

Then, the carriages collided again.

As his coach hit the bridge once more, Devereaux felt the wooden rail break cleanly in his hand. The trestle rose high above him as he tumbled downward, and the horses pulled the carriage back securely onto the bridge. Continuing to fall, ever down toward the roaring river, he was consumed by a flash of deepest regret. There would be no proposal to the school now. Worse, unthinkable even: there would be no trip to the Pyrenees for the Devereauxs; no atonement for his many transgressions; no opportunity to finally offer his wife the life she most wanted—and deserved. And all for what reason?

Approaching the rocks below, Jean-Philippe Devereaux gave a last mournful howl.

"Elizabeth…!"

CHAPTER THREE

"Won't you please reconsider?" Luc Masset pleaded. The stout, gray-bearded gentleman put an arm around the woman in his sitting room, his deep brown eyes brimming with concern. "I am afraid you will come to regret this day."

"I already regret this day," answered Elizabeth, rising from her seat. Smoothing the skirts of her blue traveling outfit and tugging the bolero into place, the tall, slender woman looked around the sitting room for the matching bonnet. How sad to leave here, she thought, breathing in the aroma of baking bread and Madame Marie Masset's lavender perfume. This family had provided one of the few places she felt at home in this dismal country, a rare oasis in all of France she felt she belonged. Much more a home than the villa she shared with her husband. "Regret that my marriage—my attempt to make a life here—has come to an end and I must try to begin again."

"Philippe adores you," said Marie. Luc's wife rose too and took Elizabeth's soft hand in her weathered ones. "At least stay here with us until you can speak to him."

Elizabeth looked from one Masset to the other. These people had opened their door to her, time and again, as she looked for her oft-missing husband. At first, it had been a fearful wife who called on the couple who knew and loved Philippe as they would a son of their own. Then, as the outcome never varied—that romantic intrigue rather than personal danger had befallen him—humiliation replaced her fear. More than an academic colleague, Luc Masset was Philippe's mentor, his confidante. He saw the pain his younger friend had caused Elizabeth to suffer over the years, saw his inability to comprehend her devastation at his wanderings. The Massets saw her fear eventually slide into anger, then apathy. Surely, they couldn't be shocked her spirit finally sought escape.

"The time for talk is over." Elizabeth found her hat on the sideboard and secured it to her chestnut chignon, her blue eyes resting on the oil portrait of the three Masset daughters mounted on the wall above. Although hardly close to the eldest girl, Elizabeth considered the younger ones to be like sisters; but she couldn't bear to see them before departing. There was no time, no purpose in dwelling on the few things that made life here bearable. "Besides, I can hardly speak to the man while he sleeps in Paris with yet another woman. A most satisfying tryst, I must believe, since he didn't return last night as scheduled." She sighed. "This drama has become all too familiar over the years. I am tired and bored of the script."

Marie rustled behind Elizabeth as she headed toward the front door. "Every marriage has problems," she said, glancing back at her husband. "Luc and I, too, had our troubles. We overcame them to find our marriage stronger than it could have been before. Please. Stay and fight for yours."

"I haven't your strength, Marie," Elizabeth said after some thought. "Nor your faith. I no longer believe my marriage to be worth the fight." She paused again and dropped into the armchair by the door, twisting the blue kid gloves in her lap. She wanted to be on her way, to be done with this place. But her love and respect for the Massets compelled her to make them understand why she had to leave, to accept defeat. "I gave up a life of my own back in America. Hardly a career of consequence…but I felt useful, at least."

"You have a life here, Elizabeth," said Marie.

"I am not without blame, I know," Elizabeth continued, looking absently out the window as the lamplighters went about their chores. "If I couldn't be an important part of Philippe's work here, I wanted nothing from this place. The trivialities of choosing the perfect goose to serve for dinner could not equal the life I had back home…or the more meaningful one I expected to find here. And I've never let myself, or anyone else, forget that.

"Something in Philippe made you give up so much to be with him," said Marie. "Those things must still be in your heart, must still be strong enough to help you forgive him."

The mourning doves cooing near Marie's kitchen window brought Elizabeth back in time, back to a porch swing on a hot summer evening in the American Midwest. A time when she basked in the attentions of a dashing French botanist devoting his life to exterminating the phylloxera that was decimating the vineyards of his country and destroying the livelihood of so many of his countrymen. "I dreamed of being involved in something that mattered. And this man's work mattered."

"Philippe is still that man," said Luc.

"Agreed," said Elizabeth. "And he still chases his noble causes far and wide, but I am part of none of them." She recalled the work that could at times bridge the ever-growing gap between them. "So many opportunities to help and perhaps even feel at home…to feel I belonged. But, as always, without his continued passion and engagement, each opportunity simply faded away. Now, we share nothing…but my bed on occasion, when a village whore is unavailable."

"Elizabeth…" The Massets shook their heads, almost in unison.

"I'm afraid this most recent assignation is the most unforgivable of all," she continued, "coming on the heels of a heartfelt vow to change his ways and the allusion to yet another intriguing undertaking we would complete together." Elizabeth sighed as tears of frustration welled in her eyes. "I'd say my heart is broken, but it's been so shattered for so long, only numbness remains."

"Please, please!" Luc pulled her up gently from the chair and guided her to the sofa as Marie brought *café* and macarons from the side table. "I will not hear of shattered hearts and deadened souls, Madame!" He turned Elizabeth to face him. "There is great love and passion in that precious heart of yours—it escapes through your eyes. Fury? Yes, I see that too. But it's that very rage and your willingness to wrestle with it that makes you the extraordinary woman you are— do not run from her!"

"I've failed to manage her—or any part of her life that matters," said Elizabeth, waving away Marie's offered sweet. "I…"

"You cannot channel that energy by running from it, *mon cherie*." Luc took her hand in his. "Tell me of the project…"

Elizabeth looked at him blankly. "The project?"

"The 'intriguing undertaking' Philippe suggests. Tell me."

"A mere bone, thrown to mollify a pathetic pet," she replied, waving her hand again. "If there was indeed an endeavor, it was not as intriguing as the trollop he brought to Paris. Philippe has made his choice. I must do the same."

"Jean-Philippe Devereaux is an imperfect man and a deeply flawed husband," said Luc, with a sternness that surprised Elizabeth. "The one perfect thing in his life is you. Please. Wait to confront him. To learn of his plans for you."

"Ah. His plans for me." Elizabeth looked into Luc's eyes and offered a tight smile. "A grand scheme, of course, one in which I serve as linchpin. An undertaking of global impact! Most wonderful of all, a plan that would take me home, where we would finally have the partnership we agreed upon so many years ago." The smile slipped from her lips. "The 'plan' was merely a recitation of all my grievances, neatly packaged as a solution to our troubles. An intriguing package, of course. But when word reached me of his traveling companion, so soon after we agreed on a new and fresh beginning, I knew the package was empty. I will not live this way any longer. Without a purpose, without Philippe's respect, I have lost respect for myself."

Elizabeth covered her face. Avoiding this very scene was why she had left without seeing Philippe. A detour past the Massets' home, however, weakened her resolve to escape entirely without farewell. Now, there was no need to continue talking, to postpone the inevitable. The Massets couldn't understand her need for something more than her husband could give her; it was something she had difficulty accepting herself. She tried to rise from the sofa.

"Where will you go?" asked Marie, grasping her arm. "Home to America? Is that where your happiness lies? What is there for you that is not here?"

"The opportunity to reclaim my position with the orchestra in Chicago," said Elizabeth listlessly. "The director has invited me to return each year since its formation. This year, I accepted. The spring season begins in a month's time. I shall rejoin them as pianist."

"Truly…?" Marie stood and looked down at her young friend, shaking her head, brow furrowed. "What grand changes do you expect to find in Chicago? How will your role be different from the one you so joyfully escaped five years ago? And your desire for respect? Can you possibly believe you will finally find it there? Now?"

"No." Elizabeth closed her eyes, a great fatigue enveloping her like a smothering down quilt. "Can you imagine, then, how intolerable my life is here? I don't return to anything at all in Chicago. I run from the nothingness I've found here." She took a deep breath. "I long to find the purposeful life I dream of. But if it exists, it seems not to be in Montpellier. The overwhelming irrelevance I feel here paints my world gray. I need to find the colors again. Philippe knows this. If he chooses to include me in his life, he will follow and prove it possible. In the meantime, I will rely on my music for healing as I find my way. You must know, this decision is not an easy step I'm…trying to take."

As Marie reached out again to her friend, there came a thunderous banging on the door. Luc admitted a young man barely able to speak for his labored breathing. He saw Elizabeth brush a stray tear from her cheek.

"You know then?" the man asked breathlessly.

"Know what, Henri?" asked Luc. Marie and Elizabeth exchanged puzzled glances.

"Professeur Devereaux," Henri gasped. "There's been an accident."

"What's happened?" cried Luc.

"A carriage accident…on the Arneau Bridge." Henri glanced toward the ladies, hesitating. Finally, he touched Luc's arm reassuringly. "Monique is unhurt," he said, then looked away. "But Devereaux is dead."

It was Luc who took charge, even before Henri's words sank in—immediately understanding swift action needed to buffer, perhaps forestall, the ugly backlash that would come once the details of the news were fully absorbed.

Indeed, Elizabeth watched events unfold around her from deep within a hazy gray bubble, a distant spectator of a baffling drama. Remotely curious, she watched Marie struggle between breaking down in tears over the sudden and tragic loss of a near-son and venting her anger and mortification at learning her daughter was one of the whores referenced only moments ago. And herself? Elizabeth could only assume from the apprehension that settled at last on both the Massets' faces that she was on the verge of coming undone.

Despite his wife's tears and his friend's daze, Luc managed to shepherd the women out the door and down to his waiting coach. Elizabeth climbed in after Marie and settled herself on the bench opposite, hands in lap with eyes averted. Images flew before her: Philippe's destroyed portrait, the steamship that was to carry her across the ocean, Monique's glaring green eyes, her piano…

The Masset carriage rumbled along the narrow, winding streets of a darkening Montpellier, the thundering of wheels on cobblestones making conversation impossible. Though there was little to be said. Yes, of course, Elizabeth understood that a stop at hospital would be the first order of business: Luc and Marie were entitled to assure themselves of their daughter's well-being. Clearly, Philippe would wait.

Philippe. Gone. The vast emptiness and finality of the word was lurking just beyond Elizabeth's ability to grasp. No further confrontations, no more betrayal, no lavishing attentions in attempts to repent. Her retreat to America would not manipulate her husband into fulfilling his promises. Now, it would be the final goodbye she was coming to realize she had hoped to avoid. Intermittent, silent tears spilled from her eyes and rolled down her cheeks, but all she could feel was numbness.

Elizabeth peered across the carriage at Marie, jostling about in the opposite seat, fading as night fell. As the woman wept soundlessly into her handkerchief, Elizabeth wanted to reach out and touch her knee, to comfort her, assure her all would be well. But she knew otherwise. There was no changing this scenario, no hope to latch onto. Marie's daughter Monique would always be a tramp and Philippe would always be dead. There was only the hospital, then the police. Afterward, especially for Elizabeth, loomed an enormous black expanse of a bleak, unknowable future.

∽

It was a shrewish Monique they found at the hospital. Apparently, the trauma she'd experienced hadn't tempered her belligerence. Even from the building's towering front steps, Elizabeth could hear the woman shrieking at those around her.

"He left us!" came Monique's hateful cry as the gravely injured Claude was carried by her cot. "He knew what was to happen and leapt from the coach to save himself!"

Elizabeth sat alone in the cold marble entryway, nestled in her isolating, sensation-less bubble. She found it easy to dismiss Monique's caterwauling and its meaning, if indeed there were any. But the sight of her husband's valet, so still beneath his bandages, strangled her heart and she found herself drawn to follow the orderlies carrying his litter. After many twists and turns down and around the dreary, sterile hospital corridors, the attendants deposited Claude in a small, white, windowless room. Once they left, Elizabeth went inside and knelt on the floor beside the injured man. Poor Claude, who lived to serve Philippe. Who would have given his life for his master. Who looked as though he still might.

For some time she sat in silence, listening to his shallow breathing, watching the twitching of his eyelids. Suddenly, his eyes opened and he looked directly at her, then squeezed them shut.

"I am sorry," he whispered weakly.

Elizabeth covered his rough, unbandaged hand with hers. "You may apologize for not resting," she replied, trying to summon a scolding voice. "We need you well and back home. Soon."

"I am not a driver," he whispered, eyes still pinched shut.

Elizabeth's lip began to tremble. Poor Claude no longer had a master. With Philippe gone, no one at the Devereaux villa needed to be dressed now. Having suffered such serious injuries, he now worried about his future?

"You are to get well. We will take care of the rest."

"I couldn't control them, couldn't avoid them," murmured Claude, moisture forming around his clenched eyelids. "I am *not* a driver."

Elizabeth patted his hand again as he turned his face away, resolving to see that he and his family were cared for, even after she left for America. Philippe would have wanted that. She certainly did.

"No, you won't have to turn chauffeur," she said softly. "We will find you a suitable position once you are well." Elizabeth looked again at the limp body on the cot, breathing in a more restful rhythm now, and wondered how extensive his injuries were, wondered if he would ever be well. Answers would have to wait for Luc, of course. The physicians would not welcome inquiries from her, a woman. But they would speak to Luc.

Elizabeth's thoughts were interrupted when Luc himself appeared and helped her to her feet. "Claude?" she asked, adjusting her jacket and shaking the folds of her skirts into place.

Luc looked down and took a breath, then led Elizabeth outside. "They cannot be sure," he said once they were in the hallway.

"I will stay with him, then. Until they are."

"This is no place for you," Luc replied, taking her arm and leading her from the infirmary. "We have other matters to attend to."

"Yes. Of course…" The merest inkling of control she had begun to feel, of hope she might be able to manage this horror, snuffed itself out as Elizabeth permitted herself to be led to the door. The next stop: the police station.

ॐ

Enveloped in the dark, somber surroundings of the prefecture, Elizabeth struggled to focus as a determined Luc and a stoic Marie beside him extricated the details of the disaster. The agent turned his back to her as he spoke and lowered his voice, recounting the episode. She felt mild surprise at her ambivalence, for once taking no offense at the customary rudeness, feeling no need to step forward and demand her right to be addressed as well. None of it seemed to concern her as wisps of sounds and syllables, sometimes words and phrases, carried to her ear: a hazardously driven carriage, a freak collision with the panicked driver leaving the scene, a passing farmer coming to the victims' aid. *Such a sad story,* she thought, *such a terrible, terrible story…*

"Perhaps a seat…?" An elderly officer came to her side, pulling a stool from behind the reception table. Elizabeth's knees buckled as he helped her lower herself onto it. Her head spinning, she tried again to hear and comprehend Luc and the policeman's conversation.

"Insufferably useless! The lot of you!" cried Luc suddenly as the agent explained the damaged carriage had been vandalized and stripped while the victims were transported to the hospital. He slammed his fist on the desk. "I demand to know what steps are being taken, as we speak, to produce their stolen belongings!"

His best coat? It would have been with him and would now be unavailable for burial, Elizabeth thought. *A pity. Such a pity…*

Suddenly, her thoughts became razor sharp, and she homed in on the conversation and the reason they were there. Burial. The enormity of the loss advanced ever so slightly and attempted to wash over her, but she couldn't succumb, couldn't drown in it. Not yet. She had to move, to act, to understand the full horror of this new reality. The ever-simmering rage began to bubble to the surface. Standing up unsteadily, she made her way to the desk and faced the agent.

"Where is my husband?" she demanded.

"Unknown," said the officer to Luc. "We wait until the swollen river surrenders him. The swift current, at its strongest so early in spring, makes recovery…difficult."

Elizabeth leaned toward the officer, but he would not make eye contact. She reached out and grasped him by the arm.

"You…wait?!" Elizabeth cried, as the agent finally turned and acknowledged her. "A demolished carriage, ransacked. A dead man, missing. It appears a great deal of police work is to be done, Monsieur!" Her voice rose, in volume and pitch, attracting the attention of the officer's colleagues and others conducting business at the adjoining telegraph office.

Luc rested his hands on her shoulders, easing her away from the desk.

"Yet you wait!" she continued, furious as she pushed Luc away and stood her ground. "Pardon my ignorance, sir, I am not native to Montpellier. But I must ask: Are you truly our last resort? Is there no hope of competence here, amongst the police?"

"Elizabeth, please." Luc looked to his wife for assistance, as Elizabeth turned to address a second officer, joining the first.

"Perhaps you can offer some small hope that this agency is capable of…of action? Of results?" His silence and blank expression angered her further. "No? Is there anyone else?" She gestured angrily toward a tall man in a workman's coat and cloth hat who had concluded his business at the telegraph window and was attempting to push his way around them and toward the door. "I might as well rely upon this foreigner for help as expect it from you!"

Marie stepped forward, took Elizabeth's arm, and guided her toward the door as well. "Yes, Elizabeth," she said under her breath. "There is nothing to gain here. We will wait in the carriage."

The "foreigner," having reached the door first, held it wide for the two women to pass through. Luc stepped up behind them.

"My apologies, Sigerson," he said to the man as he stepped through the door himself. "It's been a difficult day…"

"Understood," Sigerson replied, removing his cap as he passed and stepped down into the street. "My condolences to Madame Devereaux."

Elizabeth stood next to the carriage, resisting Marie's urging to step inside. She turned toward Sigerson's departing figure.

"Monsieur!" she called. "My news is spread, then? What is the word?"

Already far enough away from the lamplight to be in shadow, Sigerson stopped and turned slowly to face the carriage. Luc stepped toward him with a heavy sigh and made the obligatory introductions.

"Elizabeth, may I present Monsieur Sigerson, who joins us just this week from Norway to pursue research at the school. Sigerson…Madame Elizabeth Devereaux."

"*Enchanté,*" murmured Sigerson, keeping his distance. He raised his voice to answer her question from afar. "I am afraid I know nothing of your husband's accident other than from your…conversation inside." As Elizabeth took a breath to say more, he stepped even farther away and bowed his head. "Now, I'm sure you are anxious to be home with your household at this difficult time. Again, my condolences."

He turned on his heel and walked quickly away.

"Yes," said Elizabeth, indignant at the dismissal. "Thank you for your…concern."

Once she was finally settled inside the carriage, the rage ebbed once more and a quivering lip returned.

"However rude, the man is right," Elizabeth said, accepting Marie's handkerchief. "I can only return to the villa now. I cannot grieve, cannot lash out, cannot escape. I can only wait—much like the helpless prefecture—until the river releases my husband." She sighed. "And me, as well…?"

ঔত

The small white villa with its stuccoed walls and wooden shutters emerged from behind the trees, every window emanating a golden glow created by the gaslights within. *What a sweet, hope-filled home it appears,* thought Elizabeth as the

Massets' horses pulled the carriage up to the ivy-covered gate. It crushed her heart to face such a scene in light of the day's events—and the news she was obligated to deliver to those inside.

Just this afternoon, Elizabeth had abandoned the house and her hopes for it, fully knowing she might never see it again. Now here she was, back within hours, but not at all on the terms she had hoped might be: in a new, legitimate partnership with her husband, taking on the world together. She peered through the carriage window, picturing herself on the porch swing with Philippe, sharing ideas about his latest passion, while watching in the front garden as a little boy or girl of their own explored the world for the first time. How she wanted to simply sit and imagine what might have been ahead for them. To forget what was. Most of all, she wanted to avoid having to break this spell and go inside to break the hearts of the people there. The Devereaux household, those who took care of her and Philippe, who tried to help her make this villa a home, was now so broken—much more permanently than the damage she had inflicted by her departure this afternoon.

Before she could bring herself to move, however, the door flung open and Yvette stepped outside and peered toward the carriage. The young housemaid pulled a cape over her dress and prepared to head down the stone path toward the road.

"Monsieur Luc?" Yvette called, her voice hoarse and weak. "Monsieur?!"

Blinded by the light streaming through the door, Elizabeth could barely make out her maid's face, but she could hear her anxiety—her fear. Poor Yvette, left in charge of the house, waiting for her master to help her cope with her mistress's abandonment. Of course she would cry out for

Luc rather than her lady. The thought jolted Elizabeth into action. She pushed open the carriage door to step out.

"Yvette!" she called.

"Madame!" The wail that emanated from the woman was otherworldly and shook Elizabeth to her core. Extricating herself from the carriage, Elizabeth pushed through the gate and took the woman in her arms.

"Yvette. I'm here."

"Professeur?!" the housemaid cried. She looked into her mistress's face in the light, saw the tears forming in her eyes. "Please. No!"

Elizabeth turned Yvette around and guided her toward the steps to the villa. "Inside," she said. "We'll talk inside."

"Oh! Please, no!" Yvette dropped to her knees, sobbing in anguish.

"You must be strong," Elizabeth whispered to her maid. "You know I look to you, always, to get us through…never more than today…"

Luc and Marie appeared beside them. He gently lifted the maid from the ground and took both women by their arms. "We shall all get through this together. Now…into the house with the two of you. The staff awaits."

Inside, they all stood in the parlor, every one of them, waiting to welcome back their mistress. Lucien, the young stable boy, pale and shaking; matronly Cook, uncharacteristically distant and removed. Claude, of course, was missing. *Did they even know about him?* Elizabeth thought. But there the rest of them stood, just as they had done earlier in the day when she'd said her goodbyes.

Sad and regretful, then. Each one of them had clearly been sorry for her decision to leave…but Elizabeth was sure her staff weren't devastated by her departure, even expected it perhaps; wondering, she assumed, why it'd taken her so long. It was more pity they felt for her, she imagined, being privy to what any household would of what went on between husband and wife. Ultimately, Elizabeth knew, it was Philippe who commanded their deepest loyalty. They revered him and would count on him to make it all right. She even suspected they would willingly accept one of his paramours in her place. They had merely waited for their master to return so they could go on with their lives as he directed.

Yet here they now stood, waiting to take their direction from her instead. Now, at her return instead of his, she saw the true devastation in their eyes, in their tears.

"It is horrific news," Elizabeth began, as Luc and Marie shepherded everyone into the parlor, encouraging them to take seats on the sofa and armchairs—unthinkable on any other day. She headed toward Philippe's leather chaise, but pulled out the piano bench instead. "Yet, I'm afraid you must already know."

"Cook came back from market this afternoon," said Yvette, "telling such an awful tale: Professeur dead, Claude in hospital…" Her voice quivered. "But then a gentleman called, expecting Professeur to be here. It gave us hope… hope that the word was untrue…"

"But it *is* true," said Elizabeth softly. "I am so sorry…he is gone." She took a breath to steady herself. "It's unforgivable that you learned this way. If I'd been here… So unforgivable of me…"

Yvette burst into renewed sobbing as Lucien covered his face with his hands. Even Cook's eyes welled up as Elizabeth's words extinguished the last embers of hope. The story was true: Professeur Jean-Philippe Devereaux was dead.

"What gentleman called?" Elizabeth asked suddenly.

"Said he was from the school," said Lucien, looking up. "Never laid eyes on him before today. Said he was to meet with Professeur today, here. Waited for a time. We hoped…"

"What did he look like?" Elizabeth probed.

"Older," said Lucien, concurrent with Cook's "Young!"

"Tall, wearing a greatcoat," said Yvette. "He carried a walking stick."

"Slim? Portly?" The consensus narrowed down to "a big man."

"What could he have wanted from Philippe?" Elizabeth wondered aloud. "What was his purpose…?"

"He wanted to discuss Professeur's trip to Paris," said Yvette.

Elizabeth thought for a moment. "He was from the university and knew of Philippe's work. A colleague perhaps?" Then, looking at Luc: "A visiting researcher, perhaps? Your friend from Norway seemed impertinently aware of my obligations at home."

Luc shook his head. "Sigerson engages no one." He turned back to the staff. "This gentleman left no card?"

They all shook their heads. There was nothing to help them identify the man or his intentions.

Elizabeth groaned and dropped her head into her hands. *All they have now is me,* she thought. How could she help these people when she couldn't even help herself cope with this unfathomable tragedy?

Marie looked around the room at everyone in tears and stepped from behind Elizabeth's bench into the middle of the parlor.

"Our hearts are broken," she said to the staff. "But Madame needs your help now. Mourn in your own way, but be strong. Your responsibilities are to this house…and to this woman. *Comprenez-vous?*"

"Of course, of course," said Yvette, as she rushed to kneel at Elizabeth's feet. "We are here, Madame. We will manage together."

Lucien and Cook joined Yvette to gather around their mistress and hold onto each other through their tears. All at once, Elizabeth felt confusion and overwhelming grief, yet awash in love…and the smallest inkling of hope that she might survive. At least until morning.

"In what scheme was he embroiled this time?" Marie Masset demanded of her husband. Having seen Monique at the hospital, the police at the prefecture, and Elizabeth safely home, the Massets were alone at last in their own home, left to make sense of the tragedy that had befallen them all.

Marie's hands trembled as she grasped Luc's arm and turned him to face her. She glared at her husband through the tears she couldn't stop, anger beginning to overwhelm the grief she felt for Philippe, the disappointment in Monique, the concern for Elizabeth.

"What debacle did he bring upon himself…and Monique as well, for heaven's sake…!?"

Fury rose up in her as Luc shook his head. He had nothing to offer that would ease her mind.

"Answer me!" she cried.

"I simply do not know, *mon amour*," Luc whispered, reaching out to guide her toward the parlor sofa—the soft refuge they sought during their most difficult times. "I am as ignorant as you of what happened today and why."

Marie pushed him away. "Nonsense! You knew he was in Paris—and you know why."

"Yes," Luc admitted, throwing himself onto the sofa, alone. He rubbed his eyes in exhaustion. "I knew Philippe went to Paris…"

"Did you know, also, that our daughter would be his courtesan for the expedition? *Mon Dieu!*"

Her husband threw his hands up in anger. "As far as his agenda and his sleeping arrangements, I had no knowledge of his plans."

"I wonder…" answered his wife, staring icily at him as she paced up and down the floor, handkerchief at the ready. "Nothing is ever simple with Philippe, and he confided in you the details of his maddest schemes. You had better think long and hard about the details of this particular scheme, Monsieur. There is more trouble to come, I am certain of it. There always is…" She stopped and eyed him directly. "I hope to God you knew nothing about Monique joining him. If I weren't so frightened for her, I'd have thrashed her right there in the hospital. And you as well if you condoned the venture!"

"Marie…Marie," Luc murmured. "Come. Sit beside me. I know you are worried about Monique and Elizabeth. I know you grieve for Philippe. In the morning, clearer heads will be better able to find answers." He sighed deeply. "If there are any. I am afraid this is all simply a horrific accident. He was involved in nothing more mysterious than a task that had grown tedious. He was looking for progress, for resolution. If only…" He dropped his head into his hands.

Marie stopped her pacing and truly looked at her husband for the first time since they had gotten the news. At last, she saw the desolation that consumed him, the physical and emotional fatigue, the deepest sorrow. She sat down on the sofa beside him and, putting her arms around him, brought his head to her chest.

"I am so sorry, my dear," she whispered. "I've let my own grief and fear keep me from allowing you to grieve as well." She kissed her husband's bowed head. "Now. Tell me: 'If only'…what?"

Luc got up from the sofa to walk the floor himself, only to collapse into the armchair after a few steps. "If only…I might have accompanied him on the trip myself. Perhaps I might have prevented the accident, somehow…"

"You? Considered joining Philippe in Paris? Whatever for?" Marie looked across the room at her husband with narrowed eyes. "Ah. You know nothing of his agenda, yet might have accompanied him…?"

"He asked me to secure a meeting with an acquaintance there. Why he asked me…?" Luc shook his head. "I wrote the necessary letter, of course. But had I gone in person…"

"What acquaintance? For what purpose?" stammered Marie, her voice rising.

"Chanute—you know Chanute," said Luc. He rubbed his eyes and stretched his neck back to stare at the ceiling. "We met him and his wife at *Société Chimique* in Paris… years ago."

"Yes, of course," said Marie, calmer now, thinking back. "The chemist. And Anne. She was lovely… American, of course, with her atrocious French. Not like Elizabeth." Marie shrugged her shoulders as Luc shot her a scolding frown. "Lovely, all the same. I wonder if she accompanied him, to visit his family here perhaps…?"

"No, no," said Luc. "Octave is a true American now, after all these years. There is no one here for him. He was in Paris for professional pursuits, I'm certain."

"Why would Philippe want to meet with Octave Chanute?"

Luc threw his hands up in the air once again. "Who could know what Philippe had on his mind at any given moment? And as for Chanute? They are birds of a feather! Octave is an even more brilliantly bestrewn intellectual than Philippe. God alone could imagine a conversation between the two!"

"Could Philippe's latest plot have involved chemistry somehow?" Marie mused. "Why not consult with you?"

"I have no answers for you, Marie!" cried Luc in frustration. "Only more questions of my own!" He took a deep breath and continued. "But no, it wouldn't be a matter for a chemist, if he sought out Chanute. Octave has abandoned the science—he is now among the world's most renowned structural engineers. But why involve me at all? In fact," Luc growled as his expression turned angry, "why not have his *wife* arrange the meeting? Elizabeth knew Chanute in Chicago—he is a patron of the orchestra. Indeed, why not bring his own *goddamn wife* to Paris rather than my daughter—and not get himself killed in the bargain!"

Marie shook her head, as confused as before. "Philippe asked you to arrange a meeting with an acquaintance of Elizabeth's? None of this makes any sense!"

"Nor to me!" cried Luc. "His story was that Chanute would remember him only as the pianist's escort. He wanted a *professional* referral. Imagine!"

Luc leapt from his chair and began his pacing at last.

Realizing she'd pushed her husband as far as he would go, Marie rose from her couch and embraced him.

"My dear Luc," she said. "You are our anchor, aren't you? Our rock. Forgive me. Let's go upstairs to bed. The morning you hope will clear our heads is nearly here. We must rest and be strong for Elizabeth."

Luc turned toward the stairs and sighed again. "Yes," he said dully, "now we must be concerned with Elizabeth."

Chapter Four

Another day, survived.

Elizabeth wasn't certain how she'd managed it, but she sensed days had passed since she'd retreated into her bedroom sanctuary. Her only awareness was of lying on her feather-down bed as the sun made its way across the sky—and of growing apprehension when it disappeared for excruciatingly long periods, leaving her to a dark room swarming with even darker demons. And her demons only grew more ominous with the passing hours, refusing to retreat even as dawn broke anew. Her stomach knotted as she faced another long night ahead.

How many days? she wondered. The two teapots on the sitting room sideboard testified that she would be heading into her third morning since the Massets had settled her as best they could, leaving her entrenched in her cocoon. Even before the bedroom door was closed, she recalled, the deluge of emotions kept in check those first few hours broke free. Had she truly spent nearly three days struggling in vain to compose herself, to stop the tears and the self-recriminations, to form a cogent thought?

At first, it was the grief that overwhelmed her, wracking her body with sobs, spilling tears for Philippe and all she had hoped for their lives together. All of it now truly, finally lost.

Before self-pity could take root, however, contempt plowed its way forward. Contempt for herself, now suddenly the weeping widow merely hours after having chosen to abandon the man—even taking the time to stand before their dearest friends to enumerate his shortcomings. And it wasn't only Philippe she had left behind. Her household, too, suffered her selfish neglect—left alone without direction, only to learn of their beloved master's death from the village washwomen.

Even when Monique came to mind, Elizabeth couldn't summon the anger to derail her bitter monologue. How could she fault Philippe for choosing to leave his selfish, demanding wife at home for a holiday with the beguiling Madame Picard? Elizabeth understood how she, as his spouse, represented obligation and responsibility to her husband, while Monique and the others satisfied his need for excitement and passion. *Each for her gifts*, she thought dispiritedly.

In fact, that Philippe and Monique had been lovers came as no surprise at all to Elizabeth. Not so for the Massets, she recalled, almost in pity. Had they been willingly blind to their daughter fluttering around Philippe at every opportunity, much to his blatant enjoyment? Mademoiselle Masset had once informed Elizabeth that she and Philippe were meant for each other, despite his impetuously bringing home an American wife. Even after she seemingly fell for the sophisticated and wealthy businessman Stephan Picard and became a married woman herself, Monique Masset Picard had made it clear she meant to have Jean-Philippe Devereaux in the end.

And she did.

Elizabeth fended off another outburst of tears by attempting to focus on her responsibilities, on the tasks to be completed as she waited for Philippe's body to be found. Putting the villa and staff in order must come first, she supposed, for Claude, especially. She would have Yvette bring his wages and offers of assistance to his wife in the village. At last: A decision.

Rolling to the edge of the heavy cherrywood bed, Elizabeth pushed a tangled mat of hair from her face. She shuffled over to her dressing table and peered into the mirror. Looking back at her was a pale, gaunt woman, her blue eyes puffy and bloodshot. Slipping down onto the bench, she lit the candle and picked up the silver brush from the table. In the light of the flickering flame, she began to work through the tangles in her thick chestnut hair.

Long, soft strokes of the brush brought the highlights in her hair to prominence, red to match a smattering of freckles. "Speckles," her younger brother John used to say. "Speckled like a bird's egg." John loved brushing her hair when they were little, Elizabeth remembered with a smile. Perhaps there *was* something to return home to, something she felt entitled to enjoy. Initially, running from a failed marriage, she would have been taken in reluctantly. Now, though, John and his wife, Emma, would have no qualms about accepting her as a widow.

A widow.

Would she, as a widow, still be welcomed to perform with the orchestra in Chicago? Of course not. Elizabeth knew there would be little interest at Orchestra Hall for encouraging a bereaved woman to join their company. No matter. Her passage across the Atlantic was indefinitely delayed anyway as she waited for Philippe to be plucked from the river. Whatever awaited her in America, there was no reason to imagine any path forward until she was at liberty to plan for one.

The tangles brushed from her hair, Elizabeth puffed out the candle and stumbled back to her bed. She curled under the quilt, hoping for sleep, and praying to keep the demons from tormenting her, even for a few moments.

An hour later, however, she was still haunted by the harsh, unrelenting critique of her choices. Again, Elizabeth crawled out from under the covers and hunted through the bedstand drawer for a match and her cigarette case. No need to resist the tobacco now. While her husband relished his own pipe, his nose wrinkled at her cigarettes. The memory brought a sad smile, recalling that she smoked to excess on the evenings he was absent, taking pleasure in his disapproval when he returned. She continued her search for a match.

A book...unused stationery...a gun. Elizabeth picked up the cold, shining weapon by its pearl handle and examined it thoughtfully; it was clean and loaded. She retreated back under the down coverlet, recalling an incident she thought long forgotten.

Philippe had given her the derringer, misinterpreting her concern about being alone at night. Target practice was a low priority, she told him when he offered instruction, as her father, a military man, had made sure his daughter's shooting skills were top-notch. Especially at close range. Philippe hadn't gotten her meaning at first—that *he* would have been her target of choice—but, finally, they both shared a hearty laugh. It had even generated a cleansing discussion of their differences, giving her great hope. For a while at least.

Elizabeth pursed her lips as her thoughts returned to the present and an even closer-range target than her unfaithful husband had been. Cradling the pistol to her chest, she stared ahead unseeing, considering an alternative path out of the hell she now occupied.

Clean and loaded.

She pried open the chamber for confirmation, snapped it shut and cradled the gun again, unshaken by the alarming thoughts that arose from deep in her soul. A single shot through the heart would surely end her wait for release. Her finger tensed on the trigger. No more regrets about the career she had given up, however unrewarding; an end to the fruitless pursuit for some greater purpose in her life. The chamber began to turn. No more heartache about what had been lost and what might have been. Just one shot needed. Then they could throw her and Philippe down the same hole and let husband and wife spend eternity working out their problems.

Elizabeth shuddered. *Eternity.* The coward in her could not take control now, she thought. People still relied upon her.

As she placed the gun back into the drawer, a box of matches materialized near the back. She plucked a long, thin cigarette from her case and lit it. Drawing the mellow smoke slowly into her lungs, she was relaxed by the smell of the tobacco as much as by the deep breath. Thoughts of her future edged their way into her consciousness and took hold at last. She had to find the courage to face it.

What to do with the house, and all within it that made it a home? She looked around her own elegantly furnished room—the Louis Quinze chair, the moiré draperies, the silk woven rugs. Beautiful trimmings of the house Philippe had designed to enchant his new wife and keep her content. All so much less meaningful to her than his own presence and commitment, however. Glaring evidence of the lack of understanding between them that had plagued their life together.

That much easier to part with, Elizabeth resolved. She could certainly use the francs it would generate. Sell it all when Philippe's affairs were settled. With Philippe the last of the Devereaux line, the dispersion of the family's considerable assets was her decision alone. But no—there *was* family: the household staff who had cared for them these past years. They would make use of whatever she left behind, she knew.

Yet another decision made.

Nearing the end of her cigarette, Elizabeth considered stepping downstairs to the parlor. An hour at the keyboard—the piano rescued from her poker-wielding rage by the wise Yvette—always calmed her mind and soothed her body. Although never truly moved by music himself, Philippe had instructed the builders to make the room the model of acoustic perfection. And they had succeeded. Her performances there sounded as full and rich as at any concert hall, the chords dancing about the room with those following. The couple's happiest moments together had been in the parlor, filled with colleagues from the school come to hear Philippe talk of his work and to relax as Elizabeth played. A brief thrill brightened her heart as she thought about the duet of her own composition, just completed.

But as she stubbed out the cigarette, snuggling back down into the bed seemed to be the best course of action. Her piece required an accompanist, she thought glumly, a violinist in this case. A violinist with all the passion for his violin that she had for her piano. Elizabeth smiled sadly. How she wished Philippe had played. They could have shared so much, so deeply, if music had been part of their lives together. Perhaps her writing the piece was wishful thinking. Wishing, perhaps, there might be a passionate accompanist someday. And a true partner, in life and love as well as in music…?

But not tonight. Now, all Elizabeth wanted was to sleep, to escape her thoughts, her shortcomings, herself. Whatever delusion had driven her to strive for some meaning, some purpose in life was now exposed as a pipe dream, a castle in the sky. Tonight, her only desire was to escape her demons long enough to rest.

Still later—well after midnight—the tinkle of breaking glass awoke Elizabeth from a fitful sleep. At first, she was confused to be torn so suddenly from wrestling with Monique Masset, to awaken and find her fingers pulling at her own hair. In her dream, the two women had been fighting to join Philippe in his carriage, kicking and clawing each other to get to the coach first. But he had taken off without them. With a heaviness in her chest, she recalled that he had, indeed, left without them both.

Now she heard nothing. But Elizabeth knew the sound had come from downstairs and not from her dreams. She shoved the billowy quilt aside and stepped onto the icy floorboards, first one foot, then the other. Choosing her path carefully, avoiding the boards that squeaked and groaned loudest, she picked her way around the bed and into the chilled and darkened sitting room. Making her way past the chaise and the desk, she reached the opened door. A low scraping sound came from below as she passed through the door to the hallway leading toward the staircase. Someone was entering the villa by the side entrance, near the kitchen.

Elizabeth stepped back into her rooms to get a candle. She would not be terrorized by the local ruffians who vandalized carriage, stable, and home all around Montpellier. She would confront these cowards who attempted to intimidate a woman, suddenly bereaved and alone. They would not go unchallenged here.

Upon returning to the bedroom, however, Elizabeth paused before her bedstand, matches in hand. Coward or no, the intruder might have an accomplice—and they might be armed. She gently placed the matches back in the drawer and eased the derringer from it instead.

Making her way back down the hallway, the cold pistol in hand, Elizabeth could hear muted voices coming from the study. The muffled sound of splintering wood told her the intruders were breaking into Philippe's desk. Her heart pounding in her ears, she tiptoed toward the top of the stairs. Yvette had drawn the thick draperies across the windows and turned down the gas before retiring. All was inky blackness below.

"Who is there?" she demanded boldly, grasping the smooth wide banister for courage.

The murmuring and the splintering stopped.

"I am armed!" Elizabeth called, somewhat less bold. Her shaking fingers managed to cock the pistol in substantiation.

Silence blanketed the house for endless minutes, the clock in the parlor sounding off the seconds. Then, the door to the study burst open; the dark outline of two figures moved quickly toward the steps. Before she could react, a blast erupted from below. The rooms downstairs lit up in the briefest flash, momentarily revealing one intruder already on the staircase. Elizabeth instinctively dropped to the floor at the sound of the shot and pointed her gun down the stairs. The staircase squeaked and groaned as both intruders made their way toward her for a second try. Panting with fright, Elizabeth wrapped her arm around the banister's spindles for stability and imagined her father's calm voice in her ear, repeating the proper sequence during pistol practice. Major Douglas Wellington had believed full-well his daughter would need to be a skilled shot; tonight was not the first time he had been proven correct. She held her breath and fired into the blackness below: Once. Twice.

A startled cry came from mere inches away—the first man had been just before her as she crouched on the top step. He toppled backward, arms and legs sprawling in every direction, taking his associate down the stairs with him. Elizabeth heard them scramble for the front door, the pebbles crunching under their feet as they ran toward the road. She remained crouched at the top of the steps, frozen in place.

Before long the silence was broken by a familiar voice.

"Madame! Madame!" Yvette was making her way through the dark from her own room at the back of the house. "Where are you?" The maid ran about the lower rooms, turning up the gaslights, searching desperately for her mistress. "Are you hurt?"

"Yvette," called Elizabeth, "I am all right." The violent shaking in her hands told otherwise.

The bedraggled Yvette rushed back into the entry and stared up at her mistress, her mouth gaping in alarm. Looking down at her nightdress, Elizabeth saw a spattering of blood along her sleeve.

"I am unhurt," she insisted as her stomach lurched. "This must have escaped the veins of one of our guests."

Yvette bounded up the stairs. When she reached Elizabeth, the maid grabbed her arms, patted her head, touched her cheeks. "You are not harmed," she pronounced. "But so cold!" She moved to guide Elizabeth back to her bedroom.

"I would welcome a wrap," Elizabeth said, her entire body now consumed by the shaking. Nevertheless, she pulled away from Yvette. "Bring one downstairs and I will survey the damage."

"You have neither eaten nor *moved* for two days," scolded Yvette as Elizabeth started down the steps. "Your face is whiter than ash. Back to bed before you faint on the staircase. I will bring your tea."

"I would welcome a wrap…downstairs!"

"Do not enter the kitchen!" the maid called helplessly as Elizabeth continued her descent. "Glass is everywhere!"

Elizabeth tiptoed around the mud the men had left on the carpeted steps. A big man and one smaller, the footprints told her. From the amount of dirt left behind, they must have sunk deep into the garden before entering the house.

The marble floor of the entry hall was painfully cold on her bare feet and Elizabeth's shivering approached spasms. Before she could wish for them, Yvette appeared with her heavy dressing gown and fur-lined slippers. Stepping into the warmth of the slippers and wrapping the gown close about her, she continued to the left and stepped into the study where her husband had often worked late into the night.

With one sweeping glance, Elizabeth took in this room her husband had left only days before and was overcome by his presence. As she scanned the dark wood and muted colors he preferred, the mellow smell of his tobacco filled her senses. Picking up the black clay pipe he had carelessly tossed on the desk before leaving for Paris, she again felt the tightness in her throat and the burning in her eyes she had endured the last few days. Elizabeth cradled the pipe in her palm as she dropped into the armchair at his desk. The comfortable old, worn mahogany armchair, completely discordant with the elegant marble desk, was Philippe's favorite, suffering the angry crashes of his temper and enjoying the absent caresses of his pensive moments. It was here in his study that Philippe was most himself, Elizabeth always said, most the man who had charmed her with his attentions and awed her with his brilliance. Whenever she wandered in and lit the fire to sit with him while he worked, she was most reminded of the talks they'd had back on her father's porch, when he'd convinced her to return with him to France.

Indeed, one evening, they'd sat here for hours, almost until morning, discussing her time with the Chicago Orchestra and her work there, the relationships she'd developed and how they might play into an endeavor he was planning. He'd teased her about Theodore Thomas, the German who'd immigrated to the U.S. and founded the orchestra itself; perhaps she would emulate Thomas by doing the same in France, he'd suggested. She was tickled to learn how Philippe had admired from afar one of her benefactors, Octave Chanute—a chemist who now devoted his life to building bridges and facilitating train travel. She recalled Philippe gently suggesting that Chanute consider the implications of deforestation along the rail routes.

But whenever she asked Philippe about the project subsequently, he would wave his hand in irritation, saying he had no plans, at least none formed enough to explain. Right before leaving for Paris, though, he had suggested the time for explanation was at hand. She would never know, now. How sad such a thing had kept her from her husband during his final days.

Resolutely replacing the pipe on Philippe's humidor, she chuckled darkly. No, it was not insignificant research that had kept them apart. It was a very significant and spiteful Monique, a woman malicious enough to arrange for a telegram to be sent to her lover's wife to document her victory.

As Elizabeth pushed herself away from the desk, her eyes confirmed what her ears had suspected earlier: the intruders had broken into the locked desk and overturned the boxes containing Philippe's correspondence. She looked around more carefully and noticed paintings taken from their places on the wall. Objects that might have hidden something were taken up, examined, and tossed aside.

"Despite the damage they caused, they didn't take much," Elizabeth told Yvette, who had appeared in the doorway. "Will you permit me to see how these gentlemen gained access, now that I am properly shod?"

Yvette stepped away from the mahogany door as her mistress moved back into the entry. Elizabeth scanned the marble floor as she walked, seeing nothing but more mud tracks like those left on the steps. Upon reaching the kitchen, she observed the expected globs of mud and pieces of the glass pane, shattered during the clumsy break-in. Hardly "everywhere" as Yvette proclaimed, a pile of shards had been formed as the opening door swept the glass into a corner. Nothing in this room had been touched, she noted; the intruders had gone directly to the study. Determined, focused housebreakers—if unsuccessful ones—Elizabeth thought. She had seen enough.

"Yvette," she called, slowly making her way toward the stairs. The maid appeared at her elbow. "Please have Lucien spend the rest of the night here on the sofa. We will both rest more easily knowing he watches for our friends' return."

"And then we will contact the police?"

Elizabeth paused, thinking back to her recent experience with the constabulary. "I do not believe that will be in the least bit helpful, Yvette," she said, ignoring her maid's puzzled expression.

As Yvette threw on her cape to rouse the stable hand, Elizabeth longed for the warmth of her bed. The shivering had not stopped, even with her warm robe; she felt weak and lightheaded. Hugging herself, tucking chin to chest, she began ascending the stairs. The crisis now passed, Elizabeth was angry again. What recourse did she have for this violation? Her brush with the local police at the prefecture, and the indifference and incompetence displayed there, had done nothing to reassure her that she could rely upon the agency. What an ordeal to suffer, now of all times. She truly wanted to quit this place.

Suddenly, her eyes fixed upon a small white card lying on the staircase, covered with mud. Picking up the torn scrap, Elizabeth sat down heavily on the top step and studied it. It was a fragment of Philippe's calling card. Elizabeth knew Philippe hadn't dropped it there before his trip; Yvette wouldn't have allowed it to lie there for days. Their midnight visitors must have taken it from the study.

Heading back down the stairs, she went into the study and again opened the rifled drawers of Philippe's desk. They were empty. Righting the boxes that had held his correspondence, she found the papers themselves missing. She flung open the doors of the armoire. Bare. Pulling out the drawers of the secretary, she found those also wiped clean.

It took a moment to sink in.

Every document relating to her husband's work had been taken.

Having dealt with demons of a very real nature during the night, Elizabeth was at last exhausted enough to earn a few hours of dreamless sleep. Rest, however, would remain elusive.

As the sun inched its way above the distant tree line, revealing a crystal-clear morning, she surrendered the effort and climbed from her bed. After pulling a robe over her nightdress, she tiptoed out of her room and into the hallway overlooking the parlor below. Her attempt at stealth was for naught, however, as her maid was already on duty, climbing the stairs bearing her mistress's *café*.

"I am sorry you don't rest, Madame," said the maid as she reached the landing. "A terrifying night, on top of…" Poor

Yvette. Still trying to maintain some order in her own mind and heart as well as in the house. "*Café…?*"

Elizabeth smiled wanly, passing the stairs and stopping in the doorway to her husband's rooms. "In here. Please."

Stepping warily into the room, Elizabeth steeled herself against the waves of emotion she knew waited to strangle her heart. Taking in the dark colors of the walls, carpets, and furniture her husband had chosen, she saw that here too all was just as Philippe had left it, the morning they'd said goodbye. Frozen in a moment when so much had seemed possible, her anguish began to resurface until the uninvited memory of the fateful telegram broke the spell. Perhaps, as it always seemed, none of it had ever been truly possible.

She shook her head to clear her mind of the relentless doubts that plagued her and began pulling boxes from under the four-poster bed, portfolios from the mahogany cabinets, books from the wall of shelves, and more papers from a trunk tucked up against the footboard. After some time, hours it seemed, Elizabeth finally settled on the floor to sip her lukewarm *café au lait* and look around in dismay at the boxes, bags, and trunks containing her husband's personal papers scattered around the room.

What did she hope to accomplish? If there were indeed some intriguing evidence of a world-shattering initiative, ripe for the picking—for the pilfering?—it would surely be here among the papers Philippe had kept closest. But now, with the sparkling morning light beaming in, Elizabeth could no longer fathom that armed men would burgle her home merely for records of her husband's work. Could she have simply interrupted them as they rummaged through the first room they found, looking for valuables? But why indiscriminately clear the room of old paperwork? If they were, indeed, coming for some valuable research, what clues did she expect to find here—and would she recognize the clues if she stumbled upon them?

Before long, she came to understand it was to satisfy her own curiosity rather than find motives for the previous night's break-in that compelled her to begin. Sitting among Philippe's papers, seeing his handwriting, touching his books, breathing in his scent…Elizabeth realized it wasn't questions about the burglary at all that had brought her here. Questions about her husband, her marriage, and the life that was so abruptly, so permanently snatched from her, those were the ones that needed to be resolved. Looking back, perhaps, to find a way forward?

More mysteries, however, more questions, were raised by her search than were answered. Thoughts of the break-in left her mind as Elizabeth was made ruefully aware of how much she did not know about Jean-Philippe Devereaux. Sorting through the contents of his cabinets and boxes, she found herself amazed time and again at her discoveries. So many areas of interest she knew nothing about, boxes and boxes of books she never knew he'd read, souvenirs from places she never knew he'd visited.

A stack of canceled train passes for destinations throughout Ohio and North Carolina puzzled her most; she'd only known of his time in Chicago. Her confusion turned to hurt when she found a recent souvenir: an entry receipt to the 1893 Columbian Exposition, just the previous year. They had visited Chicago together, to welcome John and Emma's new baby girl, Louisa. But Philippe had gone to the World's Fair without her, leaving her at home to stew in bitterness at his penchant for vanishing on a whim.

Vexed anew, Elizabeth abruptly replaced the train tickets and receipt. No need to dwell on what she'd hoped for in that other lifetime. He'd left her behind on so many occasions, in so many ways. Finding more evidence and additional occurrences changed nothing.

Elizabeth's own love of books drew her to look with enthusiasm at the boxes of Philippe's volumes. History was her husband's passion outside of his work and she found dozens of volumes about war and politics and economics—Italy, Germany, Switzerland represented among them. His keen interest in Germany, of course, was understandable; dear friends in Alsace still lived the trauma and upheaval of the war, decades prior, that made them subjects of the German Empire. Among the books she also found notes Philippe had written to himself; names of people, it seemed. Perhaps connections to make during his visits to Germany as he investigated the source of the recent cholera outbreak? The paper those notes were written on intrigued her immediately: thick, smoothly woven paper with the stamp of The Charité, the University Hospital in Berlin. *Sebastien... Otto...Humboldt Platz...Picard...* She chuckled darkly to see that last name listed. Monique Masset's husband, Stephan Picard, was Alsatian. Had Philippe sought his counsel in managing the woman?

Elizabeth sat back on her heels, fondly recalling the handsome, delightfully attentive Stephan Picard. Not a member of the academic community, Picard was a successful businessman who saw to the procurement of many of the university's materials and product needs. He had often been a guest at the Massets' dinners and *soirées*. It was only shortly after Elizabeth arrived in France that Picard had won Monique's hand in marriage. What an unlikely pair, she'd always thought of the Picards: he so warm and personable, she so angry and self-centered. Perhaps it was because of the oddity their union presented that Elizabeth was so intrigued by him and always delighted when Stephan made an appearance at a gathering. More likely, she admitted, it was that he inevitably made his way to her side to commiserate as his wife fussed over Philippe, never failing to charm her with his glowing compliments and lighthearted banter on their shared burden. She thought back to their last meeting, just weeks ago at the Massets' home.

"Madame Devereaux!" he had cried upon seeing her, taking her hand and brushing it with his lips. "May I distract you from my wife's games by escorting you for a breath of air?"

Elizabeth had gratefully accepted the invitation and the glass of champagne Stephan had picked for her from a passing tray. They stepped out onto the back terrace and toasted the nearly full moon.

"You never seem the least bit troubled by her behavior," Elizabeth had said, puzzled. "I envy you your indifference."

Stephan smiled briefly, then brushed back his blond hair and focused his deep topaz eyes on her. Her heartbeat quickened as she recognized something familiar in them. Disillusionment? Melancholy, perhaps? "She is a challenging woman, Elizabeth," he said at last with a sigh. "Single-mindedly focused on what she wants, willing to take whatever steps necessary to get it. I, no less so, I suppose. We are ideally suited…. Heaven help us." He drained his champagne glass.

"Do you fear losing her?"

He cocked his head to the side, his brow furrowed. "Lose her?" Stephan followed Elizabeth's gaze into the parlor where Monique sat, enrapt by Philippe debating his colleagues.

"To Devereaux?" he asked. Realizing she meant exactly that, he let out a sonorous belly laugh, loud enough to bring the parlor conversation to a halt. "I know, I know, your husband plays games of his own. Mere recreation! How could you not recognize his devotion to you? He could never take the games seriously. And risk losing *you*?" Picard smiled and reached for her hand. "I am dismayed their...interactions trouble you."

"Again," she replied, "I envy you your indifference."

Frustrated by repeated advice to accept Philippe's "interactions" as simply a game, she had taken special pleasure in the urgency with which her husband had joined them on the terrace, once he became aware of her *tête-à-tête* with Stephan.

The bittersweet memory brought Elizabeth suddenly back to the present. She looked down at the notepapers in her hands. So much had happened in just a few short weeks. Had Stephan been informed of the accident? How could he look away now from his wife's capers? No matter. There would be no more parlor chats and recreational interactions, now. And she must focus on the task still before her.

Next was a box of papers, with a script in Philippe's own hand and it made Elizabeth's heart swell with pride: his brilliant treatise on phylloxera—the destructive infestation that had wiped out so much of France's wine-producing vineyards over the past twenty years. Ensuring that the cure her husband helped develop was made available to the vintners of the Languedoc region was something Elizabeth had hoped to be part of after their marriage. Phylloxera had been the topic of their first ongoing conversation.

Again, Elizabeth found herself returning to the warm summer nights the couple spent sitting on the hard, dusty wood of the porch steps, gazing at the endless field of stars above them; he explaining the intricacies of the problem, and she marveling at his approach to solving it. How valued she felt as he earnestly explained that grafting healthy American vines onto the diseased plants in France would help them grow strong and begin to fight against the blight. His concern for the vintners and his pride in taking on the crisis were what had intrigued Elizabeth Wellington about Jean-Philippe Devereaux; they were what made her believe he could guide her to a much more meaningful life in Montpellier.

Elizabeth sighed deeply and tried once again to fight back against the reminders that she had continually fallen short in realizing her own dreams. But the smile returned as she came upon a playful essay involving a child's toy. Not a piece of research at all, but an account of the Devereaux's honeymoon trip to the foothills of the Pyrenees, where she had flown a kite. What an exhilarating experience that had been! Reading, she could again feel the wind in her hair and the thrill in her heart as she at last got the kite into the air. She could even hear Philippe laughing with pleasure at her glee, cheering her on. And she could feel again his strong arms secure around her, his rough hands on her skin as he made love to her there on the hilltop overlooking the village. An equally exhilarating experience.

With a lump in her throat, Elizabeth tucked the piece into the pocket of her robe. Next, she came upon a small journal, also in his handwriting, that returned her to Chicago once again. Elizabeth was delighted to find that it documented his time there, immediately before they left as a married couple for his home in France. She read tales of the people she'd introduced him to, his impressions and conversations with people who comprised and supported the orchestra. While performing merely for the pleasure of wealthy, influential people seemed trivial and could never compare to what Elizabeth hoped to find in France, Philippe had taken the time to interrogate and know all those who came to hear her, delving into their interests, their accomplishments, their own hopes. He had been fascinated by them, by their passions and gifts. Now, she was fascinated, even awed, to learn from his words how their gifts had inspired his own.

Poring over each document, Elizabeth was at a loss to find anything here in her husband's work that would inspire burglary. What her investigations *were* inspiring, however, was a new appreciation for who Philippe was and how he worked. Perhaps, even, how she had indeed helped him in his pursuits, although unbeknownst to her. Then, she thought back to the night before he left for Paris. *"…your diplomacy, your connections…"* he had said, crediting her with some ability she had yet to grasp. Suddenly, she needed to know more. More about his work and how she might have helped him. And, possibly…to determine what his latest grand scheme for them had been?

Elizabeth clambered up from the floor and scurried back to her own room, leaving the debris of her husband's papers in her wake. Shedding her dressing gown and nightdress, she reached for her riding outfit. When she heard Yvette removing her *café* from Philippe's room, she called to her.

"Have Lucien bring Cheval to the front garden! I am bound for the university!"

Chapter Five

At daybreak, the University of Montpellier, too, came slowly to life. Lecturers prepared their remarks as students put finishing touches on work to be presented. Word continued to spread about the tragic accident that took the life of a much-loved and much-maligned member of their community. Especially in the university's Institute of Botany, administrators adjusted to a new reality…

A tall gentleman with a long overcoat draped over his thin frame approached the curator's desk at the entrance to the Institute quarters. Offering the most charming countenance he could muster, he addressed the young scholar seated before him.

"My apologies for the intrusion," he said. "I am hoping you might direct me to the offices of Professeur Jean-Philippe Devereaux."

"Yes, of course, Monsieur," the young man began, then faltered. He looked down sullenly at his hands. "You know, of course. About…?"

"About…?" repeated the gentleman, with a puzzled expression.

"Professeur is…gone."

"Disappointing," the man replied. "I wished to discuss an aspect of his work that mirrors my own. Is there a place where I might familiarize myself with his research while I await his return? His office? The libraries?"

"I so regret to say that Professeur Devereaux was killed in a horrific accident, mere days ago."

"Good heavens! I am so sorry to hear. My deepest condolences."

The gentleman frowned deeply, his eyes bursting with sympathy and heartfelt emotion. "How difficult this loss must be for you. For the Institute." And in a lower voice, "For the university."

"Yes, indeed," said the young man softly. "So much to do, so much work ahead of us…"

"However will you manage?" asked the gentleman, just as softly. He shook his head sadly, contemplating the injustice Fate had forced upon them all. He pulled a card from his pocket. "Who will step in and continue Devereaux's important work?"

"As though such a thing would be possible…" began the scholar dismally. "There is no one. No one with Professeur's scope, his vision. No one at all…"

The gentleman let the silence linger.

"Of course," the younger man continued at last, almost reluctantly, "Monsieur Gregoire will be charged with making what sense he can of our efforts. He *may* be of some assistance…"

"Gregoire…?"

"Yes. The Professeur's associate. I believe I saw him heading for the libraries as I came to the front entrance. Perhaps you might find him there. Perhaps he might speak with you…"

"Thank you, sir," the gentleman said with a slight bow of his head. "Again, my sincere condolences on the loss of Professeur Devereaux. A brilliant man. Such a loss…"

Sigerson continued on his way.

❧

Despite Elizabeth's impatience to unearth more evidence of her husband's intellectual pursuits, Yvette would not permit her mistress to leave the house without a proper breakfast, insisting it would be the first solid food she'd taken in days. Once restrained, decisions about household matters, including an update on Claude's stable yet still fragile condition, filled much of her morning.

Later that afternoon, Lucien finally brought his mistress's white Morgan horse around to the front garden gate for her ride into Montpellier. A crisp breeze, cool despite the strengthening spring sun, rustled the ivy-covered fence as he brushed Chevalier down with careful, loving strokes. When Elizabeth stepped out onto the villa's front step dressed in her riding boots, jodhpurs, and cropped jacket, the stable boy flustered as she addressed him.

"Are you well, Lucien?" She brushed back his sandy hair to touch his cheek. "You're so drawn. You got little sleep after our waking you last night, did you?"

He hesitated. "No less than any other night…since…"

"Poor Lucien," Elizabeth said soothingly. She lifted his chin so he would look her in the eye. "I know how fond you were of Professeur. And he was as fond of you—you took good care of him. I know you'll miss him."

"And Claude, too, Madame," Lucien added. "Cook says he won't be coming home, he's too badly hurt. Why has this happened to us?"

"Where does Cook get her information?" Elizabeth asked sternly, although knowing the woman could very well have her story right.

"She's been sneaking into the infirmary, in the evenings." Lucien adjusted the horse's saddle and continued brushing. "She says when he dies, it'll be down as murder. Says it *was* murder with Professeur."

Murder?! "Cook has stones in her head," said Elizabeth, after a moment of stunned silence. "Claude will be home with us soon."

"Pardon, Madame, not home with *us* at all," Lucien muttered, his strokes no longer careful or loving. Chevalier stomped on the budding narcissus, trying to skitter away. "You were leaving us, too. *Are* leaving us. You and Professeur were family…"

Clearly, Cook's tales of murder hadn't made too horrifying an impression on young Lucien; it seemed his deeper concerns were for his broken and mourning family. Elizabeth hugged him fondly. "I am proud to be part of your family," she said, deliberately ignoring his concern about her impending departure. Lucien flushed with pleasure, nonetheless.

How strange to realize, only now, that he had valued her, too. How much she had taken for granted here. This young man, who knew as much as anyone about her, and her home life, didn't think her a failure. He saw her as family. As did Yvette. Then, as if on cue, the maid scurried out onto the whitewashed porch with the expected disapproving glance at her mistress's attire. She threw a heavy cloak about Elizabeth's shoulders.

"You draw unwanted attention to yourself in a man's riding habit," chided Yvette as Lucien busied himself adjusting the saddle straps yet again. "You are alone, now. You would do well to fit in."

All the warm thoughts Lucien had conjured dissipated as Elizabeth dug deep for the patience to cope with her overprotective maid. At times, she welcomed Yvette's assumed guardianship. Today was not one of those times.

"I will never fit in here," snapped Elizabeth, mounting the horse roughly. "And my interest lies merely in taking a comfortable, unencumbered ride into the village. I am not concerned that my appearance is inappropriate to one newly widowed."

Elizabeth snatched the reins roughly from her stable boy's hands, but reached down and tousled his hair. What a sweet, devoted young man, she thought, so much like her brother John when he was growing up. She vowed to be sure he, too, was taken care of when she left. Yes, these people had all been her family here in France. Lucien, Claude, Yvette, even Cook. They would all be cared for when she was gone.

"Madame?" Lucien spoke up hesitantly. Elizabeth paused and turned the horse toward him. "The police, Madame? May I report our intruders to the police?"

She looked skyward, took a deep breath, and repeated what she had told Yvette the night before: that it would do no good. She paused as his face fell. "Ah, do as you wish," she said with a shrug.

Finally seizing control of Chevalier from the boy, Elizabeth kicked the horse into a quick gallop and headed up the dirt path toward the road.

"Alone at last, my sweet Cheval!" cooed Elizabeth to her mount as she eased him back into a walk. "Time for some exercise for you and some air for me."

The half-hour trot north into the village of Montpellier was an uneventful one, except for the thoughts and arguments swirling around in Elizabeth's mind. One week ago, she fully expected to be on her way to America by now.

How long ago last week seemed, she thought, navigating the horse around the muddy puddles that were beginning to harden in the shade of the olive trees she passed. Elizabeth nodded politely to a man dressed in the dark, loose clothes of a vintner, riding in the opposite direction. He raised a weathered hand to his wool cap and pulled it a notch farther down over his eyes.

"So sorry for your loss, Madame," he mumbled, inching his horse onto the stones that lined the earthen path so Elizabeth and Chevalier could pass. She nodded her thanks in return.

Despite the oddly cool temperature for March, the gnarled olive trees were beginning to bud, sending their snappy fragrance wafting through the crisp air. Elizabeth drank in deeply of the breezes that skimmed her cheeks and refreshed her, suddenly feeling less anxious about being out in public, asking questions, even seeing Luc. Perhaps she was ready to take on her new persona.

The widow Devereaux. As a couple on horseback appeared heading toward her, it was Elizabeth's turn to move off the path. Again, she accepted her neighbors' condolences. Would it be any easier to turn to her brother as a widow than as a woman who had left a man he said she should never have married? However bitter John was over his sister giving up her career to join his teacher in France, he would welcome her home again now. Elizabeth would turn to him and his wife as soon after Philippe was buried as possible. While the orchestra may or may not be open to her—she couldn't know until she arrived there—she needed time to heal. Being with John and Emma and their little toddling Louisa would help, and she felt an overwhelming desire to feel the love and care she knew she would find at home with them.

Her discoveries this morning, however, continued to intrude at the edges of her thoughts. Learning more about Philippe's work, about her possible involvement in it, and perhaps the plans he had…Elizabeth believed the knowledge, perhaps the evidence of his faith in her, could help her healing, could perhaps suggest the meaning and purpose she felt missing in her life. She meant to grasp at the fleeting hope the notion gave her.

Now, she had to make quick work of it all this afternoon. America—home and family—awaited.

Clopping through the lush, tree-lined outskirts of the village, then down the narrow, twisting, cobblestoned rue de l'Université, Elizabeth arrived at the school itself. Relieved of Chevalier by the school's stable boy, she headed toward the imposing main building and its entry, surrounded by the palpable energy of students and educators at work. A glimmer of excitement sparked her spirit.

Even when simply stopping to visit her husband, she had always felt a certain sense of belonging here, a warming welcome—if not by the male academics, at least by the atmosphere of intellectual pursuit. The worn stones of the building's facade, the foot-beaten steps, the creaky, heavy oaken doors all gave her the feeling of being in the presence of something bigger, something more important than the unremarkable existence she'd come to live in Montpellier. Even now, walking up and down the maze of corridors toward the library, the sense of underlying anticipation and intrigue grew inside her. Surely, evidence of Philippe's last venture must be hiding on the shelves, just waiting for her to discover it.

As she stepped through the dark wooden arches of the library entrance, the muted sounds of scholarly investigations and the scent of volumes old and new filled her senses. It was some moments before Elizabeth even tried for the attention of the lending desk assistant. Waiting for her request to be filled, she hardly noticed the barely hidden glances at her riding attire: scorn from a lady happening by, leers from the gentlemen patrons. At last, the research assistant returned from fetching Professeur Devereaux's work on file. His look was one of annoyance.

"I'm sorry, Madame," he said. "All of the Professeur's materials have been withdrawn from the shelves. There is nothing for me to give you."

"I don't understand."

"The books, pamphlets, and research papers written by Jean-Philippe Devereaux are gone," the assistant explained slowly, condescendingly. "There is little more to say."

As he moved to help the student next to her, Elizabeth seized his arm. "Gone? But why?" she persisted, her heart racing. "Why would they all be gone?"

With an exasperated sigh, the assistant searched listlessly through a drawer beside him and pulled a card from it. "Perhaps you might ask Monsieur Jon Gregoire. He is the evil culprit who has absconded with the material."

Elizabeth recognized the name of an undistinguished colleague of Philippe's. "I see. Borrowed." *Not stolen at all*, she thought. "Monsieur Gregoire has borrowed the papers."

The student grimaced a sarcastic smile of praise for her deduction.

"*Merci* beaucoup *pour votre aide*," she said to the assistant, with equal sarcasm.

How bothersome, thought Elizabeth as she left the library and wandered once again through the dark and majestic halls of the school, trying to remember which corridor would lead her to Philippe's rooms. Why would

Gregoire choose this moment to go over his colleague's work? The man will be assuming Philippe's role now, she reasoned, and would very much need to know as much as possible about the work his superior had conducted. She did not envy the man. Philippe thought Gregoire a fool and considered the man's own post beyond him. Perhaps not odd at all that the man would want to live and breathe Philippe's words.

Finding the door to the new Institute of Botany, Elizabeth tapped on the etched glass. There was no answer. Before turning to leave, she absently tried the knob and found it unlocked. Pushing gently on the door and stepping inside, she was surprised to see the very Jon Gregoire who filled her thoughts, sitting at her husband's desk.

"Monsieur…?"

"Good afternoon, Madame Devereaux." The portly Gregoire shoved a handful of papers into his valise. "I am sorry for your loss," he grunted, pulling himself up out of the creaking chair with the greatest effort, "if you'll please excuse me…" He attempted to step around her and out into the hallway.

"Thank you, Monsieur," Elizabeth replied, sliding herself into his path. "May I ask your purpose for being in my husband's office?"

"It is my office now, Madame. Your husband no longer has need of it. Uh…rest his soul."

"Nor has he need for his notes, or his published work," Elizabeth said, intently studying his expression. "Is that why you collect them?"

"With all due respect, I am now charged with making sense of the mess he left behind," said Gregoire, beads of sweat forming on his brow from the exertion of standing. "I cannot begin until I decipher what it was he tried to accomplish—and with whom he allied himself." He shifted himself toward the door."

"Just one more thing, Monsieur," said Elizabeth, backing her way to block the exit once more. "You will return the papers taken from this office? The library will track down Philippe's published material, I assume. However, I will need to see his private notes as soon as you've finished with them."

"This office was wiped clean, Madame," Gregoire said, pushing his unwieldy body by her at last. "I found it to be as empty as he was." His voice trailed off as he rumbled down the dim hallway.

"Wiped clean? By whom I wonder?" Elizabeth muttered as she closed the office door behind her.

More dark labyrinths, more hidden doorways. *Wherever was the confounded chemical laboratory?* she fumed silently to herself. And why had Gregoire denied taking Philippe's papers? Why had he cleaned the library shelves of Philippe's work?

"Luc Masset," said Elizabeth quietly as she miraculously stumbled upon the sterile room of chemicals and instruments. "A familiar face in this den of silverfish."

"Madame Devereaux!" Luc got up from his desk and embraced her. "Elizabeth... How do you manage? Once Yvette got you in her clutches, she shooed us away and would let no one near you."

"I manage," she began in a demure undertone. Only one student occupied a table at the far end of the laboratory, but she did not want to be overheard. "I have yet to cope with this horror. But recent circumstances have served to distract my attention."

Luc waited patiently during her dramatic pause.

"I need your help, Luc," Elizabeth said. "I am searching for evidence of the initiative Philippe had in mind for us. I know I discounted the endeavor, before…before we got the news." She shrugged her shoulders listlessly. "Now, I wonder what he had in mind, what role I might have played. It might be the last I have left of him…"

"My dear, dear little one," said Luc soothingly, guiding her to a nearby table. "If the project was on his mind, there would be no evidence of it yet, here."

"Well, yes," she agreed. "Even so, my inquiries at the reference library have produced nothing; the worm Gregoire has taken everything off the shelves. I search more for notes or references to Philippe's work that may be, or may have been, at the school."

"I am quite sure there is nothing other than his published works to be found here, even if they are in Gregoire's possession. Philippe would have kept his most precious, valuable records with him at home. If you find his papers among his personal belongings at home, you will find everything of importance to his work."

Elizabeth sighed in frustration. "I had hoped there would be something here," she said. "A good deal of his papers are…gone. I'd hoped to find some clues here to what they might have contained, in the library or his office."

"Gone?" Luc exclaimed. "Whatever do you mean, gone?"

Elizabeth took a deep breath and held it, knowing her news would not be calmly received. Finally, she exhaled and answered him.

"We had a break-in last night," she intoned dully, looking away. "I interrupted the burglars in their work. They had only time to stuff items from Philippe's study into their bags. Nothing of monetary value, but of great value to me as I attempt to learn of his plans."

She eyed Luc warily as his eyes widened in astonishment and disbelief. "A burglary?! *Mon Dieu*—and *they*?! How many? Were you hurt? What happened? What could they have wanted with Philippe's papers?"

"We are all safe," Elizabeth assured him. "What, indeed, would anyone want with his papers? Local ruffians at work? Times *are* difficult. But today I am finding comfort in learning more about Philippe's research and his plans. Why, suddenly, is there no evidence of his life's work?"

As Luc began to answer, a tall brawny man, clean but more raggedly dressed than the teachers and professors about the school, poked his head in the door and looked at them questioningly.

"Yes, Olivier!" Luc called to him. "What is it?"

"Monsieur Masset, Monsieur Beault must speak with you," Olivier replied, then disappeared.

"I must go…briefly," said Luc. He placed his hand over hers. "I can hardly conjure documents that captured the dervish swirling inside your husband's head…but I shall ponder your plight. You will remain here until I return?"

"Yes." Elizabeth managed a thin smile. "Despite your pessimism." She sat down at the table. Luc, too, forced a smile and went to answer Olivier's summons.

A minute passed. Two. Elizabeth's head pounded, her ears roared, conflicting thoughts clamored in her brain. Philippe dead, but still missing; she a captive, unable to move on with her life until he was found and put to rest. And then? Could she bring herself to leave France before exploring the possibility she may have been helping him organize his thoughts as he approached some problem? A problem she was meant to help solve?

Elizabeth felt a dispirited darkness envelop her as she bitterly admitted the answer was yes. What did it matter the contribution she might have brought, the value she might have added to Philippe's plans? Without him, or some surrogate, she would have no agency to bring whatever it was to fruition. All she felt capable of was escape—to home or anywhere else safe from this horror, where she could try to begin again. Nothing, she resolved, could keep her here a moment longer than it took to find and bury her husband. Her *murdered* husband, Cook's voice interrupted. Because of his work? But what work—and why?!

Elizabeth brought her hands to her head. How long would she be destined to grapple with such outlandish scenarios? How could she leave without finding a resolution to her delusions? *Resolution?* She chuckled grimly, chiding herself for imagining she might have the ability to resolve anything at all! If Luc claimed to know nothing, what hope of resolution could she find on her own?

Resting her head on the table, Elizabeth groaned, the sense of being trapped consuming her—trapped in her mind as well as in France. Images of a life haunted by the events of the past few days swirled around her. She saw herself obsessed, searching for answers that would never be found, asking help of people who would never provide it. All she saw before her was a bleak future and her inability to change it. Fear, hopelessness, and anger overwhelmed her. Without thought, Elizabeth lifted her head, snatched a beaker from the table, and threw it across the room.

The vessel shattered against the wall, sprinkling bits of glass over the work of the forgotten student.

Startled, the man snapped his head up, seemingly unaware that he was not alone. Elizabeth stared into the eyes of a man much older than the typical student; at least 40 years of age, she guessed. Although not at once handsome, the dark, meticulous hair and thin, piercing face gave him an appearance that intrigued her, and was somehow familiar. She was riveted by the intensity of his gray eyes as they locked onto hers.

"An American with a temper," he said, finally releasing her gaze. Looking neither annoyed nor amused, the man stood up tall—at least six feet—and carefully picked pieces of glass from his coat.

"An Englishman with a gift for observation," retorted Elizabeth, embarrassed by her behavior and even more so by his witnessing it. She pushed herself quickly from the table and gathered her things.

"Englishman…?" repeated the man in surprise as Luc Masset reentered the laboratory.

"Oh no, my dear!" cried Luc to Elizabeth. "Again, Monsieur Sigerson visits us from Norway. You made his passing acquaintance mere days ago, outside the prefecture, I'm afraid. Sigerson, may I formally present the most beautiful…"—he eyed the glass shards—"…and fiery Madame Elizabeth Devereaux."

"*Enchanté*, Madame." A polite smile flashed briefly across the visiting researcher's face. "Again, my sympathies."

Although claiming to be Norwegian and speaking in near-perfectly accented French, Elizabeth was certain Sigerson was British. Pasty-white skin at his hairline told her his tanned complexion was unnatural, obtained from extended exposure to the sun; a man much more accustomed to the fogs of London, she surmised. A starched collar and smooth chin belied his attempt to appear preoccupied by academic pursuit. After a pause, she extended her hand in greeting.

"My apologies for…dropping the beaker over your work, Monsieur. Tell me, what brings you to Montpellier, so far from the beautiful fjords of Norway?" This last part spoken with cutting emphasis.

"Coal-tar derivatives, Madame," Sigerson replied curtly as he took her hand briefly, then turned to gather his belongings from the table. "Now, I must be the one to apologize, for I have passed more time here than I wished. Good evening to you both."

"One more thing, Monsieur," Elizabeth said quickly. "Were you by chance acquainted with my husband? Perhaps you visited my home the day he died?"

"I regret I did not have the pleasure of making his acquaintance, Madame."

"I see."

Snatching up his bag and overcoat, the researcher bowed his farewell, leaving Elizabeth and Luc alone in the laboratory.

"Much too regal," mused Elizabeth. "Too self-possessed for a Norwegian."

"Madame, Madame," cried Luc, laughing. "Your stubbornness will be the end of you! You search for secret documents—you badger me when I cannot produce them. You mistake poor Sigerson for an Englishman—you demand that he be! Come, have supper with old Masset. Such a young, beautiful lady at his table would be a delightful gift."

Searching her mind for the reason she could not dine with Luc, Elizabeth came up empty. Yvette was right: she was alone, with nothing to go home to. Her failure to keep Philippe happy made her wonder if it might always be so. She thought of the odd researcher and sighed heavily, startled to realize she regretted not being young nor feeling beautiful.

Elizabeth then thought of her books and the piano she turned to again and again when she felt so utterly alone as she did now. Even imagining herself at the keyboard or paging through her precious volumes failed to create a spark within her, leaving her feeling as though the last dying ember of her spirit was simply beyond rekindling.

"Elizabeth." Luc's voice softly cut through the darkness. "I know this is an impossibly difficult time. But please, do not deprive us of your company so quickly. Marie and I have been overcome with worry about you."

Elizabeth smiled wanly. If her books and music failed her, perhaps company would keep her from the abyss. Being with Luc Masset, basking in his lavishing attentions, was all any woman could want; perhaps only the motherly presence of Marie Masset would improve the scene. As she took Luc's offered arm, the messenger Olivier shuffled his way into the room as he had before.

"Pardon," he said. "I have been asked to inform you that Madame's presence at the mortuary is required. Professeur Devereaux has been found."

CHAPTER SIX

Yet again in the Massets' elegantly appointed carriage, Elizabeth and Luc were rattled across the cobblestones of rue de l'Université, then onto the smoothly paved boulevard de l'Hopital. How odd, Elizabeth thought, peering through the window at the lamplighters beginning their rounds, to be summoned to a hospital, a place dedicated to preserving life, to see a dead man. What matter where Philippe was? He would still be dead, and she would still have to identify him. Whether she did so in a hospital or in the village marketplace, the anguish would be the same.

As the carriage jolted to a stop outside a darkened door on the side of l'Hopital General, Elizabeth took a deep, shaky breath. She tried to envision herself climbing back into her seat, the late afternoon sun completely set, this ghastly task complete. But as she resumed her uneasy breathing, she knew it all lay before her. Philippe lay before her. The man she had vowed to love forever—and then vowed to leave. Now she had to look down upon that man in death and feel the pain and regret of not having found some way to forge the partnership she was coming to believe they both had so dearly desired.

If only someone else would do this part. If only she could just turn and run, leave it all behind her.

Luc helped Elizabeth down from the carriage, then guided her up the small, half-height steps to the door. The crisp spring air carried the aroma of crocus to her nostrils and tempted her to remain outside, among the budding display around the door. Luc's hold got slightly firmer as she hesitated, and suddenly, they were inside the building.

"This way, Monsieur," said the attendant when Luc informed him who they were. Elizabeth silently thanked the young man for not acknowledging her, however such slights typically infuriated her. Today she hoped to fade into the walls, hoped they would forget her, hoped this ordeal would all end somehow without her participation. It almost seemed to be happening just as she wished.

"Where was he found?" Luc quietly asked the physician who came to escort them to the morgue itself. "Who brought him here?"

"A younger man, not of the village," came the reply. "He'd been fishing in the river, on holiday. Found the body lodged in the reeds where the river turns sharply. Surprising the authorities did not find it earlier…" The man continued on in grisly detail, describing the broken and decayed condition of the body, the second-rate recovery methods. At last, Luc silenced him by inclining his head toward Elizabeth.

"Yes, of course," the medic murmured. "Forgive me."

The trio continued down a long, dark hallway, in silence but for the thud-thudding of their boot heels. Attempting to forget their mission, Elizabeth concentrated on her surroundings, noticing the layers of dust on the gas lamps overhead and the sharp, sickly smell of chemicals that assailed her nostrils. Housekeeping here would not be a concern, she realized forlornly. No one with reason to walk these halls would be offended by the cobwebs or the stench. Their minds would be occupied by more dreadful chores and responsibilities. At the door of the morgue, Madame Devereaux and Monsieur Masset were asked to sit and wait as the coroner finished preparing the body for identification. Madame was appreciative of yet another reprieve.

Then Elizabeth suddenly found herself holding a pouch; in it were the items Philippe had with him when he was found. She sank into the offered seat and began to untie the leather strap around the burlap bag, aware of Luc sitting nearby in support yet looking away in discretion. Her stomach knotted. But how could examining the common, everyday things Philippe had owned upset her now? She'd been at that very task all day, hoped she'd become hardened to it already.

Elizabeth paused, recalling another time she was asked to examine a dead man's belongings: her father's. That experience, shortly before she met Philippe, had shattered her. With her brother away at college, it fell to Elizabeth to go through the many things that had made that man the father she adored: his pipe, his books, his diary. A locket with her late mother's picture had only intensified her sense of loss. She had not been in the bowels of a musty mortuary that time, she remembered, but in the hot sun outside a military encampment. Could this time be as traumatic as then? With her father, at least, there was no corpse to identify; the natives who had allegedly killed Major Wellington had not left a body behind. At least the feeling of abandonment was less today. Her father's death had left her truly alone for the first time in her life. Her husband's passing only finalized the loneliness she had felt for years.

Returning to the present, Elizabeth saw a gold, deeply dented pocket watch spill out of the bag first—a wedding gift from his bride. Adhered to the inside cover of the watch would be a picture of Elizabeth; she felt a small sense of satisfaction, imagining Monique Masset seeing the image of her lover's wife whenever he consulted the time. Unable to force it open, she continued to the remaining items. An unfamiliar brown leather pocketbook, bought in Paris, perhaps; a few francs; and some notepaper with smeared scribblings were the only things left of her husband.

"Can this be all?" she murmured. Luc did not respond. Elizabeth tucked the items into her own handbag, becoming aware of another, deeper level of emptiness descending upon her.

Finally, the coroner was ready, and they were summoned inside. Three bodies, respectfully covered with white sheets, lay upon slabs in the wide, sterile room. Becoming absorbed in considering the sickness or accident that took their lives, Elizabeth reluctantly followed Luc and the coroner past the first two shrouds to the third body, the one that concerned them. She steeled herself as the doctor roughly pulled the sheet back from the dead man's torso. Gasping, she looked down at the swollen, starch-white face staring up at her with lifeless eyes. She buried her head in Luc's shirt.

"His eyes," she whispered. Philippe's blue eyes had been the most striking she had ever seen. She couldn't look into them like this, gruesomely sunken and clouded.

The coroner passed his hand over the corpse's face and the eyes were closed. Luc eased Elizabeth around to look at the body again. This time she noticed the bruises around the face, the misshapen head. What a horrible fall it had been, she thought, hoping he hadn't suffered the pain these injuries evidenced. Even his strong, square jaw was askew. She reached out and touched his black hair, his beautiful thick hair. Her lip began to tremble.

"Is this your husband?" asked the coroner brusquely. Elizabeth heard nothing as she ran her eyes along the dead man's wrinkled, mottled skin, reaching for a scar that had so disturbed her proud husband. Philippe was sensitive about the ugly mark on his shoulder, evidence of a riding accident years ago. His wife had teased him, claiming to find it a welcome sign that he was not perfect, a mere mortal. *How very mortal,* she thought sadly. "For the official record, is this Jean-Philippe Devereaux?"

As Elizabeth took a breath to say that it was, she realized the scar was not there. There were no marks on this body, no signs of the surgery Philippe had undergone. Although similar in appearance, this man could not be her husband.

"Elizabeth?" Luc guided her toward the room's only chair and undid her scarf. "I'm so sorry, my dear, but the doctor needs to hear you say that this man is Philippe. Just say the words for him and we can leave and then this nightmare can come to an end. Elizabeth, do you hear me?"

Still stunned, Elizabeth managed to focus on her friend and realized Luc believed the body before them was Philippe's. He would not think of the scar. The distorted features of the corpse certainly resembled her husband; indeed, until failing to find the familiar mark, she too was convinced. Now, whether or not the law ruled Philippe officially dead rested solely upon her identification.

"No, no, no!" cried Elizabeth, dropping her head into her hands. *What of his belongings?* she thought. *How could this man have Philippe's things?* But were they his things? She wasn't even sure! What was happening?

"Sweet Elizabeth," whispered Luc, taking her in his arms and rocking her gently. "Such a horrific end...our dear Philippe!" He broke down into tears himself.

Over Luc's gasps she heard the coroner repeat his question once more and she knew she had to act. Something terrible was happening and whatever it was, whoever was responsible, Elizabeth was shaken to her marrow in terror. She must get away to safety—immediately—and she saw escape before her: escape from France, escape from this atrocity and its relentless unfolding. Elizabeth took a deep breath and raised her head.

"Yes," she said to the coroner, softly and without regret. "This is my husband, Jean-Philippe Devereaux."

∾

Back in Luc's carriage, Elizabeth rested her head on the windowpane. She tried not to think of the man in the mortuary, who he was and why he seemed to have Philippe's belongings. The thought terrified her. When the attendant had presented her with a package containing "Philippe's" clothing, she told him to burn it. She did not want to know if this man also wore her husband's clothes. The only thoughts she would allow herself were of sitting on the deck of a steamship headed for America. Even if troubles of another kind waited back home, they couldn't be as horrible as those she knew here. She was determined to end her time here quickly, making plans to bury the body she'd identified as soon as was practical. No project or plan of Philippe's, however meaningful, was worth remaining here to investigate. Not when some grisly plot seemed underway. She couldn't be caught up in it any further.

"We will take you home," Luc was saying, composed and supportive once more. "I assume you would shudder at the thought of spending the night with us."

"I will stay in my own home tonight," Elizabeth concurred, resolving to ride Cheval back even though her head spun with lightheadedness. Still, she would see herself lying in a ditch beside the road before sleeping under the same roof as the Massets' eldest daughter. "I will accept your offer for supper, however; at least a nibble to sustain me for the ride. I am not long for this place, my friend. Once Philippe is put to rest, I shall leave for America."

"We will discuss your plans over a hearty meal, then," Luc said. "It is never wise to make significant changes during a crisis. You need to settle yourself for a bit, bring some order back into your life."

Elizabeth stared ahead in silence. A cool glass of wine would bring all the order she needed at this moment. Considering the vintage and how to include a cigarette in her orderly scenario, she was lulled into thinking the morning could very well bring a day where she might gain some control…of herself and her life. Arranging her departure would be her highest priority.

"And what of your many questions this afternoon?" Luc asked suddenly in a mischievous tone. "You would leave Montpellier without solving your little mystery? Without uncovering Philippe's scheme or determining why some local ruffians would want his scrap papers? Surely, this curious cat could not abandon such a puzzle!"

"I do not care who wants Philippe's scraps, if indeed that was the intent of the burglary. I do not care why. I want to be home." Elizabeth regretted the harshness of her voice, but it wasn't to be hidden. Better, too, to display the harshness than the fear.

Luc patted her knee and sighed deeply. "Forgive my selfishness. This has been a frightful time, I know. You are indeed entitled to be home with your family. That is where you *should* be. You need them now."

Elizabeth was silent. Wanting nothing more than to flee, she was nonetheless haunted by her deed at the morgue. Unwelcome thoughts barraged her mind. Where Philippe? What would happen when his body finally surfaced? The police would surely question her, demanding she explain how and why she could have made such a mistake. But she would be long gone by then, Elizabeth decided with surprisingly little guilt. Long gone. Selfishly dismissing thoughts of an anxious family, waiting in dread for news of a missing father or brother, she pretended to have no answer for them. At least, no answer that would further her own purposes—or keep her safe from an unimagined terror that lurked beyond her ability to fathom.

Then, even more appalling thoughts took over.

Did someone intentionally stage the recovery of Philippe's body? Rather, a body they wanted to be identified as Philippe's. Why? To have her and the authorities believe he was found and end the search? Had they found the body themselves—*was* it his watch?! —and there was reason to want it left undiscovered? To cover up that he had, indeed, been murdered? None of it made sense in the least! Why… Elizabeth's heart stopped cold. A loud ringing tolled in her ears and her fingers and toes became tingly. She felt herself sliding down the smooth leather of the carriage bench.

Her next sensation was of Luc's arm around her shoulder and the taste of brandy on her lips.

"Madame!" said Luc, taking a swig from his pocket flask himself before re-plugging it and replacing it in his coat. "Such a delicate flower you've become… We must feed you at once or you will fade away before our very eyes!"

Elizabeth resettled on the bench, forcing herself to consider again the thought that had nearly put her into a dead faint. "I suppose…" she began, hesitating as she attempted to keep her panic under control. "I suppose it was foolishness to hope he might have survived…"

Luc squeezed her hand and nodded. "I, too, held out hope," he said softly. "Everyone has assured me—police, medics, family—it was impossible. The river is too shallow under the Arneau. From the bridge's height, he would have been dashed onto the rocks from wherever he fell." There was a catch in Luc's voice as he stifled a sob. "You saw him…"

Yes, I saw him, Elizabeth thought. *I saw someone.* Somehow, hearing that her husband couldn't have survived such a fall did nothing to allay her fear or guilt. Something was very, very wrong.

It was not long before she felt the carriage jolt to a halt; within moments the driver was opening the door and helping her down. Luc followed. As if in a dream, Elizabeth floated into the inn and was seated at a table set for supper. Before she realized it, a glass of Vouvray chenin blanc stood before her, awaiting her appraisal.

"To Jean-Philippe Devereaux," toasted Luc softly. "A brilliant man with a set of very human shortcomings. May he rest in peace."

"To Philippe." Elizabeth raised her glass in the name of her dead husband. *And to the unfortunate man who takes his place tonight*, she thought with a cringe.

Luc shrugged his shoulders as his nose wrinkled in reaction to the bitterness of the wine. "I am afraid it will be some time before we can once again take a fine vintage for granted here. Shall we try something else?"

They decided their luck would probably remain the same.

The meal passed quickly as Elizabeth picked at the steaming pheasant before her, concentrating her attention on the wine carafe and the noisy antics of the pub patrons. At first, believing no heartache too great to be eased by a shared glass of wine, however inferior, Luc indulged her. But as his dinner guest silently sipped away glass after glass, he became concerned.

"Your plans to ride home become less realistic with each taste, Madame," he chided her gently. "I will have to send you away in my carriage and have your Chevalier boarded in the village for the night."

"I am perfectly capable of riding, Monsieur," Elizabeth retorted, although finding it necessary to carefully enunciate each word. "In fact, I feel so physically adept, I may just decide to entertain this peasant crowd. Introduce them to the ethereal beauty of chamber music, perhaps." She glanced toward the piano at the center of the pub. "Elizabeth Wellington Devereaux gives a farewell concert."

"You've had a great deal to drink, Elizabeth," cautioned Luc. "Perhaps it's time…"

He was interrupted by a visitor looming over their table: his daughter, Madame Monique Picard. After acknowledging her father with a curt nod, the young woman gazed down at Elizabeth with an insolent sneer.

"Monique, dear," said Luc, looking about for her husband. "You shouldn't be here, unescorted. If Stephan is still away, will you come home with me?"

"I regret your learning about Philippe and me in this way," Monique said to Elizabeth, ignoring her father. "I'm sure it came as a tremendous shock. Had it not been for this tragedy, we would have revealed ourselves to you upon returning from Paris."

Elizabeth sighed deeply, annoyed by the intrusion upon her tipsy contemplation of the intended concert.

"Why, yes, Monique," she replied at last, looking suddenly puzzled and taking another sip of her wine. "It did indeed come as quite a shock. I truly thought it was Simone who joined Philippe in Paris; I am certain she was to accompany him. Were you a last-minute stand-in?"

Monique's face flushed scarlet. "Philippe and I were in love!" she cried. "He was about to leave you."

"Monique…" Luc tried again.

"Of course, of course," Elizabeth said with a smile, waving her hand dismissively. "In truth, none of his…diversions…kept him from coming home, no? Philippe leave me? For you?" She summoned up her heartiest laugh as Monique turned her back and scanned the room. "And Monique? Please don't breathe a word of our talk to young Simone." Elizabeth glanced toward a table near the fireplace where the girl sat at that moment. "She's so sweet and sensitive. It would crush her to know Philippe spent time…with the likes of you."

"Go home, Elizabeth," hissed Monique. "You were never welcome here, least of all now." As she stomped toward the fireplace to confront her "rival," Elizabeth stole a quick look toward Luc.

"I apologize," she said.

"The girl has been a heartless shrew since that Alsatian she married spends more time abroad than at home," replied Luc in absolution. "She wanders off by herself for weeks, even months at a time. I don't know her anymore."

Elizabeth mumbled unintelligible words of reassurance. They both smiled. "Now, for my recital?"

The weary piano in the center of the inn parlor was hardly the magnificent instrument that stood in her home; the keys were chipped and gouges of wood were taken from the boards. But, while the wine might have slurred her speech and clouded her sight, it only loosened her fingers and freed her hands. Performing flawless glissandos to familiarize herself with the feel of the keys, the heavenly sounds Elizabeth Devereaux brought from the piano evoked a respectful silence from even the villagers who had only come for their nightly fill of ale.

As she played, Elizabeth's spirit left the foul-smelling pub, nasty Monique, and unfriendly France itself, to wander on the cool shores of Maine in the United States, as she had done as a child, vacationing with her parents. The pounding chords of Chopin's *Polonaise* accompanied the surf as sea met the rocky New England coast in the recesses of her mind. Then onto the *Minuet* by Mozart and she was suddenly being swirled around a ballroom by a tall man in evening clothes. Her eyes shot open, unable to identify her dance partner.

As Elizabeth finished the piece, her eyes came to rest on a familiar face: Sigerson, the Norwegian researcher. He sat alone at a small table with a pint before him, untouched. His dreamy eyes were fixed on her, his lips set in an introspective smile. As the final chords faded, Elizabeth watched her admirer start, as if breaking from a trance, and give his ale the attention it was due.

With the brief performance over, the pianist returned to her table to take another drink herself, but thoughts of her audience of one remained. How pathetic, Elizabeth thought as she swallowed another mouthful of the bitter wine, to be so touched by the admiration of a stranger. Philippe had never looked at her as that man had. Not because he was lost in her music, not because he thought her beautiful, not for any reason at all. Though she had longed for it to be so, Elizabeth had to admit, neither had she ever looked so at Philippe.

"Elizabeth, you have passed beyond the point of enjoying a mediocre bottle of wine," said Luc, putting the carafe out of her reach.

"I am enjoying both the wine and the company," she said. "And the company is enjoying me." She leaned conspiratorially toward Luc. "I believe your researcher friend Sigerson is smitten by me."

"Sigerson?! Now I *know* you've had too much wine!" Luc chuckled heartily. "Were you a particle of coal dust, I might consider the claim. But that man is as cold a fish as I have ever come across. I assure you, he notices nothing beyond his lens—not even a woman as beautiful as you, my love."

"Well," replied Elizabeth, between spurts of giggling, "perhaps if I sharpened my *repartée* on the subject of coal tar…"

They both laughed: he at the idea of her attempting to catch the notice of the contemplative academic; she, uneasily, that such an idea would occur to her at all. Suddenly, Luc's eyes shot toward the door; Elizabeth's followed. For no reason she could explain, her heart sank. The object of their amusement was leaving the pub—with Monique Picard hanging on his arm.

Elizabeth pursed her lips and reached for her wine glass. Luc quickly filled it from the water pitcher, and she peered at him over the rim as she sipped. After some moments of deep breaths, Elizabeth replaced her glass on the table and dabbed her eyes, horrified to realize she'd started to cry.

"I have a confession," she said at last. "Please don't judge me as harshly as I deserve."

Luc put his hand over hers. "Please, Elizabeth. You've had a harrowing week…and much wine this evening. You need to end these recriminations—and to end this day." He pushed his chair from the table and began to rise.

"It was not Philippe at the mortuary!" she blurted—and the floodgates burst. Elizabeth buried her face in her handkerchief, trying to muffle her sobs.

Luc stopped halfway to standing, then slowly returned to his seat with a heavy sigh. He sat patiently while Elizabeth wrestled with her crying jag and tried to catch her breath to speak. As the minutes passed without success, he leaned forward and took her hand in his.

"Elizabeth," he said. "Please come home with me. Marie would give the world to have you with us. She…"

"I said it was him, but it couldn't be…it's impossible!"

"I know…I know," Luc said soothingly, handing her his own fresh handkerchief. "It's just too horrible to comprehend. Too unthinkable to accept."

"No. You misunderstand!" She took a deep breath. "It wasn't Philippe's body. It was some other man, someone without a scar. I said it was Philippe because I was afraid. I have to escape, to get away! But where is Philippe? What if he is still alive? We must find him!"

Luc's eyes widened in horror as he watched his friend unravel before his very eyes.

"Elizabeth!" he cried. "Where do you get such ideas? As much as I had prayed for some miracle, I saw Philippe on that slab. It crushes my heart—but it's true. He's gone."

"No. That man hadn't the surgical scar that was on Philippe's shoulder. It was not my husband's body."

Luc bowed his head and reached out to take Elizabeth's hand yet again. "I'm so sorry. If only it could be true. In actuality, the damage done to his body, especially to the skin, after a brutal fall and days in the river…"

Elizabeth sat in silence, dumbfounded. Luc didn't believe her! How could she undo what she had done without his help? "He had no scar."

"So much could have shifted, broken down, washed away. Please. Let's not dwell on these gruesome details. I only wish what you say could be true."

Taking a deep breath and blowing her nose into Luc's handkerchief, she wondered, even hoped: could he be right? No matter; he wasn't giving any credence to her claim. And whether Luc was right or not, Elizabeth knew she had already given her friend cause to be deeply concerned for her state of mind—and continuing along these lines would bring about more problems than assistance.

"Grasping at straws, I suppose," she said, wiping her eyes. "I know you don't blame me."

"Not in the least, my dear," said Luc, rising once again. "Not in the least."

CHAPTER SEVEN

Not long after Monique and Sigerson made their exit and Elizabeth made her unaccepted confession, she found herself outside the inn, awkwardly attempting to mount her horse. Despite the exhibition she presented, she was grateful to be on her way.

The wine and the pub had lost their appeal. The alcohol had turned against her, making her feel as though she moved through quicksand, her extremities unable to efficiently obey her commands. The inn's patrons, too, had turned on her—the one who intrigued her having chosen the company of the one she loathed. Then, trying to unburden her guilty conscience, her dearest friend merely made her question her own sanity. At last, finally managing to place herself in the saddle, she was at least thankful for her riding outfit and for not having to watch the spectacle she presented.

"You are well enough to ride?" asked Luc, sounding anxious as he was forced to witness that very spectacle. Without a moon, the narrow roads were nearly invisible; the misty rain that had fallen while they were inside might even have made them dangerous in spots. A stiff gust of wind carried an oddly familiar odor and even greater apprehension. "I implore you, again: please come back to the house." He paused. Sighed. "It appears that Monique will be occupied elsewhere this evening."

"I am quite all right," insisted Elizabeth. She leaned forward and patted her horse's neck. "Besides, Cheval knows the way better than I. My task will be only to hold on and let the cool night air clear my head." She smiled and blew a kiss to her friend. As she trotted down the road, she could not see him shake his head sadly.

"'Til tomorrow," Luc murmured, "which will bring you more than an aching head, I'm afraid. Arrangements must be made…"

Chevalier, as foretold, had a successful time navigating the slick and muddy paths, luckily for his woozy mistress. He trotted gently toward home, through the trees, the rutted paths and underbrush, all with the smoothest movements to keep his rider situated. Elizabeth, contented by a wine-infused bloodstream, bobbed and rocked with her mount, dreaming of the breathtaking views enjoyed as a young girl riding through the countryside on outings with her family. The endless, infinite sky; the wondrous, mysterious mountains and bluffs; the icy splash from the cold-water springs after a sweltering climb.

A trip to her girlhood home in Illinois would come soon, now. She would head there in hopes of gathering the strength to make a new life for herself. But could she leave Montpellier and its secrets behind and truly embrace that quest? Shut out her seemingly unhinged belief that it was not her husband she had identified at the morgue? Elizabeth shook her head, trying to clear her thoughts. She had started this day hoping to learn more about Philippe's work and how she might have contributed. But there was no project, no great global initiative. Was there? Just a fat, lazy academic hoping against hope to learn how to fill a role far beyond his capabilities…

With that thought came the inkling of a burden lightened. No project, no villains searching for Philippe's work. No nefarious agents presenting dead bodies for inaccurate identification. Her thoughts jumped once again to her departure.

"Oh, Cheval," she said. "If only you could navigate the labyrinth of my scattered brain as well as you manage these paths!"

Chevalier clopped on.

Nearly home, Elizabeth felt a cold blast of wind intrude upon her fuzzy-headed reveries, and she was suddenly startled to notice the brightening sky. It *couldn't* be morning. She fought frantically to recall the events of that evening. Despite the lengthy supper with Luc, it didn't take all night. Further, she was heading south—the sun would not rise dead ahead. At last, her faculties now razor sharp, she noticed that the light was moving in quick spurts, first advancing, then receding. Something was terribly wrong. She kicked Chevalier into a quick gallop to reach the clearing.

She was staggered by the scene: the house ahead—her home—was engulfed in flames.

"Yvette!" cried Elizabeth. She pushed her horse for all he was worth, willing him to run even faster. When they reached the path leading to the front door, Chevalier reared up and rotated on his hind legs; he would go no farther. Elizabeth slid off his back and tumbled to the ground, picked herself up and pushed her way through the gate. "Yvette!"

As she approached the front door, the heat became too intense, the smoke too powerful. Elizabeth ran to the side. With the fire concentrated in the front of the house, the kitchen door was the only chance of gaining access. For the second time that evening, she was grateful for her unconventional choice of attire. Elizabeth grasped the porch rail and kicked at the board Lucien had nailed to the window to replace the glass broken the night before. The wood cracked. Two more swift kicks splintered the board, enabling her to reach through and unlatch the door.

Smoke surrounded her, blinded her, and took her air. She stumbled forward and fell to the floor. Coughing, Elizabeth crawled sightlessly on her hands and knees, feeling her way toward the entryway and Yvette's bedroom. Then, she heard choking sounds behind her. *Yvette!* Elizabeth had fallen over the maid upon entering the kitchen. Breathing in more of the deadly smoke, she was just able to stand up, crouch over the unconscious woman, and with a strength that surprised her, lift Yvette and carry her into the cold night air.

"Breathe, Yvette! Breathe!" Elizabeth shouted as she laid her maid on the cold ground, safely away from the blaze. She grabbed the young woman by the shoulders and shook her. "Please breathe! Please be all right!" Elizabeth sat on the ground and held Yvette's head and shoulders in her arms. The woman suddenly began to gasp for air. She coughed once, twice, then vomited—all over her mistress.

"Thank God!" cried Elizabeth, hugging Yvette as she choked, attempting to take in air. "Where is Cook? With her sister tonight?"

Yvette nodded weakly as she pushed herself away from Elizabeth. Resting on her hands and knees, the maid took deep, luxurious breaths.

"Lucien," Yvette managed to blurt out before another fit of coughing, then sobbing.

"Lucien?" repeated Elizabeth. She jumped up and ran for the door again but halted and turned at the sound of Yvette's voice.

"Dead."

"I can find him, too," replied Elizabeth weakly, turning again toward the house. She did not move, however; Yvette's face told her it would be of no use.

After some moments, the maid was able to speak again.

"Not by fire," she said, her words punctuated by coughing and gasping. "He tried to stop them. They killed him."

"I don't…"

"They came back to finish their work. He tried to stop them. They killed him. They set the study afire."

They. The men who had broken in last night, the ones Lucien had watched for until morning, and about whom he had begged her to call in the officials. Elizabeth sank to the ground in horror as the reality hit home.

"Where is he?" she asked dully, feeling the bile build in her throat.

"He found the men in the study. I saw one crush Lucien's skull."

Yvette struggled to her feet, fighting with the folds of her nightdress. Tears leaving white traces down her soot-stained face, she stumbled toward the road. "They will come for me, too," she said in a monotone. "I must get away. My brains can be spread about as easily as Lucien's…"

Elizabeth crumpled further to the ground, hands to face, hardly aware of Yvette, of the cold, even of the fire. Lucien! The sweet boy who had cared for Chevalier like his own child, who had looked up to his mistress and had trusted her. Beaten to death, defending her property because she would not go to the police with him and insist on their protection. Lucien…

Yvette!

Elizabeth snapped her head up and saw the dazed young woman stumbling down the road, away from the village. She realized they could both be in danger, now. *They* might still be nearby, waiting to see their job complete. Swallowing the panic, Elizabeth clambered to her feet and sprinted after Yvette. When she reached her, she grabbed the maid's arm.

"Are you able to ride Cheval with me, Yvette? We'll head back into the village and find a warm place to stay. Come, let me help you into the saddle."

Yvette looked at her mistress with unfocused eyes. "I have friends here, Madame. The villagers are my people. You go stay at the hotel with those who are worthy of your company. They will find you and beat you to death. As for me, I will be safe, hiding among the peasants."

Her words stung like an icy slap, but Elizabeth took it without flinching. More fuel to the fire she tormented herself with made no difference now.

Yvette had turned from her mistress and was erratically shuffling down the road in her bare feet, still headed away from the village in her confusion. Elizabeth reached her and grabbed her by the shoulders.

"You will come with me, Yvette d'Etiveaud," she said sternly.

"I will be safe, hiding among the peasants…"

Elizabeth raised her hand and struck Yvette's face with a sharp slap, and the maid sank to the ground. The woman appeared to be unconscious for a moment and her mistress feared they were no better off than before. A minute later, the sounds of soft weeping came from the huddled mass in the mud.

"Madame," Yvette whispered. "Please forgive me…I…"

"Get up, Yvette," Elizabeth interrupted her. "Get up on Cheval. We must take you someplace warm." As the maid coughed and vomited once more, her mistress's confidence in getting the woman to the village sank further.

At that moment, a horse-drawn cart came into the clearing and Elizabeth reached down to seize the moaning, weeping Yvette and run for cover, but it was too late. The driver pulled up next to them, bundled in an overcoat, face shadowed by the brim of his hat.

"Is she hurt?" he asked in a stoical voice, looking down at Yvette. Then, glancing toward the burning house, "Is anyone inside?"

Elizabeth looked up into the cold eyes of Monsieur Sigerson. She felt the hairs on her neck stand on end and her mouth go dry.

"Yes, and yes," she replied curtly to control the tremor in her voice. "The first situation requires immediate attention, if you are willing to provide it. The second is beyond intervention."

Sigerson quickly jumped down, picked Yvette up and effortlessly swung her onto the seat beside his own. "Madame," he said, eyeing the white horse in the distance, "I will drive this woman to the physician in Montpellier. You will follow?"

"No, Monsieur," said Elizabeth, deciding Yvette shouldn't suffer a drive back to the village. "My maid needs to get warm immediately. Once she is safe, we can summon medical attention. In which direction are you headed? Surely, we can find someone to care for her without taking you out of your way."

"I am headed west, toward the cottage I have taken about a five-minute ride from here," he said slowly. "There are no homes along the way. You will find no help in that direction."

Elizabeth's pulse quickened: he lived so close, and yet she had never seen him before. Suspicion began to mingle with an intense curiosity. Could his presence—here in Montpellier, now since Philippe's death—be coincidence? She had little faith in coincidence. Why, then, was such an outrageous plan formulating in her mind?

"So close! How fortunate!" she heard herself say. "I will wrap Yvette up there and give her something warm to drink while you get help. We are lucky indeed that you happened along."

Monsieur Sigerson did not concur.

"Madame," he called after Elizabeth as she trotted toward Chevalier. "Such an arrangement would be completely unacceptable. I occupy the cottage alone. There is no household staff to attend to…ladies." This last word spoken as though he'd been asked to accommodate an infestation of vermin.

"Oh, no matter," Elizabeth called back from the saddle. *Definitely British*, she thought. "We hardly need a tea laid out." She kicked Chevalier into a gallop and headed west, ignoring her qualms about the consequences this latest decision might bring.

The sole resident of the cottage less than a kilometer away, with his tearful passenger, was compelled to follow.

Indeed, the Norwegian's home was a very short distance away. Arriving before its resident and her patient, Elizabeth turned Cheval back in the direction she had come and watched the flicker of the dying flames that had just destroyed her own home. The home she had poured so much love into, hoping love would grow from it in return. The beautiful garden she had tended, the piano she had neglected these past months. Everything that had been good and bad about her marriage, her life here, gone with the ashes that were beginning to drift back to earth. And worst of all, Lucien, she thought, her throat constricting.

Suddenly, Elizabeth's back went rod-straight in the saddle as the realization struck: They—last night's housebreakers, Lucien's murderers—*were* looking for something of Philippe's. They hadn't gotten what they wanted and returned, killed Lucien as he tried to stop them, then burned the house to cover the deed. The thought took her breath away.

Elizabeth gasped, trying to slow her racing heart, to quell the rising fear. As she dismounted her horse, horrific thoughts, scenarios, and speculations about these men swirled inside her head. What had they sought? Something valuable enough to warrant taking a life! *"It'll be down as murder when Claude dies,"* Cook had told Lucien. Had Cook's talk of murder been more than just talk? Had Claude seen something before falling from the carriage? *Philippe's* murder?

Then her mind turned to the body in the morgue. If these men had killed Lucien and burned her house to destroy the evidence of their activity, wouldn't they do whatever necessary to hide evidence of Philippe's murder, as well? Perhaps even plant his belongings on another man, hoping to end the search for the body that might implicate them in the crime?

As Elizabeth attempted to make sense of her spine-chilling thoughts, she heard Sigerson's cart in the distance clattering toward her, and a frightening question fought its way to the surface: Was Sigerson one of them?

As Sigerson and Yvette rounded the bend and pulled up in front of the cottage, Elizabeth saw her maid hunched over, holding on to the boards tightly. Her face showed pure relief as she recognized her mistress waiting for them.

"Madame!" Yvette tried to climb from the cart and fell out. Elizabeth helped her to her feet. "Madame...I am sorry...Lucien..."

"I know, Yvette," said Elizabeth, embracing her. "Thank God we have you safe." She felt a tightness in her chest and a momentary feeling of panic as she eyed their scowling savior. One of the perpetrators? Whatever the case, he seemed amenable to getting the doctor for Yvette, and the two ladies dissolving into tears could only discourage that willingness.

"Yvette, Monsieur Sigerson will retrieve help. He is our neighbor—*my* friend in the village." She lifted her maid's face so Yvette could see her attempt at a teasing smile, then whispered, "We will be safe here."

Elizabeth herself was not convinced.

CHAPTER EIGHT

Sigerson stared sightlessly before him, his brow furrowed in anxiety as he bumped about in his cart. *What bad luck to have encountered that pair,* he thought, as his horse maneuvered the grooves and channels in the rock-hard mud. The local police pounding on his door to question them could not be allowed. His only option was to fetch the doctor and get the women on their way as quickly as possible.

Nearing the turnoff that would take him north toward the village, the researcher glanced toward the smoldering Devereaux villa. Surprised that the blaze seemed to have burned itself down, curiosity replaced his apprehension, and he turned his horse and rumbled the cart down the path toward the house. Upon reaching the charred gate covered by crumbling, browned branches, he was met by two men who appeared from the side of the structure. Sigerson pulled up the horse and sat frozen in his seat.

Police.

"Who are you? Do you know the occupants of this house?"

"I am Sigerson," he replied. "I live a bit down the road. Heading home this evening I came upon Madame Devereaux and her housemaid. They had just escaped from the building; one was overcome by the smoke. I took them to my cottage and am now going for medical assistance."

"You don't appear to be in much of a hurry," accused one officer.

"The maid's life is not in danger," he replied, "but she does need to be seen by a physician." Certainly, one who had the lungs to moan and wail as that woman did during their short ride together could manage a few moments more, he thought. "With the officials here, I thought this might be the best time to search for a brooch Madame Devereaux believes she dropped in the mud before departing."

"Have your look around, Sigerson," said the policeman, glaring with narrowed eyes, "then be on your way. A young man died in this fire. We can't have curiosity-seekers poking around."

"You say Madame Devereaux is with you?" interrupted the second officer.

"Only for the moment, sir," the researcher replied quickly. "Once the physician sees the maid, they will be on their way."

The second officer seemed satisfied and the first officer repeated his order. "Do what you came here to do and be on your own way, then."

Sigerson nodded and jumped down to begin his "search." He threw his overcoat back into the cart and slipped a leather bag over his shoulder. Heading for the house, he kept his eyes riveted to the ground as he walked. Upon reaching the side of the smoldering structure, he found an officer examining a badly burned body. The "Lucien" the maid sobbed for, the researcher concluded.

"Died in the fire, indeed," scoffed Sigerson under his breath, noting the condition of the dead man's head. A double-edged sword, perhaps, police incompetence. Anyone with eyes to see would know a falling beam could not have inflicted such damage; it was only too clear that those blows, coming from every angle, were delivered with the guidance of human hands. The policeman looked up at him with a scowl. Sigerson quickly made the sign of the cross. "Poor Lucien."

Continuing around the house, Sigerson found himself at the kitchen door. He extracted a lens from inside his pack and examined the wood installed to cover the broken window. Put in just before the fire, he concluded, seeing a shiny bent nail and shards of glass lying on the ground, on top of the disturbed mud. The makeshift window had been kicked in during the blaze, probably to rescue the housemaid. A resolute woman, that American.

He slipped inside the broken door and entered the kitchen. Fallen beams blocked his path, forcing him to climb over the wreckage to reach the entryway. Here, at the front of the villa, the destruction was total. No hope of reclaiming even an inkwell from the study, Sigerson observed. He climbed past the ashes of the room, across the cracked marble entry floor, and over the collapsed staircase. What he found in the parlor stopped him cold. He shook his head bitterly and gave a heavy sigh. Madame Devereaux's once-proud grand piano lay crushed beneath the debris of a fallen wall, the wood charred, the keys scorched and scattered.

A metallic glint from beneath the pile caught Sigerson's eye as he moved into what remained of the parlor. He made his way through the rubble toward a tin box; his eyes lit up as he opened it. A book and several sheets of paper were inside, intact. The man glanced through them quickly, then stuffed the box into his bag with a satisfied grin. His work complete, he laboriously retraced his steps to exit the ruined house.

Now, to find the physician, who must be compelled to return with him to claim the women who had claimed his home.

Although Yvette whimpered pitifully on Sigerson's sofa, Elizabeth decided she was coming around nicely. No more admonishments, no veiled accusations. The maid was content to weep until more tea was served, drink it, then resume her tears. Elizabeth again tucked the dressing gown their host had laid out around Yvette and curled up in the armchair opposite the now warm and glowing fire.

As she closed her eyes Elizabeth's mind again sprang into action and seized unsanctioned control. Unwelcome images—of her house ablaze, of Lucien falling to the floor mortally wounded, of the icy regard with which Sigerson had looked at them—flew hauntingly before her eyes. Worse, her frightening speculations were forming into terrifying conclusions: Rather than accidental, Philippe's death was to keep him from fulfilling his plans; her home was burglarized to confiscate records of his work, apparently without luck since the burglars returned tonight to finish what they started; they killed Lucien when he tried to stop them, then burned her house to the ground. Elizabeth's eyes shot open, coming again to the most chilling of her conclusions: somehow, Sigerson was involved.

She needed to get Yvette away from here, and soon. Unfortunately, Sigerson himself was the very means for their escape.

Elizabeth leapt up once again and began to pace about the room. Out of the corner of her eye, she noticed a brown glass humidor with a wooden lid resting upon the mantle. Peeking in, she found the jar filled with loose tobacco and several rolled cigarettes. She breathed in the sweet, musky aroma of the rich leaves and felt herself relax, just a smidgen. Plucking one cigarette out, she placed it between her lips, lit a taper in the fireplace, and brought the flame to the cigarette's end, inhaling deeply. How breathing in more smoke after clawing her way blindly through a burning house could be a comfort, she couldn't fathom. But a sense of calm did indeed come over her, and she was finally able to overcome her racing, fearful thoughts.

With each smoke-filled breath Elizabeth's thoughts became more and more orderly, with indignation and rage replacing her fear. Arsonists and murderers had taken Lucien, perhaps Philippe; they must be punished. With little confidence in the police, how could she possibly see that it happened? Where even to start? She looked around the cottage. Certainly, if Sigerson was involved, she could learn more here.

In the dimmed gaslight and flickering hearth, Elizabeth at last began to survey her surroundings. The cottage itself was spotless, yet shabbily furnished: an old, threadbare rug covered the stone floor and worn draperies hung from the windows. Only the forlorn sofa Yvette occupied and two badly used armchairs before the fire provided seating. No personal articles or mementos were about, leaving her to recall Luc saying Sigerson had only recently come to the village. A small door from this parlor area led toward the back of the house. Elizabeth tried to open it, but it was stuck. Not locked, she determined; jammed. She knew the vintners' cottages she had visited used this room for storage. What might Sigerson have stored here? Pondering whether or not to force the door and leave evidence of her prying, she leaned too heavily on it and it gave way under her weight. The decision made for her, Elizabeth peered into the darkness, took a deep breath, and stepped in. What she saw made her gasp.

A *music* room! A small spinet piano sat in the center, a sofa to its left was placed up against the window. There was no other furniture, nor could any have fit, so small was the space. As Elizabeth ventured closer to the piano, she noticed a violin tossed carelessly onto the sofa and a flute caught between the cushions. She wrinkled her brow at the shameful treatment of the instruments. Perhaps Sigerson had let the cottage from someone at the school? Someone in the School of Music, she decided, who should know better! She backed her way out and returned to the parlor.

Moving back into the entry, she stood before the staircase leading to the second floor. A single door at the top of the stairs led to a bedroom; Elizabeth had seen their reluctant hero duck into it before departing to fetch the doctor. If any place in the house would provide clues to this man's identity and motives, it would be there. She parted the curtain on the front window. It would be an hour or more before he returned. Ignoring the briefest moment of unease, she climbed the steps. Reaching the second level, she found the door slightly ajar and pushed on it gently.

A bit more comfortable, this room, thought Elizabeth as she poked her head inside. The bed was covered in a simple afghan. The nearby armchair was somewhat less worn than those of the sitting room. A nightstand and armoire completed the furnishings. Unlike the fireplace downstairs, she observed, this fire was frequently lit.

Then, she saw the picture.

Elizabeth stepped into the room and nearer the fireplace to pick up a small portrait, tucked behind some correspondence propped against it. She was fascinated by the tiny mahogany frame and the picture of an attractive woman smiling coquettishly, formally dressed, with dark hair swept up under a stylish hat. This beauty was no mother or sister, she thought to herself with a smile. His displaying it, however haphazardly, certainly didn't fit the image Luc painted of the man: the researcher taken only by the objects of his lens. When Elizabeth returned the picture to the mantle, she examined the envelope that had rested against it—an unposted letter addressed to Jon Gregoire at the Institute of Botany. Her heartbeat quickened. Sigerson denied knowing Philippe, and yet he had business with Gregoire? The securely sealed envelope frustrated her desire to investigate further. Elizabeth turned to the plain wooden armoire near the window. Unlocked, it threw up no barriers to her explorations. She seized the cool brass knobs and pulled.

The clothes that filled the wardrobe fascinated her and heightened her suspicion of their owner. Elizabeth picked up an English tweed walking jacket from the floor of the closet. Tucked into one pocket of the coat was a matching tweed cap; the other pocket contained a pair of rich, black leather gloves. She found it easy to imagine the too-well-manicured academic in these fine clothes. The apparel certainly gave credence to her speculation that he was British. A British gentleman.

What to make of the rest, however, was beyond Elizabeth. Costumes? A white cotton robe, one that might be worn in the hot sun of the Middle East, was flung over the rod; a heavy fur-lined coat, the one item that warranted a hanger. Then she saw what looked like a large hat box shoved to the rear of the armoire. Elizabeth crouched down, pulled out the box, and removed the lid. It was filled with pots of face paint, glasses, mustaches, wigs. Not costumes. Disguises!

Elizabeth sat back on her heels, her mouth agape. Could Sigerson be *hiding* from someone? To judge from the clothing, his evasion took him from one side of the world to the other. What had brought him to the south of France? Then again, perhaps he wasn't in hiding at all. Disguises would make him invisible, anonymous, if he were here to steal something…or to murder someone? Could these pieces be his means, his tools, for absconding with Philippe's work? And was he now preparing to join with Gregoire in his efforts? Or had their affiliation already been forged?

Searching the pockets of the various garments in the armoire yielded no answers. Elizabeth was moving to look through the nightstand when she heard Cheval neighing and stomping on the stones outside. Someone was coming. Scurrying from the room, she flew down the stairs, and headed for the kitchen hearth—the area farthest from the road.

The dark hearth was dimly lit by the dying fire Elizabeth used earlier to warm Yvette's tea. She poured some for herself and sat down at the long oaken table with the brew before her. Seconds later she heard the front door swing open. Sigerson stepped inside, followed by the village physician.

"The lady is in here," said Sigerson, indicating the parlor. Within seconds, he appeared before the kitchen hearth.

"You retrieved the doctor quickly," said Elizabeth, trying not to grimace as she sipped the icy tea. "You must know his haunts."

"In fact, he found me," Sigerson replied, eyeing the mug in her hands. "Dr. Moulin was called upon to tend to your stable hand; I met him not far from your home. After certifying that the young man was indeed dead, the doctor accompanied me directly here. Your maid is no worse?"

"Yvette has rested fitfully," said Elizabeth. *Why does he study me so?* she wondered. "No matter. Thanks to your timely appearance and willingness to assist, all will be well."

"Of that I am sure, Madame," said Sigerson with a quick, less-than-sincere smile. He leaned against the worn, creaky sideboard, looking at her intently as he dug a cigarette from his coat pocket. Although rattled by the intensity of his stare, Elizabeth managed to return it.

After some moments, Sigerson released her gaze and turned to one of the cabinets she had not plundered looking for Yvette's tea. From one shelf he took a dark bottle and, seating himself on the bench beside her, poured its deep golden liquid into two glasses. "Perhaps a sip of warm sherry, rather than cold tea, might help your own rest."

Elizabeth's eyes lit up in appreciation and relief as Sigerson put a match to the table lamp. Her overindulgence at dinner this evening seemed a lifetime away, and sherry would calm the jitters she was unable to shake, especially having been nearly caught digging into this man's belongings. Or perhaps it was what she uncovered that added to her uneasiness? Ignoring Sigerson's observation that she had not sat there in his absence over a warm drink, she reached for a glass.

Sigerson held his glass over the lamp, warming its contents, and Elizabeth did the same. She held the warmed sherry in both hands before drinking, then raised the glass. "To Lucien," she said sadly. Emptying the glass in two quick pulls, she realized it was the second time this evening she had toasted a dead man.

"Lucien," rejoined Sigerson, sipping lightly from his own drink.

The liquor warmed her body and clouded her head quickly. Elizabeth didn't want to think about Lucien or about Philippe. Didn't want to grieve for what she had done or what she had lost. She needed to know more about this man before her.

"May I ask a question, Monsieur?"

"Of course," Sigerson replied warily. He glanced up the stairs at his bedroom door as she poured herself another glass of sherry.

"What attracts you to Monique Masset?"

The researcher cocked his head to the side, considering her question. At last, he chuckled silently and leaned back to toss his cigarette into the fire. "I am not *attracted* by her talents in the boudoir, if that is your speculation. Although I understand that would be a typical reason most men might…escort her from the pub on any given evening."

"Why, then, did *this* man escort her from the pub on *this* evening?"

"I thought Madame Picard might possess certain information of interest to me."

"Hmm…" Elizabeth tried to imagine what Monique could possibly know that was of value to Sigerson; certainly, not new theories about the properties of coal tar. Could he have been asking her about the accident? About why Philippe was in Paris? "And does she?"

"She does not."

At this point, the doctor entered the room, interrupting their conversation and preventing her from asking more. "Mademoiselle d'Etiveaud is able to travel," he said. "Perhaps I may take the ladies to a friend's home?"

Elizabeth immediately thought of Luc, who only a few hours before had begged her to stay with them. Thank God she'd refused him. She would have lost Yvette as well as Lucien.

"Thank you, Doctor," she said. "Luc Masset of the rue de l'Université is a dear friend who would take us in. We would be most appreciative for transportation to his home."

Elizabeth gathered herself hurriedly, realizing that Luc would be frantic if word of the fire had reached him. As she started rising from the table, her eyes caught a layer of fine, black dirt covering Sigerson's trousers, no longer hidden by his coat as he got up from the bench to make room for her to pass. She studied him up and down, now noticing the slightest traces of black dirt smeared around his hairline. Concentrated there as if in an attempt to remove it.

Could it be soot? Soot, as from a fire? *Her* fire?

Her heart racing, her mouth dry, she wondered: had it been there before? She met Sigerson's eyes once again. All humor, real or imagined, had vanished; the cold glare of earlier had returned. Suddenly, her idea of coming here to learn about Sigerson seemed foolish, even dangerous. She must get away as quickly as possible. Upon standing, however, the room spun wildly before her, the sherry uniting with the wine of earlier to rob her equilibrium. She fell hard back onto the bench.

"Careful, Madame," said Dr. Moulin, taking her arm in concern. "You have experienced a great trauma."

"What ails me is poor judgment," she replied, glancing toward Sigerson. With that, Elizabeth cautiously got up from the bench and headed toward the brighter light of the sitting room, one foot placed carefully before the other. She turned and paused before her host, reaching down to take his hand. "Thank you, Monsieur. We are deeply grateful for your assistance."

"Not at all," he replied curtly.

Elizabeth's knees weakened as she looked down at her own hand, now also soot-covered; the smell of sulfur filled her nostrils. She stumbled from the room as quickly as her intoxicated body would allow, wondering how she came to be clutching three of Sigerson's cigarettes.

❧

The Massets' home in the rue de l'Université was a tall, narrow stone structure like most of the houses near the school. As Dr. Moulin's carriage made its way down the slick and winding cobblestone road, passing only the occasional reveler reeling from the nearby pub's bounty, Elizabeth peered from within. She saw a candle glowing through the draperies of the deeply recessed windows of the house's upper floor. Someone in the family was still not home for the evening. She well knew who, and was both thankful and amazed that Monique had found a companion after being disappointed by Sigerson. At least Elizabeth might cause less alarm to the Massets if an anxious parent was still awake, keeping watch.

Elizabeth stepped limply from the carriage and slowly climbed the stone steps to the front door. She looked down at herself. The spotless riding habit she had worn at dinner only a few hours before was stained with soot and reeked of vomit. Perhaps alarming the Masset household was unavoidable, after all. She grasped the tarnished brass knocker and banged it twice.

Some moments passed before her knock was answered by Marie Masset. Her sleepy, irritated expression at being awakened turned to alarm as she saw Elizabeth standing on her front steps.

"Elizabeth!" she cried, seeing the mess of the younger woman's clothing. "What has happened?" Marie grabbed Elizabeth's shoulders, pulling her into the foyer.

"No, Marie," said Elizabeth, mustering what little calm remained within her. The presence of a motherly face and caring arms primed the floodgates for bursting, for releasing the anxiety Elizabeth had contained until now. "Yvette is hurt. We need help."

Marie swept her dressing gown around her and hurried down the steps. "Bring her in here, Doctor," she called, recognizing Moulin's carriage. She swished her way back up to the door, pulling Elizabeth inside with her. "You are safe now," she said. "We will take care of you. Whatever has happened, we will manage it."

"No!" cried Elizabeth, her voice rising in panic. "It cannot be managed. You cannot fix what I have done…"

"Jean-Luc," called Marie to the upper floor in a cool, unruffled voice. "Please come down, my dear. Elizabeth and Yvette are here. They need help."

Dr. Moulin guided Yvette into the parlor and the maid looked about her, relaxing as she recognized the Masset home. "Many thanks, Dr. Moulin," said Marie as the physician left the house. "We will be sure to consult with you on their condition in the morning."

Luc at last came hurrying down the stairs, his nightshirt billowing about him. Daughters Annette and Nicole skirted by their father and rushed toward their visitors. The adolescent girls looked horrified to see Elizabeth huddled on the sofa, trembling and silent.

"Elizabeth!" they cried together. "What has happened?"

Their father gently pulled them from her. "Elizabeth and Yvette would be much more comfortable in some fresh nightclothes, don't you think? Please go upstairs and select something from your wardrobes."

The girls reluctantly turned away and headed slowly toward the stairs. Luc sat on the sofa next to Elizabeth and hugged her tightly. For the second time that evening, she buried her face in his shirt and let the tears fall.

"You are safe here," said Luc, stroking her hair. "Tell me what has happened."

Elizabeth took a deep breath and lifted her head to respond. "There was a fire. Lucien is dead." She took another breath, trying to control the terror, even the guilt, that threatened to consume her. "It's my fault…" She tried again to speak, but couldn't manage to choke out the words.

Luc looked at the faces of the women around him. His daughters standing frozen by the stairs, his wife at Elizabeth's knee, and Yvette. He looked at Yvette for a long moment.

"Tell me what happened," he asked the maid. "What of this fire?"

"Men broke in last night," Yvette began. Luc nodded that he was aware of the incident. "They returned tonight to finish their work. Lucien surprised them. They killed him and set fire to the house."

"And Madame believes herself to be responsible?" Luc asked, glancing at Elizabeth.

Yvette twisted her hands in her lap nervously, tears spilling over. "I grieve for a friend," she replied at last. "I said unkind things. Madame was very brave. She saved my life."

"Girls," Luc said to his daughters, "please help Yvette change her clothes and put her to bed in the blue room." As Annette and Nicole helped the maid up the stairs, Luc bowed his head to touch Elizabeth's. Marie sat at her feet, hands on her knee.

"Please speak to us, child," Marie said. "We can help."

"I wouldn't ask for help," said Elizabeth regretfully. "He begged me to involve the police…even went to them himself. But what would they have done for a young stable boy? Nothing. I should have asked for their help. Now Lucien is dead."

More tears. Luc and Marie waited as Elizabeth struggled to calm herself.

"Do you believe making a report to the local prefecture would have resulted in a sentry posted outside your door?" he asked her at last. A deep breath and more sniffling from Elizabeth. "Yes, reporting the incident was the right thing to do. Would it have prevented what happened tonight? Unlikely. You must understand that."

Elizabeth looked up at Luc as he brushed the tangled auburn hair from her swollen face. Was it possible that she couldn't have prevented what had happened to Lucien? The overwhelming anguish of responsibility eased ever so slightly.

"Monsieur Sigerson came to our aid," she finally managed to say, her words nasal and thick. "He took us to his cottage in his cart and went to fetch Dr. Moulin."

"Sigerson?" asked Luc, frowning. "Again, the Norwegian from the laboratory?"

"He happens to live not a kilometer from my own home…what is left of it."

"He doesn't strike me as the type to act as Good Samaritan."

"Nor did he…at first," said Elizabeth. "But I feared for Yvette. Not knowing the extent of her injuries, I seized the first opportunity to get her someplace warm. Monsieur Sigerson was that opportunity." She shuddered, recalling his cold, distant eyes and soot-covered clothes, her fear of him and why he was here.

"Heaven help the person you 'seize' for any reason," said Luc with a smile, hugging her fondly.

"He disturbs me," Elizabeth began, taking the handkerchief Luc offered her and dabbing her eyes. She considered how much to reveal at this moment. Luc would still be shaken by her claim the body she had identified was not Philippe. Now was not the time to introduce more conspiracies—that she suspected he had been murdered, that Sigerson was involved. "Why was he there, at my burning home? Why is he here in Montpellier at all?"

Luc looked at her with a furrowed brow, shook his head. "He is in Montpellier to explore the derivative properties of coal, my dear. You know this. And you yourself tell me he is your neighbor…little mystery that he would happen by on his way home from the village, no?" He raised his chin and frowned more deeply. "Has he done something to cause you to fear him?"

"No…no," she replied, realizing she had nothing definitive to evidence the man's ill intent. That he had costumes in his armoire and wore sooty clothing proved nothing. That he corresponded with a vile faculty member was no crime. "I see monsters and mysteries in every dark corner, I suppose. And yet, last night's vandals returned, killed Lucien, and burned my house to the ground. Monsters seem to follow me about, Luc. Whether or not Monsieur Sigerson is one of them…" She shrugged her shoulders.

"Well, he seems to have dispatched his charitable deed with honor, arranging to get you here safely," said Luc. "Now, no more talk of this horror. You must rest. And here is my littlest cherub with your nightclothes."

The Massets both kissed Elizabeth's forehead as Nicole appeared with a white cotton gown in her arms. "You will sleep in my bed," said the young girl, taking Elizabeth's trembling hand and leading her toward the stairs. "It is all ready and waiting for you."

CHAPTER NINE

The next morning dawned clear and mild, finally typical of a mid-March Montpellier day. Outside, the sun baked the roads into softening and perked both the plants and the population. Girls pushing flower carts and farmers offering their fruits and vegetables lined the narrow, meandering cobblestoned streets. With the return of the sun, the flowers seemed a bit brighter, the fruits juicier on this beautiful spring morning.

The warmth and light that washed into Nicole Masset's bedroom, full and strong, was not as welcomed by its occupant. Elizabeth Devereaux, huddled in the center of the big feather-down bed, fought to shut out the blinding, intrusive sun. Feeling a gentle touch on her arm, she pried open her sore, puffy eyes to see the blurred outline of Nicole standing by the bedside.

"It is breakfast time, Elizabeth," said Nicole gently, "considerably past, in fact. Please try to come down and have something to eat. Papa has brought you croissants and cheese. He knows you favor them."

Croissants and cheese. Elizabeth had no hope whatsoever that her aching head and queasy stomach would accept any such combination.

"I am afraid I won't be joining you for breakfast," she managed to mumble, turning her face away from the girl with a grimace.

"Papa insists. He is most anxious about you."

Of course he is, thought Elizabeth. She had appeared upon his doorstep in the dead of night, looking like a chimney sweep and smelling like the gutter, then proceeded to lose her mind in his parlor. *He must wonder if a call for hospital attendants will be required.*

"This is all so awful," said Nicole quietly, sitting down gently on the edge of the bed. She placed her hand on Elizabeth's. "First Philippe…now this fire."

Elizabeth closed her scratchy, burning eyes again. The sweet girl—with her mother's sleek dark hair and her father's caring brown eyes—was skillfully giving her a chance to share her distress. But Elizabeth wasn't ready to unburden herself just yet.

"It is as if I listen to another woman's story," she replied, shrugging weakly. "I feel as a paying spectator, mildly curious about how the performance will end."

Elizabeth rolled slowly to the side of the bed and sat up. Not so bad. She eased herself to her feet, wise Nicole at her elbow, and stepped ever so gingerly across the braided rug toward the washstand. Reaching the basin, Elizabeth dipped the facecloth into the water and held it to her forehead. The cool water both soothed and refreshed her. Perhaps she might live.

At Nicole's gentle urging, Elizabeth prepared for her appearance at the breakfast table. Easing into one of Luc's dressing gowns to cover up Nicole's too-short nightdress was her most ambitious undertaking. A half-hearted attempt at the hairbrush brought the young girl to her side again.

"Do sit down, Elizabeth," Nicole insisted, taking the hairbrush in hand. "You can't leave your beautiful tresses in these tangles." She began to pick at the red-brown strands of her friend's hair with the brush bristles. Elizabeth dutifully obeyed and made herself comfortable on the ottoman before the mirror.

"I must look a fright," she said, drawing the gown closer around her and lowering her head to stretch her stiffened neck.

"Why must you leave us, Elizabeth?"

Elizabeth sighed heavily. "I don't belong here, Nicole."

"You *do* belong here. You belong with us."

"You and your family always make me feel welcome," she agreed. "But the feeling evaporates once I step outside your door. I cannot be who I want to be here…or even find out who that is…"

With her hair still in knots, Elizabeth slowly stood up and hobbled over to the basin for another cool swipe of the washcloth. At last ready to leave the bedroom, she felt somewhat confident of reassuring the Massets she was alive and well; that is, as long as no one insisted she add cheese to her croissant.

Down the narrow hallway and toward the head of the stairs, Nicole led her ailing guest ever closer to the morning room and breakfast. Elizabeth clung to the mahogany railing as her bare feet found the first step. Down, down, down. One step at a time. Back down the stairs she'd climbed last night, into the parlor where she'd tried, for the second time, to confess her mistakes. Then, to the table, where she would ask for help in making amends?

The table was laid out for morning *café*, although the bright sun shining into the cheery room came from so high in the sky Elizabeth knew it was much later in the day. Again, with Nicole's assistance, she settled herself into a chair and poured some of the steaming brew. Much more soothing than the cup of cold tea she had taken at Sigerson's, the warmth of the *café* made Elizabeth feel calmer, a bit more in control, and a bit more ready for Luc, who soon came in and seated himself at the table.

"How do you feel this morning, *mon cherie?*" he asked, kissing her hand in greeting. "I have a mind to take a leisurely walk through the gardens of l'Peyrou and would be most pleased for you to join me. I am afraid we have arrangements to discuss."

"Yes, arrangements." Identifying a corpse, of course, was not the end of this nightmare; it was merely a prelude to the most dreadful scene of all. Now, she must plan to bury the man she had claimed was her husband. How she wished for Luc's confidence that the man was truly Philippe!

True or not, Elizabeth considered her good fortune, if that was what it truly was—luck that the unhappy fate of this man in the morgue would combine with the sloppiness of the local police to provide the opportunity for her to escape France. Or was it a sinister plan to remove her from the scene? Whether it was Fate or someone's evil scheme that had brought her to this moment, last night's brief resolve to take vengeance surged once more, fighting with the ever-growing fear that the police would discover her lie to the coroner; fear that the murderers would come for her; fear, even, that she would never forgive herself for pushing on to clear her path for home. She sighed deeply and tried to give the croissant before her its proper attention and was surprised to find it well received by her stomach. Perhaps a chunk of cheese needn't be ruled out so hastily.

"As for how I'm feeling, I am at a loss for words. Please pardon my overindulgences." Elizabeth tore a piece of her croissant. "As for the process of coming to understand and cope with the atrocities of the past week…I will be much more successful if I keep my head about me."

"Beating yourself will not do here, Madame," Luc chided fondly. "It has been a terrible time."

"I accept full responsibility for my behavior," she said, feeling a dull pain in her chest. "Actions committed and omitted."

"Dear, dear Elizabeth," murmured Luc, sipping from his cup.

She looked at him suddenly. "Yvette? Where is Yvette this morning?"

"Yvette is remarkably improved today, having only an ugly cough and a head full of singed hair to show for her experience. She and Annette and Marie have gone to market this afternoon. Little Nicole would not budge from the house until she knew you'd eaten." He smiled fondly at his youngest daughter as the girl beamed over her own cup.

"You took care of me when Mama and I had the influenza," Nicole reminded Elizabeth. "You gave me tea and broth and kept me in clean linens and nightdresses. I knew just what to do."

"I was in good hands, indeed," said Elizabeth as she attempted a smile at her young caretaker. The warm glow from the love she felt was short-lived, quickly replaced by the once-again growing outrage at the crimes committed against her and hers. Murdering arsonists took Lucien, her husband and his precious work, her home, she reminded herself. They must be brought to account. In this village filled with such carelessness, where the police might very well have presented her with the wrong corpse to identify—how could she expect justice to be served? Were the murderers to go unpunished while she lived in fear? Her eyes widened in a jolt of confident determination. With the previous night's clarity of mind, her vow of revenge transcended the fear. She lifted her chin defiantly as she peered at Luc.

"Yes, we should take that walk."

"Our home is yours for as long as you wish," said Luc, taking Elizabeth's arm and guiding her through the great Arch d'Triomphe. They strolled down the path of l'Peyrou, toward the wide-open spaces of the beautiful promenade overlooking the village of Montpellier.

"I will not displace Monique." *Although the witch was maneuvering to do as much to me,* thought Elizabeth. She physically squirmed, knowing the gaudily adorned bodice and skirt Marie had left out for her to borrow had been pulled from Monique's wardrobe. "I would appreciate your keeping Yvette with you, however. I will stay at the inn."

"It is with the greatest relief that I report my eldest is at last with her husband," said Luc, sitting down on a stone bench near the gardens and running stiff fingers through his thinning hair. "Stephan has returned from Alsace, and they are once again together in their rooms on the rue Baudin. I had high hopes that married life might calm my daughter. And yet, each time he leaves her for any length of time, I again become the tormented father, again feel responsible for her behavior."

"The beautiful and caring Annette and Nicole should convince you Monique's behavior does not reflect her upbringing," said Elizabeth. "You and Marie have much to be proud of."

Luc smiled faintly and stood up, extending his arm for Elizabeth to join him. In silence, they headed out on the broader promenade and circled the statue of Louis XIV on horseback. Then, knowing it was her favorite spot, Luc guided Elizabeth toward the lower promenade, where water trickled from a small fountain in the middle of a duck-filled pond.

"I would consider it a gift if you stayed with us," he said at last. "I am very frightened for you. That those fiends returned to finish their work alarms me."

Elizabeth smirked. "Yet I survive, no?"

"Hmm," replied Luc with a smile and turned his face up toward the sun. "Yes, I suppose you do."

They found another stone bench near the fountain and sat for some time, lost in unsettled thoughts. The sun had no warmth for Elizabeth today, did not bring the cheeriness it once did. Feeling the eyes of those who pranced by in their Sunday finery—the plumed bonnets, swishing taffeta skirts, tapping walking sticks—she avoided their stares. The beautiful fountains and gardens were mere mockeries. How she loved them when she'd first discovered l'Peyrou, loved sitting here thinking about her hopes as a new wife, and someday as a mother. How the gurgling and trickling of the water from the fountain had suggested such beautiful melodies to her ear; the bold and delicate garden colors revealed the nuances of a sonata to her eyes, sprinkled with the gleeful chirping trills of the finches and the mistle thrush. How this place had provided the hope of finding something new here for herself when her initial dreams seemed impossible. But now, with Philippe gone, what little chance she had of finding her purpose in Montpellier was lost as well. The idea that she might have come so close, that Philippe might have devised an initiative that would bring them together, only made the pain greater, the loss deeper. Suspecting someone had killed for information about a potential project continued to fuel the fierce battle between her anger and her fear.

The anger was winning.

"I must ask your help on another front, Luc," said Elizabeth at last, knotting her gloved hands in her lap. "The men who killed Lucien and destroyed my home: they must be punished."

Luc's jaw tightened, but he said nothing.

"I mean to see that it happens," Elizabeth continued, more harshly than she intended. "After last night, I do believe they came for Philippe's work. When I interrupted them at my home, they returned and took what they wanted and burned the house to cover themselves." She ignored Luc's violently shaking head, raising her voice so he would hear. "I will determine what it was among Philippe's research they sought and find out who they are. I will see them pay for what they have done."

"This is madness!" cried Luc, jumping up from the bench. "The police are in the business of hunting down thieves and murderers. You have had the closest brush with these monsters allowable. I will not sanction your attempt to identify them and their motives—and by God I'll not lend my assistance. Please, no more of this nonsense."

Luc shook his head a final time and set off at a quick pace. Clearly, her request was rejected. Elizabeth hurried after him, stirring up the starlings who had watched the altercation from the plane trees. He meant it when he said he was frightened for her, and she heard the full force of his fear now. Still, there was no hope of success without his help. At this juncture, however, retreating somewhat seemed necessary.

"I must at least know what they sought," Elizabeth tried again, attempting to catch her breath as she trotted along beside him, her skirts tangling around her ankles. Their footsteps crunched the gravel as they walked on, slower now. "The project…our project, the work Philippe believed would bring us together. Whether or not it was what the brutes came for, I must know…it's all I might have left of him." Luc stopped in his tracks. "Perhaps you can tell me who helped Philippe in his work," Elizabeth continued softly. "Surely, questioning some of his former colleagues would present no danger."

Luc turned her to face him, his eyes squinting in the sunlight. He looked at her silently for some moments. "Is it not enough that my three daughters live only to put more white hairs on my head and deep lines in my face? I must suffer your stubbornness as well? Your curiosity will be the death of me, Madame," he said, embracing her tightly. Then, he tucked her arm in his and proceeded at a more leisurely pace up toward the promenade.

"I must know."

Luc sighed. "*No one* could fully know Philippe's mind, or his pursuits. His areas of study touched so many disciplines. All his work is publicly available. No one would need steal…indeed, murder for it."

"What of something that hadn't been made public yet?" Elizabeth bowed her bonnet to a disheveled vintner she had tried to help years ago. He lifted a grimy hand to his cap in response. "Something that might gain respect for an academic who had no hope winning it in his own right, perhaps."

"Madame Devereaux!" Luc's eyes widened as he stopped cold. "Can you possibly believe someone at the school would take advantage of your husband's death to further his own career? Think of what you're saying!"

"I know very well what I'm saying," Elizabeth said, lifting her chin and returning his stare. "I have no doubt someone would try to take advantage of Philippe's death. I'd even wonder if someone might have *caused* it." There. She'd said it aloud.

"Do you realize…" Luc stopped in midsentence as he himself appeared to realize what she was implying. "You accuse Gregoire! You believe Jon Gregoire murdered your husband and your stable boy, then burned your home? *Mon Dieu!*" He clapped his hand to his forehead.

"I accuse no one," Elizabeth replied quickly. "And yet, Monsieur Gregoire should be questioned about the papers he took from Philippe's office yesterday."

"You saw him take something from Philippe's office?"

"*Gregoire's* office, now."

"The man has the ambition of a toadstool," muttered Luc, "and half the intelligence. He is not capable of masterminding such a scheme."

"Gregoire was thrust into a difficult position when Philippe returned home from America," Elizabeth said. "A desperate position, perhaps. Philippe, suddenly his superior, wrote papers beyond his comprehension and Gregoire was unable to shine on his own merits. Isn't it possible he became aware of a dynamic new idea Philippe had conceived and aimed to claim it as his own? Wouldn't the threat of being pushed, yet again, farther from the limelight be enough incentive for him to act?"

"But so boldly? So mercilessly?" cried Luc, shaking his head. "Whatever could Philippe have devised that would push Gregoire to such lengths?"

"Ahh." Elizabeth said dully. "The very question that began our conversation yesterday at the laboratory. It is as if I'm caught in a never-ending loop. Just as a girl practicing the piano, when I thought I'd reached the end of a sonata, the coda appears, and I must go back to the beginning and start again." She smiled ruefully. "I was too impatient, of course, to appreciate it heralded a breathtaking, dramatic finish. Might such a finish be ahead of me now?"

Luc paused mid-step, his shoulders slumped. "You win, Madame," he murmured. "I can bear your persistence no longer. We shall visit Gregoire and demand he tell us all."

"When?"

Luc took Elizabeth's hand and led her to another bench along the walkway. "Your next concern must be Philippe, my love," he said softly, tucking a stray strand of chestnut hair back under her hat. "In two days' time you bury your husband. This puzzle will wait."

"Of course." Luc could not understand that she felt no urgency regarding Philippe's funeral, that she felt little obligation to the body now being prepared for burial. Admitting she couldn't dismiss the idea her husband's body was still a captive of the Lez—or disposed of to hide the evidence of his murder?—would not help her cause now. She'd shared enough insane theories for today; she needn't recall yesterday's.

"After the funeral, of course."

"Perhaps…" said Luc suddenly, his brow furrowed in thought. "You might consider writing to your friend in Chicago, Chanute, and asking if he connected with your husband in Paris."

"Octave Chanute?" asked Elizabeth with a smile. "He and Philippe were to meet? Why ever…"

"Ahh," said Luc, mimicking her. "We arrive yet again at one of your codas! Perhaps Chanute can give you a clue about what was on your husband's mind."

Elizabeth smiled, a bit wistfully. "I can very well imagine what was on Philippe's mind when he sought out Chanute—hero worship! And no surprise he kept his plans from me: I tormented him mercilessly about his blatant adulation of the man. When I introduced them at a gala for the orchestra, Philippe was like a shy acolyte at the feet of a wizened master." She felt a warm glow at the memory of how excited Philippe had been to meet her patron, barraging the engineer with questions—about the bridges he built, the growing train networks he managed, the impact the rails' progress might have on the surrounding woods. "There was no research, no project discussed. Chanute is no academic. Philippe was simply enthralled by the man and his ability to bring ideas to reality. Everyone always is."

"I see. Well then…" Luc said as they began their long walk back to rue de l'Université. "There is a harmless fellow who might give you information you haven't found at home. Olivier is one of the messengers about the school; he brought us word that Philippe's body had been found. He lives outside the village, a few kilometers west of your villa. He served as a clerk for Philippe, performing odd tasks and the like. Perhaps he might give you a broader idea of the research that was conducted. What little Gregoire offers us will concern the Institute of Botany, I'm certain."

Elizabeth nodded her head in silence. She had no interest in the minutiae a clerk might glean while running errands. Gregoire held the key to her puzzle, she was certain of it. Knowing the insidious academic would volunteer nothing, she believed his secrets would be the most valuable information of all.

Luc must help her to uncover them.

෮෯ර

The Arneau Bridge was an imposing wood and stone structure, looming high above the River Lez, far north of Montpellier, near Montferrier. Long in disuse as the railway became the more comfortable, preferred method of travel from Paris to the south, the bridge served only the sheep herders and the farmers who walked home from their work in the vineyards and fields each evening.

Most recently, however, the overpass saw a great deal more attention than it had in decades. An unusual parade of carriages had crossed over early one evening during the previous week. An unfortunate collision had occurred, driving one carriage into the rails, breaking the guards in two places. Later came the official investigators and their conclusion of an accidental collision—and an accidental death.

Now a most unofficial-looking person investigated.

A tall, thin man with a leather bag slung over his shoulder appeared on the bridge, his long woolen coat flapping about his calves as he minutely examined each of the boards. Up and back, again and again the gentleman trotted, stopping, studying, collecting invisible objects and tucking them into his pockets. Then he trained the same attention on the yet to be repaired guardrails. Suddenly, he dropped down to his belly and hung his head over the edge, craning his neck to see beneath.

It was Sigerson.

Peering through the lens he drew from his pocket, the researcher studied the buttresses below the deck as his coat-tails snapped around his head in the wind. Seemingly satisfied, he pulled himself up, adjusted his clothing, and dug into his bag to pull out several large river stones. Out, too, came a canvas sack into which he piled the rocks. He balanced the bag in his hands and, after some thought, frowned and scooted off the bridge to collect more stones. Finally, the sack was filled to his satisfaction, and he tossed it over the rail into the water. He watched carefully as the canvas took on water and was eventually weighed down by its burden. He checked his pocket watch, and with a nod bounded off the bridge.

Now, the rushing river would be the object of his study.

Climbing agilely down the rocky, slippery embankment, Sigerson quickly reached the water's edge and plunged in up to his calves. Oblivious to his soaking boots, the researcher sloshed back to shore and carefully made his way along the bank, taking in every detail of the scene before him like a bloodhound hot upon a scent. Walking slowly at first, he broke into a trot at times and doubled back often, his eyes darting in every direction. Stopping here and nodding; darting there to scratch his head, then continuing. Finally, stopped by the silt and debris of brush that had gathered in a sharp bend in the river's flow, he dropped to his knees—his coat hopelessly sodden—and once again brought out the lens.

This time, he was not satisfied.

Sigerson shook his head in annoyance, as though disagreeing with an ignorant colleague. "Impossible…" he muttered aloud.

He climbed through the reeds and onto the shore, working his way downriver on the rough and craggy pathway. Picking up his pace, he covered almost a kilometer before stopping. At this point, he waded into the river past his knees. Dropping on all fours, Sigerson moved his arms about, searching so deep he had to crane his neck to keep his head above water. He stood up, shaking his head in frustration. Back to shore and again downstream for another kilometer. He repeated the process as before. Again, he was dissatisfied. Downstream another stretch, another search through the murky water. This time, he plunged his head deep down into the river. When he came up for air, he pulled a shredded leather garment with him.

Sigerson stood up tall, water and mud dripping from his hair and clothes, and stared blankly ahead. After some time, he let out a low whistle and turned his eyes skyward. With a heavy sigh, he waded wearily back to the shore, shrugged off his sopping overcoat, and sat down hard on the ground. Finally aware of the condition of his coat, he realized with dismay there would be nothing but ruined cigarettes in the pockets. No tobacco to bring order to his racing mind. With no other choice, he breathed in the fresh air of the beautiful day and admired the sapphire blue sky. A breathtaking blue, he thought. Like Elizabeth Devereaux's eyes.

Sigerson's head shot to the left, as though to admonish whoever had placed the unbidden thought into his brain. It surely wouldn't have come from his own mind. While he could understand Madame Devereaux being in his thoughts when she seemed always in his path—at the laboratory, the inn, her burning home—that the sky itself should remind him of the woman was bewildering.

And yet, of little concern. No reason to even speculate upon the meaning of such thoughts. The woman could be nothing but the source of a puzzle to solve. Particularly given his situation—and what he now suspected of hers.

CHAPTER TEN

As much as Elizabeth wished for the funeral to be over, the two days since her walk with Luc passed so quickly, she felt completely unprepared for the event and her role in it once the day arrived. Indeed, the sight of the black horse and carriage that came to collect her and the Massets for the procession filled her with dread.

The long trail of horses, carriages, and mourners also draped in black resembled an inky, feathery snake winding its resolute way down the cobblestone streets of Montpellier. The late Professeur Jean-Philippe Devereaux's caisson led the procession; his widow followed in the first carriage, accompanied by Monsieur and Madame Jean-Luc Masset; the younger Masset daughters followed; and they, in turn, were followed by the many dignitaries of the school and the village. Dozens of mourners attended the coaches on foot as they inched toward the cemetery. It was, indeed, an impressive tribute to a most notorious member of the community.

Who do I bury? thought Elizabeth, peering out the tiny coach window at a wrinkled old woman pausing respectfully by the roadside. She so very much wanted to believe Luc, to rid herself of the guilt she felt for claiming a body she suspected was not her husband's. But her doubts persisted.

The vandalism and torching of her home made the simplest explanation difficult. Clearly, someone was desperate to find something of Philippe's, desperate enough to commit arson and murder. While Jon Gregoire would undoubtedly be desperate to save his career, would he have the accomplices to engineer such an undertaking? He was certainly influential enough to find such assistance. How easy to imagine him ordering any measure necessary to keep her away from him and causing him difficulty. Yes, perhaps even to present a drowning victim, similar in appearance to her husband—and ensure a murdered body was never found.

Elizabeth squeezed her head between her fists. If true, she had played right into his hands, given him what he wanted. Perhaps. Yes, she had identified the body as Philippe. Yes, now she was free to bring her life here to an end and leave for America.

Or was she?

By leaving Montpellier and its secrets behind, leaving the murderers to operate freely, she would further cooperate with them. As much as she wanted to escape and move on with her life, how could she? Learning about Philippe's plans was now about more than finding her purpose. She had to identify his initiative with global implications—something that would compel someone to murder—so she could identify those responsible. And to make them pay for what they had done, what they had taken.

Overwhelming obstacles loomed, however. How long before Philippe's body was truly recovered? Even the unreliable police would come for her at some point, making her answer for her misidentification, perhaps charging her as an accomplice to the murder the body might evidence? There wasn't much time at all. She groaned and covered her face. Marie put a consoling arm around her.

Finally, the cemetery gates came into view and Elizabeth steeled herself for the unpleasantries that awaited.

The poor girls she had seen thus far had been wailing since before the procession began; she hadn't even encountered Monique yet. Elizabeth could only look to the end of the service, when she would concentrate on putting her life here in order and gathering support for investigating the whimsies of Philippe's mind in the hopes of identifying his genius undertaking. Then, identifying those who meant to stop him, bringing them to justice?

Yes, she had played into their hands, Elizabeth thought ruefully as she was helped from the glossy black carriage, but she would not abandon France until she played a hand of her own.

In twos and threes the mourners shuffled through the tall, wrought iron gates of the graveyard beside the Cathedral of Saint Anne to see Jean-Philippe Devereaux laid to rest in peace. There would be little peace for those in attendance, however. Trouble brewed even before the priest made his way to the head of the gravesite.

"I must ask you to remove your daughter," Elizabeth whispered sharply to Luc as Monique took her position nearby. "Her intrusion into my marriage was not a welcome one—neither is she welcome here."

Before Luc could act, Stephan Picard stepped forward and took Elizabeth's hand.

"My heart breaks for you, Elizabeth," he said softly, "and I deeply regret this unforgivable encroachment on your grief." He paused, shaking his head. "Please…please call upon me for whatever you need. Anything." With that, Picard took his wife firmly by the arm and led her to the rear of the gathering. Although remaining silent, Monique struggled with her husband the entire way.

The rest of the service was a blurred collage to Elizabeth as prayers were said, blessings given, and flowers tossed onto the coffin of the deceased. Finally, it was only for the mourners to file past the widow and offer their condolences and it would all be over.

With a great feeling of warmth—and surprise—Elizabeth received those who would extend their sympathies. A poor, elderly woman living near the Devereaux villa invited her to supper; the man who owned one of the largest nearby vineyards offered a cottage on his property for her use. Not all the people thought she was a failure, not good enough, smart enough, beautiful enough. Not all the young women filed out with their noses in the air, unwilling to confront the woman they had deceived. Not all her husband's colleagues left the cemetery before the prayers were even over. There were some people who cared about her. She suddenly felt lucky to have them, to know them after all this time. How unfortunate that it had to be after such tragedy for her to have finally realized they existed.

But as the final mourner passed, and Luc and Marie left her alone at the graveside, Elizabeth's mind began turning toward the difficult work before her. She bent down to snatch a stray white rose at her feet. She stroked its silky petals and took a deep breath, inhaling its fragrance before surrendering it onto the casket.

"Rest in peace, sir," she murmured.

Elizabeth turned toward the gate and found herself eye to eye with Sigerson. She stood with her mouth agape, stammering in search of words.

"He was a brilliant man," Sigerson said when it became apparent her voice had abandoned her. "My deepest sympathies, Madame. You've endured a most difficult time."

"Yes," Elizabeth replied. "Yes. You knew my husband, then?"

"By reputation only, I regret to say," Sigerson said, smiling politely.

Elizabeth smirked and looked down. "Yes, that is regretful."

"His reputation as an ingenious academician and researcher," Sigerson cut in. "I regret I hadn't the opportunity to make his acquaintance personally."

"Thank you." Elizabeth paused, wondering what Sigerson might know about Philippe and his research, what he might be able to reveal about his work. Too, she very much wanted to continue holding this stranger's attention as she had while at the piano keyboard. "Tell me, Monsieur," she said, reaching out to grasp his elbow and stepping toward the cemetery gate. "What about Philippe's work intrigued you most? The phylloxera perhaps? Or something more recent?"

With a cringe he surrendered his arm and escorted her toward the road. "My interests at the moment relate to the Professeur's work in the earth sciences."

"Of course," said Elizabeth, smiling graciously. "Coal. Derivatives."

"Coal-tar derivatives, yes."

"Oh, nothing newer then," she said with a pout. "His research in that field was long complete, even before I knew him."

"A testament to the enduring nature of his work, for it to be still so relevant today," said Sigerson, seemingly relieved to have reached the road. He disentangled her arm from his and stepped back as he bowed his farewell.

"It is so kind of you to come, Monsieur Sigerson," said Elizabeth. "I've been made to feel that I have friends here in Montpellier."

Sigerson looked thoughtful for a moment. "Yes, Madame," he said, "you may very well have more friends here than you think. Of course, it's important to decide who among them are worthy of your trust."

Elizabeth opened her mouth to ask for more of this insight, but Sigerson had already tipped his hat, turned on his heel and was walking briskly away.

"I have seen enough of this petty little village for today, Stephan," said the weary Monique Masset Picard to her husband. Her eyes lidded and her shoulders slumped, she looked around for the carriage that had left them off at the inn for their midday meal. "I must head back."

"So soon, Monique?" said Picard with an exaggerated pout, his golden-brown eyes wide with disappointment. He fussed with the button on his black sack coat and adjusted his tie. "You pay your respects to Madame Devereaux and now it's back off to perform your charitable work? You've been at it for far too long! Can you truly spare no time for the husband you've so neglected?"

Monique looked up at her husband with wide green eyes. "You know I act on your behalf as well as my own, Stephan," she said, reaching up to readjust his tie herself. "For your benefit as well as mine."

"Yes, I suppose you do," he replied. "However unseemly the benefits you acquire for yourself may be…"

The green eyes narrowed. "Your success relies on a strong presence in the communities you serve, no?"

"In the communities *I serve,* yes." Picard peered at her through narrowed eyes of his own. "Not necessarily the communities my *wife services*!"

"How dare you!" Monique cried as her husband raised his arm to signal for the carriage. A curious crowd began to form as her voice got louder. "You know how I feel…what I want. You know my dreams will never be satisfied, trapped in marriage to you."

"Trapped?" Picard's frown deepened. "I keep you well fed, in fine clothes, with beautiful places to live… A gilded cage? Perhaps. But not a locked cage. You freely disregard your vows and toy with any willing man of the village. Even expect one to take you away from me."

He chuckled to himself as Monique climbed into the carriage and banged the door in place as she took her seat.

"Elizabeth Devereaux is twice the woman you are, you spoiled girl! You thought Devereaux would leave her for *you*? You live in a dream world, indeed."

Monique's eyes filled with tears of anger and frustration. "If this fiasco hadn't occurred, Philippe and I would be far away from here," she called at his back through the carriage's open window as he walked away. No longer caring about the growing number of onlookers, she continued her tirade. "Far away! Now, I am yet again condemned to suffer you and your insults."

"Yet you stay, no?" he replied, turning to look at her from the street. "Apparently, providing the resources to support your style of living has earned me the pleasure of your continued…partnership? Can it be merely the freedom I give you to carry on your antics that earns my place in your heart?"

"Go to hell!"

Picard stepped swiftly forward, his eyes flashing, and flung open the carriage door. He reached up and grabbed Monique's shoulder, pulling her forward until his lips brushed her ear. "I have every right to thrash you here in the square as the adulterous wife you are," he hissed. "No man in the village would fault me. I'd rather suspect many to step forward with supporting testimony."

As Monique freed her arm and tried to slap his face, Picard shoved her angrily back into the seat. He began to walk away but stopped and turned to gently close the carriage door behind him, then leaned his head in through the window.

"Perhaps you ought indeed flit back to your *work*, my love," Picard said softly. "I am afraid that before long we'll see all your efforts will have been of little consequence…"

Monique tried to swing at her husband again as he banged on the door to signal the driver.

"Home with Madame Picard, Pierre," he said. "It seems she has work to do!"

After assessing the damage to her clothing and person—both minimal—Monique too encouraged Pierre to get underway. Stephan would find his own way back. As for herself, she did indeed have work to do.

CHAPTER ELEVEN

The days following the funeral filled Elizabeth with as much trepidation as those preceding it. Each knock on the Massets' door and each hand-delivered message Luc received gave her cause to shudder. Could this be word that Philippe's body had finally been found? Was this the summons to answer for claiming another's body was her husband's? Would she face accusations of being responsible for the damning evidence the body might reveal? And even when her mind was free from the inevitable retaliation of justice, or the many details needing attention to arrange her departure, it churned on the thoughts that with every passing day, Gregoire was able to move about and further his purposes without challenge—and she was helpless to prevent him. Until Luc would allow it, Elizabeth was unable to confront the man; while a guest in the Masset home, she would behave as the Massets thought proper. And it would hardly be proper for a grieving widow to parade down to the university and accuse a faculty member of murder.

And so it was that when the authorities finally came for her, she almost felt a sense of relief from her tortuous speculations and ruminations.

At the first sound of pounding on the Massets' front door, Elizabeth knew it was the police; knew in her bones that Philippe had been found and they were here, at last, to confront her with evidence of his murder, to force her confession, and take her away in irons. Sitting on the sofa, hands folded in her lap, she waited for them to come.

"Good heavens!" cried Yvette as she scooted through the parlor past her mistress, heading for the door. "Why the clamor?!" She pulled open the front door to reveal two agents of the prefecture standing on the steps, eyeing her menacingly. "Yes? What is your business here?"

From her seat in the parlor, Elizabeth could imagine the petite woman looking at the policemen with as intimidating a look as she could conjure.

"I am Officer Dupont," said the shorter of the two, stroking his graying mustache. "This is Agent Lefevre. We are here to see Madame Devereaux. Bring her here to us. Please."

Yvette placed her shoulder behind the door as she inched it toward closing. "You will have to look elsewhere, Monsieur. I do not know her whereabouts."

Lefevre inclined his head toward the door and looked left into the parlor. "Why, Madame Devereaux sits right there…" He pushed the door, and Yvette with it, back into the entry and stepped inside the house.

"You are not welcome here!" cried Yvette. "I shall fetch Monsieur Luc!" She ran down the front steps and dashed toward the school, leaving Madame Devereaux to manage the visitors on her own.

"Come, come!" said Elizabeth wearily, slumping into the cushions, resigned. She waved at the armchairs by the fireplace. "Sit. You'll forgive me if I don't set out tea…"

"This is not a social call, Madame," said Dupont gruffly as he took his seat and brought notepaper from inside his coat. "We have some questions…and news."

"Yes, I imagine you do," said Elizabeth, trying to remain calm yet unable to still the shaking in her hands. The blood pounded in her ears, and she felt her heart would burst from its efforts.

Dupont and Lefevre exchanged knowing glances.

"Eight days ago, you identified the body of your husband, Jean-Philippe Devereaux, in the village morgue," stated Agent Dupont. "Correct?"

There was no denying it now, thought Elizabeth. Her actions, her claims, were part of the public record. She'd even taken possession of the body and buried it. She couldn't say differently now.

"Yes."

"Yes…," said Dupont. "And then?"

"Then?" Elizabeth repeated, her brow furrowed. "Then…? I don't understand."

"What did you do after you left the morgue?"

Elizabeth took a deep breath. Two. Why torment her like this? "Good Lord, I went to my home!"

"But you didn't, Madame, did you?" said Lefevre with narrowed eyes and pursed lips.

Elizabeth thought back, confused. "No…" she said slowly. "No, I guess I didn't."

"Why not, Madame?" asked Dupont.

Elizabeth shook her head, tried to think. Where had she gone? What had she done after claiming the man in the morgue was her dead husband? What was the right answer? "I…don't know."

"You view and identify the dead body of your husband," said Lefevre, "then enjoy a lively evening of dinner and music at the pub. Peculiar behavior following what most of us would have found a profoundly traumatic experience, no?"

Of course! Dinner with Luc, a spat with Monique, her performance at the piano. She sighed. Certainly not behaving as though she'd just identified the broken and swollen body of her dead husband. The officers clearly knew what she'd done. Why didn't they confront her?

"I'm not sure what you want me to say," she said softly. So, they knew. It didn't mean she had to give them anything to confirm it, to do their work for them. "You say you have news?"

"Yes, Madame, we do indeed have news," said Dupont haughtily. "Which is precisely why we are here. You have some explanations to deliver."

Both officers smirked and nodded to each other as Elizabeth shifted uncomfortably on her sofa, ready to erupt. She could stand little more of their smugness, their maddening interrogation skills. Such incompetence! Why didn't they make their accusations? They were mistaken if they expected her to make their task simple.

"What would you have me say?" she asked. Perhaps she would welcome prison, protected from the idiocy she suffered daily here as a price for her freedom.

Dupont stood to his full height and stared down at her harshly, apparently hoping to intimidate. Elizabeth stood as well, rising a head taller than he. She returned his stare.

"Your villa's fire and stable boy's death were arson and murder, Madame Devereaux!" said Dupont, in a loud voice and accusatory tone. Hands on his hips, he walked toward the fireplace and posed with his arm on the mantle. There he stood, letting his words sink in.

Elizabeth's knees buckled in relief, and she collapsed back down onto the sofa. This visit wasn't about Philippe at all— it was about the fire and Lucien. The police knew nothing! She brought her hand to her face to cover her gaping mouth.

"Yes, Madame," said Lefevre, rising to join his colleague. "Shocking, no? Arson and murder. Not a pretty business at all. What do you know of it?"

"What do I know of it…?" Again, more confusion than enlightenment from these blundering fools. "Whatever would I know?"

"Well, Madame," said Dupont, "had you been in residence—as one would certainly *expect*, given your activities that day—you would have fallen victim as well. Or would you?" He squinted his eyes quizzically. "Perhaps you arranged for the fire as a means of wrapping up your husband's affairs here? You were quite vocal about your intent to leave for America, even before his tragic death, no?"

As the enormous vise of fear squeezing her heart eased, realizing she wasn't to be carted off to jail, another all-too-familiar emotion took hold: fury. She took in a deep breath, let it out slowly. No use.

"How *dare* you!" Elizabeth whispered as she stood again, taking in the two officers in her glaring sights. Now, it was their turn to be stunned. Her voice rose in volume with each word. "How dare you come here and make such accusations! Had you properly investigated the break-in to my home the night before the fire, the villa would be intact and Lucien would be alive today. Rather, because of your consistently bungling your duties, you leave the murderers and arsonists and anyone else who takes advantage of this village free to operate without risk!" At this point the policemen were inching away from her, ever closer to the door; Lefevre reached for the latch. "And you try to cover up this latest failure by accusing *me*? Because my actions are not as you believe a bereaved widow *should* behave?!"

Suddenly, the door swung open, pushing the agents back into the parlor. Luc Masset muscled his way into the room.

"What is happening here?" he demanded of the policemen. "Explain your presence in my home!"

"We were here to question Madame Devereaux about the villa fire and her stable boy's death," said Dupont stiffly. "Nothing more."

"To question me?" cried Elizabeth. "To *accuse* me of having a hand in it…" Luc's eyes widened in disbelief. "All because I had the shamelessness to join you for supper that evening."

Luc shook his head. "Gentlemen, I believe it's time for you to leave," he said, as Dupont and Lefevre hurriedly made their way through the front door. "And in the unlikely event you have a more reasonable line of inquiry, I'll thank you to be in touch with me before you speak with anyone in my household again."

Dupont and Lefevre were down the stairs before he could slam the door behind them.

∽

Days later, Elizabeth was still shaken by the policemen's visit, taking little comfort in having escaped their scrutiny. Her determination to learn of Philippe's project and punish the murderers who burned her home began to weaken as her fear began to grow yet again. How long could she possibly depend upon the prefecture's sloppy work to keep her from further suspicion? Even a force as incompetent as Montpellier's could find a body once washed ashore, could also piece together the clues its condition presented and recognize a murder. Dupont and Lefevre would be on the doorstep immediately thereafter. With her time running short, Elizabeth felt her options dwindling as well and it became increasingly difficult to keep her mind off the details of her escape. Thoughts of passage to America flooded her brain. Her belongings were few, of course, thanks to the fire; there would be little for her to transport with her on either the train or the steamship. Paris would be her first stop, then on to Le Havre for the sail to New York. Arrangements for transport to Chicago could be made more easily there than from Montpellier, she decided.

"I am so sad that you still consider leaving us, Elizabeth," said Nicole as she and Annette tried to engage their friend in a game of whist. The young women were awash in sunshine, sitting on the floor of the Masset parlor, their cards spread out before them. "Elizabeth?"

"I'm sorry?" Elizabeth looked up at the expectant faces of the Masset girls. Brought suddenly back from her near-panicked itinerary planning, she had no idea what had been said or what the cards in her hand told. "I'm afraid I wasn't paying attention."

"To us or to your game!" said Annette, laughing. "You shall be last again. But you needn't worry about Nicole. She merely continues to lament that your plans to head for home remain as before. You know we'll miss you awfully, but we understand your need to be home." At this, she shot a meaningful glance at her younger sister.

"Yes, yes, Madame Devereaux needs to be home," came a booming voice from the morning room. Luc came sauntering in and lent a hand to Elizabeth as she stood up. "But I believe she needs to make a shorter trip to the school first?"

Elizabeth's eyes opened wide and her mouth gaped in surprise. All thoughts of her trip home were pushed aside by the image of Jon Gregoire. Could it be that Luc was finally prepared to bring her to question the man about his plans for Philippe's materials? To find the evidence she was confident existed that he was keeping something from her—details of the initiative her husband planned? That he was capable of directing arson, perhaps murder?

At last, the waiting seemed over. Despite her urgency to escape France and her fear of being questioned for misleading the coroner, she couldn't pass on the opportunity to hold her husband's colleague responsible for interfering with her search into Philippe's work—and perhaps worse.

"Yes, Monsieur!" she said, holding out her hand to Luc. "To the school!"

ॐ

The paunchy Jon Gregoire was in his own sparse office when Luc Masset and Elizabeth Devereaux knocked. Even before the visitors perched themselves on the stiff, splintery seats brought in for them, Elizabeth knew she would, again, receive an icy reception from this academic. His very posture—leaning back in his chair with flabby arms crossing his broad chest—spoke a challenge.

"We are conducting an inquiry into the work done by Philippe Devereaux before his death," Luc began. "Madame Devereaux tells me you have taken all available material relating to his work into your possession. Perhaps you can enlighten us as to what areas of study he pursued?"

"I am finding little in Devereaux's work that would be of interest to anyone, truly," Gregoire sniffed. The man eyed his late colleague's widow from within the folds of his face with thinly veiled arrogance. "Except for his work on phylloxera—which was accomplished primarily with the guidance of this institute—his work had very little value. Why, even his solution to the outbreak is suspect in my mind. We have seen little improvement in the region's vineyards these five years since his return from America."

"You took papers from my husband's office," interrupted Elizabeth, refusing to let the idiot continue maligning Philippe or his work. "Tell me what you found in them."

"You may have seen me replace my own papers into my bag, Madame," said Gregoire, staring her down. "I had hoped to do some work there but found nothing of value in his office…as we've already discussed."

"Did you work with him on any projects other than the identification of phylloxera, Monsieur?" Elizabeth persisted.

"Phylloxera was the only thing the man touched of any import," retorted the corpulent man, squeaking his overburdened chair as he shifted. He looked at her through leering eyes, a tiger about to pounce on his prey. "I was not concerned with the rest of his exploits—academic or otherwise."

Elizabeth's cheeks flushed at Gregoire's mocking words and eyes. Once again, she felt the disparaging assessment of this community—yet another reminder that she fell far short of the beautiful Frenchwomen Philippe rediscovered upon his return home.

"This man knows nothing," she said, rising and turning her back to him. She yanked on her gloves.

"You may be certain, Madame, that I know at least this," hissed Gregoire. "Whatever schemes your husband involved himself in, they are no concern of yours." He stared at her menacingly. "And a word to the wise: Stop your meddling and go back to America…where you belong."

Elizabeth turned her back to him and pushed her way through the door and let it slam behind her. She rushed toward the corridor that would lead her to fresh air and sunshine. The stifling office, with its offensive occupant now being admonished loudly by Luc, was left mercifully behind.

"He loved you deeply," blurted Luc as he nearly caught up to Elizabeth, stomping toward his home. Effortlessly sidestepping horse, carriage, and street vendor, he trailed after her as she bustled down the tree-lined boulevard.

"Yes," Elizabeth called back to him. "Love the wife, *make* love to every piece of French trash to hike her skirts." When they reached the front door of the Masset home, Luc started toward the steps. Elizabeth remained in the street and turned to face him. "I do beg your pardon, Monsieur," she said, her blue eyes flashing. "I meant no offense." She turned her back to him and continued down l'Université, alone.

"None taken!" Luc called after her helplessly.

CHAPTER TWELVE

Elizabeth walked on and on, her dangling skirts and kid-leather boots failing to provide the necessary stability to comfortably navigate the rocks and ruts in the poorly cobblestoned road. She turned her ankle twice before reaching the rue Balco at the end of l'Université. Turning west onto the more carefully paved Balco, she had less difficulty heading toward l'Hotel de Ville stables where Cheval was boarding.

A group of children ran out from a house along the street playing "keep away" and caught Madame Devereaux up in their game. A little girl with long silky blond hair shyly offered the ball to her. Elizabeth smiled as she took it from her and prepared to toss it back. Suddenly, a small dark-eyed boy with a sticky, dirty face snatched it away. Elizabeth reached up high, arms outstretched, to intercept the ball on its way over her head, but she lunged a bit too far. Turning her ankle for the third time, Elizabeth fell to the ground, landing soundly on her *derrière.*

All activity on the road stopped. For an instant, there was no sound, no movement as the children and passersby gaped at the woman sitting in silk and lace, dirt and mud, in the middle of the road. And she gaped back. Finally, Elizabeth began to smile, then giggle. The children joined her, laughing in relief as their shock and worry wore away and they enjoyed the spectacle of Madame Devereaux sitting, so unladylike, in the gravel and dust of the street.

Once the beautiful music of their laughter subsided a bit, two of the children helped Madame up, but not before she snatched the ball from the oldest player. The game began anew. After several rounds, sorely out of breath, Elizabeth surrendered and continued on her way. Her spirits soared for the moment, and she stepped lively toward the hotel. Would the presence of young ones in their lives have helped? she wondered. Would being able to give Philippe children have changed their fate? Elizabeth's momentum slowed to a discouraged slog. Suddenly, a voice called out from behind her.

"Madame Devereaux!" She turned to see Stephan Picard stepping from the barrister's office, arm raised in greeting and a broad smile lighting his features. He trotted up to her and took her hand. "I'm so delighted to see you out and about."

"Monsieur Picard," she said, smiling in return. How debonair he looked in his gray tailored suit and gleaming black boots, tousled blond hair falling in his warm brown eyes. "The pleasure is indeed mine."

Picard tucked her arm around his and began walking with her. "You are stunning today in your dove-gray... where are we headed? The world is our oyster!"

"Oh, if only that were so," Elizabeth said with a rueful chuckle. "I only head to the stables to stretch Cheval's legs. I've neglected him of late."

"Surely l'Hotel de Ville stable hands are capable. Let them earn their keep." Picard stopped suddenly and looked down at her with a mischievous grin. "Join me in a glass."

"Monsieur!" said Elizabeth, astonished yet tickled by the invitation. "How kind! But I'm sure your schedule wouldn't allow for such a frivolous interruption..."

Picard laughed out loud as he resumed their walk at a quickened pace to close in on l'Hotel de Ville. "Frivolous? Your very presence would transform any encounter into an important event! If it's early for wine, I might settle for a pot of Moroccan Mint."

"Either would be lovely," Elizabeth said, lengthening her strides to keep alongside him. "I'm in quite a pique at the moment, however. I could not, in good conscience, inflict my company upon anyone."

Again, Picard laughed heartily. "Who could be more practiced than I, Madame, at weathering the storms of a peevish woman's moods?!" He stopped at the entrance to the hotel and turned her to face him. "Please, just a sip, Elizabeth," he said softly. "You've had such a wretched run—of course you're distressed! Give vent to it all. My ear and I are at your service."

Elizabeth felt a warm tranquility take over her as she accepted Picard's arm and let him guide her inside. While it always seemed to her they had little more in common than their spouses' "interactions," she realized at that moment how much of her time here in Montpellier had been tarnished by the situation—and how often Stephan's very presence would defuse her strongest, most unkind instincts. Perhaps more time in his company might have derailed her single-minded quest for Philippe's contrition? Would turning to him, to have engaged with him in the "games," have minimized the anger? Eased the hurt? No matter. It was neither who she was nor who she wanted to be. But at this moment, she was suddenly exhilarated by the idea of savoring this endearing man's attentions—and genuine concern—for the duration of a sip or two. Elizabeth even allowed herself to indulge in the delicious scenario of Monique stumbling upon them laughing over a shared glass.

"I shall opt for the Moroccan Mint," said Elizabeth as the servant girl looked to Picard for direction. "There is little hope for an enjoyable glass, at least of wine. The phylloxera remains stubborn here in the south."

"Which is why we shall have the Hugel Pinot Gris," he told the girl, sending her back into the kitchen. He lowered his voice and leaned in confidentially. "I have struck an agreement with the family in Alsace to provide the transportation of Hugel wines throughout France. A *coup*, to be sure…and, as you point out, so urgently needed here at home!"

"Bravo," she replied. "On behalf of the tortured palates throughout the country, *merci beaucoup!*"

Picard sat back in his chair and smiled, soaking in her approval. When the wine arrived, was tasted, and poured, he raised his glass. "To us!"

"To us, indeed!" responded Elizabeth, charmed. She sipped at her glass. "My goodness, it's lovely. You have done us all a great service!"

"I knew you'd love it," said Picard, flushing with pride. Then, he leaned forward and took her hands in his. "Now, please—tell me: what's happening in your life? What might I do to ease your burden?"

Elizabeth looked down at his strong hands holding hers so tenderly, looked into his eyes, so intense. Too intense. She wasn't sure she was comfortable with what she saw there.

"Are we playing the game, Monsieur?"

Picard held her gaze for a moment longer before his jaw dropped and a look of chagrin came to his face. He broke out in a wide smile as he released her hands. "Good heavens, Elizabeth, how delightful you are!" he cried. "The game! I know better than most how you loathe those who play… I would be a madman to risk your fury!"

Elizabeth smiled, too, satisfied to have made her standing clear.

"Now," Picard continued, draining his glass and refilling it. "Your plans?"

"My plans are to return to America," she began, looking into her own glass as she swirled its contents. "There is nothing here for me." Then she paused. "Except…"

Picard leaned forward, eyebrows raised.

"It's such a defeat for me," Elizabeth admitted, shaking her head. "I came here with such great hopes of working with Philippe, of helping the community, of making a difference. The cruelest part is that I might have come so close. But now, with him gone, my only future is to reclaim a position in America I never truly loved."

"Close?" Picard asked, frowning. "You know you have been right in the midst of his work throughout—perhaps not to the extent you had hoped, but part of it, nevertheless. A vital part of it."

"But there was a project," said Elizabeth, pushing her unfinished wine aside. "Something important, and I was to have a role."

Picard pursed his lips in thought. "Was it for the institute? For one of his independent projects?"

"I don't know, Stephan," she said, trying in vain to keep her voice low, and to quell the panic as thoughts of the previous weeks overwhelmed her. "But I'm afraid someone *does* know—and might want to keep me from finding out."

At this, Picard's brows arched high once again and his eyes bulged wide. "*Mon Dieu*, Elizabeth! Where do you get such ideas?"

"Murderers and arsonists give me such ideas!" she cried, gathering her wrap and trying to push herself from the table. "I am *exhausted*, continuously having my concerns—my very thoughts—disregarded as though I am a swooning damsel! Pardon my audacity, expecting to be heard…"

"Forgive me, Elizabeth," said Picard, reaching to touch her arm and encouraging her not to leave. "Of course you should be heard! Forgive me for not being more conscious of the horrific implications of all you've experienced." Elizabeth relaxed slightly in her chair. "And even the reception, the treatment you've received here in Montpellier. Of course you should be heard. Shame on me for being among those who failed to listen."

Elizabeth offered a cautious smile, charmed once again by Picard's candor. While she felt no regrets for having steered clear of the games Monique and Philippe played, she certainly wished Stephan had been more in her life, somehow. How much less lonely she could have been.

"No matter," she said at last, gathering her things again to depart. "I wave the white flag of surrender. The idea that there might have been something for me here just makes the terms of my defeat more pitiful." At this, Elizabeth finally got up from the table, thanked Picard for the wine and went on her way—to the stables and Cheval, the one male in her life who at least pretended to listen.

Now, rankled anew by her "sip" with Picard, following the anticipated dead end reached with Gregoire, Elizabeth was convinced she would find no help in Montpellier; without some assistance, her cause was lost, and she needed to end her time here. An invigorating trot with Cheval into the outskirts of the village would calm her, clear her head, and prepare her for taking the steps to facilitate her departure.

As the horse took her down familiar trails and paths, however, thoughts of abandoning her search—for a greater understanding of her husband and of his work—only increased her exasperation. It was her right to know, at least, what might have been, wasn't it? The idea that there might still be an unturned stone interrupted any attempts at lucid trains of thought. Philippe's work was still out there. Who wanted it kept quiet? Or stopped? Could the messenger Olivier, as Luc had suggested earlier, possibly know something? Shouldn't she at least peek under this one last stone yet to be turned?

Suddenly, she found that Cheval had taken her through the cool fir trees and toward the clearing near the Devereaux villa, much as they had done time and time before. This was the first occasion, however, that the horse carried his mistress past her burned-out shell of a home. Elizabeth's breath left her as the house came into view: the stone walls charred, the windowpanes broken, the plants and trees and vines burned to a fragile black paper. All gone. The sight seemed to reflect her soul: devastated, destroyed. Everything gone. The end of hope.

Intruding upon a fleeting thought of going into the villa to search for anything that might have survived, Chevalier champed at his bit and jerked his head sideways. Elizabeth gave a soft sigh, relieved to comply. She knew the horse wanted to take her from this sad, frightening scene. Vexed by unanswered questions, however, she realized that she too had an agenda still to be completed: to discover what might be beneath that one unturned stone.

Elizabeth turned Cheval west, toward Olivier's.

The feeling of having left trouble behind was only to be interrupted moments later by thoughts of the trouble that might lie ahead, even before Olivier: Sigerson's cottage. Elizabeth must pass it before she reached the turnoff for the messenger's home. Her heartbeat quickened and she urged Cheval to quicken his pace in kind. Certain the man's involvement in her predicament would become clear as she investigated, Elizabeth believed the less time she spent near him and his property, the safer she would be.

Why she was so confident of Sigerson's playing a role in the crimes committed against her, she couldn't be sure. He'd shown no more reluctance to come to her aid than any of the others in the village, yet he had done what she'd asked, without risk or harm to her. He'd been no more distant than anyone else in Montpellier. Why were her suspicions raised by this stranger? Perhaps because Sigerson *was* a stranger and corresponded with Gregoire? Perhaps because his soot-covered clothes suggested he had been in her burned home? Perhaps because he kept disguises in his wardrobe?

Or perhaps because she was intrigued by him. Deep inside, just on the verge of grasping why, Elizabeth wanted him to respond to her likewise. Unlike Stephan, Sigerson appealed to some part of her inner self, something more than the need to allay her loneliness. She wanted him to look at her with the same fascination as when she had played the piano at the inn.

Sigerson's cottage soon came up on the left. The house was dark and seemed empty; the horse and the cart he used to navigate about the village were nowhere in sight. Although eager to move on to Olivier's and learn what little he might know, Elizabeth slowed Cheval a bit and stole a glance up at the second floor. Her heart skipped a beat as the glint of a candle caught her eye. She pictured Sigerson in his room, considering his plans, his purpose here. But the light was gone so quickly, she was unsure she had seen it at all. No matter. If he were inside, he couldn't miss Cheval's clip-clopping on the stones. Apparently, he hadn't plans to invite her in for a sip of sherry tonight.

Continuing on, she lamented the rapidly setting sun and her foolishness in thinking she could arrive at Olivier's before dusk. Nearly a kilometer's trip through the woods still lay before her. It would be dark amongst the trees, in any case.

"Cheval," she said, rubbing the horse's long white neck, "yet again I rely on you to keep my head on straight. I am surely not putting it to its best use!"

She kicked the horse into a quick trot, hoping to cut down the time it would take to get to Olivier's farmhouse. It was difficult not to anticipate what the poor fellow might be able to contribute to her investigation; impossible not to hope he might be more helpful than her heart and Luc led her to expect. Olivier seemed her last opportunity to get information about what went on around Philippe at the school—and what went on around Gregoire.

Her enthusiasm waned slightly as she thought of Luc. If her impulsive decision to visit Olivier was as fruitless as she expected, he would be less willing to offer additional ideas, especially after learning she had proceeded on her own. Elizabeth would be left with no other direction to follow than toward home, to America. Olivier's inability to help her would provide the rationale, of course; it would give her absolution for heading home at last. Without Luc's backing, it would be her only option.

She had little hope, however, that her own conscience would be so forgiving.

When the Olivier home came into view to the right of the bridle path, Elizabeth saw a cottage much like Sigerson's, although carefully maintained and lovingly tended. The small gardens around the front burst with spring color, the buds having survived the frost of a week before.

Elizabeth could even imagine a light, sweet fragrance wafting up toward her. A warm, flickering candle glow emanated through the windows and almost seemed to welcome her. If only the residents would be as open to her visit…

"Madame Devereaux, do come in," said the fair, petite Vivienne Olivier, opening the door wide for her to pass through. "Our deepest sympathies on the death of Professeur Devereaux." She turned toward the stairs. "Jacques! Madame Devereaux is calling. It must be important." She indicated an armchair and Elizabeth took her seat to wait for Olivier to appear. "My dear, it's only days since you buried your husband! You must be here about something terribly urgent."

"Yes, Madame," Elizabeth said. "I need to speak with Monsieur Olivier about some of my husband's work. I've been having a difficult time finding information at the school and thought he might be of assistance."

"Surely you can help Madame Devereaux, Jacques?" asked Vivienne as her burly husband came down the stairs and collapsed into his own armchair.

"Good evening, Madame Devereaux. My sympathies."

"Thank you, Monsieur," Elizabeth said, knowing she might offer the couple her own condolences in return. With Philippe went a steady source of income for them. A mere messenger at the school had no guarantee of employment, and working in the vineyards was not a lucrative undertaking these days, either. She couldn't help but wonder how they would survive.

"I overheard you speak of your problem, Madame, but I'm sure I don't know how I can help," Olivier said, looking at her with detachment. "I merely acted as messenger for your husband, posting correspondence, delivering packages, and the like. I know nothing of the specific work he did."

Elizabeth sighed deeply, preparing herself for the process of wrestling insights from the man without him becoming resentful. Madame Olivier, seeming to notice the disappointment on their visitor's face, intervened.

"May we offer you some refreshment, Elizabeth?" she asked kindly, rising from her chair. She stood behind her husband and rested her hands on his shoulders. "Some tea perhaps?"

There was no way around accepting the invitation: Elizabeth couldn't refuse tea and then expect to be invited to stay and pump her host for information. Making the visit a social call might give him time to become willing to help her.

"Tea sounds delightful, Madame Olivier," she responded. The two women smiled and exchanged conspiratorial glances.

"Perhaps you can give my husband some details about what you need to know," Vivienne encouraged as she stepped away to prepare the tea. Left alone with his uninvited guest, Monsieur Olivier stared her down with disinterest.

"I'm sure there's nothing I can add to what you may have already found at the school," he repeated.

"That's the curious thing," began Elizabeth, as though thoroughly oblivious to his irritation. "There is nothing *to* be found. I picked through the library quite carefully. His office, too, was bare. It appears that all his work has been removed."

"Impossible," replied Olivier dismissively. "It was my responsibility to see that all his catalogued work was properly presented and accessible. His material is there."

"I tell you it is not," she said firmly. No need to offer that she was aware of who had taken it all. "From what I knew, the phylloxera consumed his time and efforts. All his findings are publicly available. Why would someone remove all the records? Is there something my husband may have researched that someone would want hidden, covered up?"

"As you are aware, Professeur Devereaux spent the first year after his return to France working with the institute on implementing the cure he developed for the phylloxera," Olivier said, staring out the window. "While there mightn't have been overwhelming support for his approach, there would be no point to covering it up. Why, it's already well-known and partially implemented."

"Perhaps there was something else," Elizabeth prodded. "A smaller interest he might have taken in something, a partnership he may have developed..."

"Oh, Devereaux's interests were broad," Olivier said with a glint in his eye. "Quite broad..."

"An *academic* interest," Elizabeth interjected. "In your dealings with him at the school, were there any smaller, peculiar projects he researched?" She thought back to the box of papers she had gone through after the break-in, the papers destroyed—or stolen—the night of the fire. What had those papers covered? "Food in the Lausanne region... kites...the chemical makeup of the Languedoc soil? Could you have any idea where any of this work led?"

"Kites?"

Elizabeth's pulse quickened. "Yes, kites. Philippe had a paper, an essay, on kite-flying in his papers at home. Did that paper have anything to do with his work?"

"What an odd subject for a paper," Olivier said, smiling. "Yes, his interests were quite broad."

"I take that to mean you know nothing about a project with kites."

"Perhaps I would, if I spoke German," said Olivier. Elizabeth waited patiently as the man paused, holding her in irritated suspense. "That man in Germany who makes and then flies in the tremendous kites? Who is he? You know the man. Professeur and he were correspondents. I know nothing of what they wrote about, but I assume Devereaux was intrigued by his work. They probably covered the kites in their letters. But since I know nothing of German, I know nothing of kites."

"Lilienthal," replied Elizabeth, deep in thought. "Otto Lilienthal."

"Yes!" cried Olivier. "Otto Lilienthal. They wrote back and forth periodically during the years Professeur was here. I couldn't know for sure, but I don't imagine there was any great research. Just a correspondence."

"Odd that I found no such letters in his boxes," Elizabeth thought aloud.

"If the boxes contained records of his academic work," Olivier speculated, "there would be no reason for these letters to be included. Again, I was not privy to this material for it was a personal correspondence, in German."

"Philippe was not fluent in German," Elizabeth recalled, her brow crinkling. "So strange that he should strike up a correspondence in that language."

"Well..." said Olivier, leaning forward with enthusiasm despite himself. "Simon Brincker is a recently graduated student of the language at the school; he worked with the Professeur last year. Perhaps he could be of some assistance."

Elizabeth nodded doubtfully and accepted her cup of tea from Madame Olivier, who had rejoined them. A student? Not very promising, she thought, sipping. "What of Monsieur Gregoire?"

"What of him?"

"Might he be of any help to me?"

"Gregoire might help clean out your pantry." Olivier laughed at his own jibe. "But as far as anything requiring reasoning and thought—I'm afraid he would be of little use."

"I know he took some of Philippe's material from the library," Elizabeth said, carefully choosing her words. "He may have worked with my husband on something of value…?"

"I tell you, the man works on nothing of value. If he has taken something of the Professeur's, it is merely with the purpose of studying it through the night. He is a fool and will be exposed as such in no time. I am surprised that he tries to remedy the situation. Do not waste your time looking to him for help."

Olivier's words surely supported her beliefs about Gregoire, but he gave her nothing more. Could facing exposure as an idiot and risking the end of his career be good enough reason for someone like him to kill? Elizabeth did consider him just the type to act so fiendishly. And yet, Olivier had given her nothing to go back after Gregoire with; Brincker was no connection.

Fretting over her disappointment must now wait while she politely responded to the social niceties interjected periodically by Madame Olivier. Yes, Philippe's death had come as quite a shock. No, she didn't plan to stay in Montpellier much longer. Yes, her brother in the United States had been informed and was already preparing to welcome her home.

"Is Monsieur Brincker still at the school?" Elizabeth inquired of Olivier as she drained the last of her tea. "You said he worked with my husband last year."

"Brincker is there," Olivier replied. "He worked closely with the Professeur last year, but I have delivered several packets to him over the previous months. Despite the many closures and departures at the school, he seems to still find work."

With her head in a muddle of discouragement, Elizabeth's thoughts turned to the dark ride home. She began to wish she had postponed this unfruitful visit until tomorrow's morning light as Luc had asked.

Chapter Thirteen

Riding atop Chevalier, Elizabeth felt much more at ease with the journey ahead. The horse seemed always to know where she needed to go and how to get her there safely. Tonight was no exception. Dodging puddles and ditches, he brought his mistress through the denser part of the woods, around the gnarled tree branches and past the eerie-sounding creatures that lived there, aiming for the clearing that would bring her to the main path. Hoping to pass Sigerson's cottage without notice or delay, she kicked the horse into a gallop.

Just before Cheval hit his stride, Elizabeth felt a fierce yank at her ankle.

Instinctively, she kicked out at what caught her, but was rewarded with a hand clutched around her knee. As her foot was wrenched from the stirrup, Elizabeth heard her skirt rip and felt her body twist off the saddle and crash painfully to the ground. Stunned, she couldn't even cry out as a rapidly spreading, stabbing pain in her shoulder prevented her from moving. Without warning, strong arms pulled her up from behind and a closed fist met her face, cutting her lip. Salty blood trickled into her mouth.

Grasping the riding crop still attached to her wrist, Elizabeth swung out at her attacker—only to slice thin air. When she heard Cheval stomping around on the ground just ahead, she realized her only hope of escape was to reach him. She managed to pull her skirts to the side and drag herself toward the horse. Elizabeth reached up to grasp the stirrup only to feel a boot kick her in her side. Again sprawled on the ground, she lay still, trying to assess her injuries. Before she could act, the arms came from behind her once more, lifting her beaten body from the dirt and pulling her by the hair to expose her neck. Her breath caught in her throat as she felt cold metal against her skin and saw the glint of a blade.

"Your investigations end here," said a man's raspy, angry voice. Not native French, she thought, just as she had when first meeting Sigerson.

Sigerson?

"No!" Elizabeth tried to call out, but there was nothing. Suddenly, Cheval reared up and ran at the man, causing him to pull his knife across her throat as he turned to run for safety. She realized this was her chance—the coward had run off, frightened by her horse. Now, she might get away.

Elizabeth pulled herself up to her knees, getting caught yet again in her flowing skirts. *These damnable clothes!* she thought, looking down at her dress. Then she saw the blood. The dark red liquid oozing from her throat had already begun to stain the bodice of her gown. *I'm going to die here,* she thought calmly. She needed to get where someone would find her before the scavengers did. Cheval seemed to have a similar notion and kept close to his stumbling mistress as she succeeded in pulling herself up and heading toward the clearing. Although Elizabeth thought to mount the horse, she couldn't even bring her arms up to grab the saddle. The break in the trees was just in front of them, she saw; no need to go too far. Cheval nudged her along, guiding her toward the cottage ahead. Elizabeth's pain faded as a dark weariness overwhelmed her. Although unable to walk any longer, she seemed unable to fall to the ground. Her vision cleared for an instant and she focused on where Cheval was leading her: Sigerson's cottage.

"No," she murmured. "It's not safe here..."

But she was no longer in control, no longer the mistress. The clouds before her eyes became darker and darker, turned red, then white. The loud roaring in her ears eased into the soft lapping of the waves at the seashore. Calmly, she gave in to the warm, dark blanket of unconsciousness that surrounded and enclosed her.

An instant later it seemed, her luxurious sleep was interrupted by the strong arms again. Wrenching her shoulders, restraining her movements, hands at her throat yet again—strangling hands. Unbridled anger and frustration fought against this attacker's finishing his work. This time she could scream, and she did so with all her might.

The man's voice seemed not so angry this time; indeed, it seemed fearful. Frightened she might attract someone's notice? She screamed even more, pushing him away, despite the searing pain the action brought to her body. She felt hot tears on her cheeks, tears of fear and the excruciating pain. Why hadn't she continued sleeping? Then, with a sudden crash, she was overcome by blinding light and searing heat. Startled, her eyes shot open to see Sigerson's face. Losing hope, she surrendered to the welcome blanket of darkness and returned to the peaceful seashore.

Elizabeth floated from oblivion unknown hours later, to find herself once again in Sigerson's cottage. Lying on the sofa in his parlor, she was aware that the fire crackled, yet her body shivered. An involuntary groan came from her lips. Not dead—a prisoner. Elizabeth tried in vain to sit. There seemed to be restraints about her body, even around her neck. The effort to move sent her head spinning, her vision clouded again, nausea overtook her. Perhaps *this* sleep would take her from this torment, she thought, as the darkness engulfed her once more.

"Madame Devereaux," called a faraway voice. "Can you hear me?"

Elizabeth could barely decipher the words, but the voice itself was somehow familiar. She fought to get to the top of the black clouds that swallowed up her brain, to push aside the now-suffocating blanket of darkness. She didn't want to stay on the seashore any longer. She wanted to live.

"Elizabeth," called the voice again, closer, softer this time. "You are safe."

She felt panic. *Was* she safe? Why couldn't she reach the voice, why couldn't she identify it? Struggling to come to consciousness, she tried to speak, but her voice was not hers. She tried to move, but her limbs would not answer. She could not give up this time; she was afraid this savior might decide she was dead after all and leave her, wherever she was. Then, she felt the taste of liquor on her tongue. The burning sensation was welcome at first, moistening her parched lips. But then, the fear again. *Sherry.*

Elizabeth tried to pry her eyes open. One eye obeyed and looked into the fierce gray eyes of her captor, crouching beside her, holding a cup. His other arm was around her shoulders, she realized, holding her up to drink the sherry that had revived her. She held her breath, confused. Gradually, Sigerson's features sharpened. Once he was somewhat in focus, she saw the anxiety in his face.

"A privilege, of course, to again be of assistance," he said, a sardonic expression quickly replacing the anxious one.

"But you will surely deplete my supply of sherry before much longer…"

"Monsieur…" she whispered, at a loss for words. Elizabeth turned her head into his shoulder. She felt as helpless as she had been out on the road with a knife at her throat.

Sigerson's body stiffened in response. Easing her head back onto the pillow, he gently withdrew his arm from around her shoulders. "Perhaps some water," he murmured, and left to get a drink for his patient.

Elizabeth managed to compose herself before her caretaker returned with a pitcher of cool water and filled her cup. Gaining some command of her body, she took the water and sipped. Sigerson kept his distance as she struggled to sit up.

"Thank you," she said quietly after managing to swallow a mouthful. "I've had quite a fright…" *Am still frightened,* she thought. *Terrified.* She sank back onto the pillow, bringing her hand to her throbbing head.

"More than a fright," replied Sigerson, sitting down in the armchair and removing a cigarette from his pocket. "A throat-slashing to boot."

Elizabeth's hand came down from her head to touch her throat, remembering. What she felt almost made her smile. The restraints she had imagined around her neck were bandages Sigerson had applied to stop the bleeding. He had saved her life.

"I hardly know what to say…" she began.

"'Thank you' was sufficient," he replied. "I hope you won't think me rude for not offering you a cigarette."

"I couldn't…" she said and stopped; the image of the cigarettes he had slipped into her hand the last time she was here popping into her head. "You guessed I smoke."

Sigerson shook his head with a smirk. "No guess. During your last visit, I smelled the remains of the cigarette you enjoyed in my absence. Tonight, a beautiful gold case with your initials gives you away." He pulled it from his pocket along with her derringer. "These fell from your saddlebag on the road near the clearing."

Elizabeth nodded her thanks.

"Now, once again I shall perform my neighborly duty and fetch your physician. You are much more in need of his services than was your housemaid."

"No!" she cried, surprising herself with the energy she mustered. "You can't leave me!" She clutched at Sigerson as he reached to take the cup from her hand, digging her fingers into his arm. "Please."

Sigerson stared at her with wide eyes. "You need medical attention," he said. "These bandages are not nearly sufficient. You drift in and out of consciousness, there's swelling around your eye, bruises on your head. I suspect a concussed brain. You need help."

"You can't leave me," she repeated, more loudly. "They will know I am alone and kill me. Please." Elizabeth began to tremble, terrified of facing her attackers again. It seemed obvious to her that the man—men?—in the woods was determined to stop her interference, to stop her from searching for Philippe's work. Surely, he would have tracked her here. She would not be left by herself.

Sigerson shook his head, confused. "You carry a pistol—I assume you can use it…"

It occurred to Elizabeth that a threat might be more effective. "I will only follow if you leave me here, Monsieur. I'll die on the road rather than wait here for the monster to finish his work."

"You are a persistent woman, Madame," said Sigerson at last, satisfied at least to disengage himself from her grasp. Falling again into the armchair, he reached down and poured himself a glass of sherry. After taking a drink, he lit his cigarette and blew a cloud of smoke into the air. "Not without a certain logic, in this case."

"Thank you, sir," she replied, laying back on the sofa.

"If you are to hold me captive, at least tell me about your assailant," Sigerson said, sitting back in the chair and closing his eyes. "You know he was not a local thug after your purse. Is it the same man who broke into your home, burned your house, and killed your stable boy?"

Elizabeth's head began to spin as the blood drained from her face. *How could he know all this?* she thought. Wasn't it just yesterday that police came to accuse her of setting fire to the villa and killing Lucien? Before then, even they insisted her stable boy had been killed by a falling beam.

"What do *you* know about my assailant?" she asked.

"Little. I do know that men broke into your house a few nights after your husband's accident and returned the next evening, bashed the head of your stable boy and set fire to your study. There are other interesting points I might mention, but I assume these are the primary facts you wondered if I possessed."

"Yes," said Elizabeth uneasily. "Those are the primary facts. How did you come by them?"

"I have my methods."

"Ah, yes. The *observant*…Englishman or some such…" she said, waving her hand impatiently. The nearly imperceptible smile that came to his lips went unnoticed.

What was it about him she wanted to ask? Something about that night, something he shouldn't have known or said or done. But her sight continued to cloud, her thoughts to muddle. She was suddenly confused as to why she was here and whether Sigerson was a friend. *He certainly wouldn't help me if he were one of them.* She brought her hand to her head once again. Suddenly, his eyebrows shot up over widened eyes—and Elizabeth realized she'd spoken aloud.

"No, Madame, I am not here to help you," he said. "I merely suggest carefully considering the circumstances you find yourself in. You've been the target of such violence. Why?"

The room spun faster around her head. Why *had* she been a target? How could *she* know? She thought anything of value had been lost—or taken—the night of the fire. But they would not assault her if they had what they wanted. Fear of another, greater sort began to grow inside her.

They hadn't what they wanted.

"Take me to the Massets'," she said, trying to get up from the sofa. "I am not safe here. I must go to Luc and Marie." Elizabeth pulled herself to sitting, fighting the nausea and the pain, but the darkness began to close in again.

"No, you are not safe here, Madame," she heard Sigerson say in a tone that chilled her. But his voice faded as she drifted into unconsciousness, and he began to speak words she did not understand. "Your involvement in this situation is troublesome and unacceptable. Go home to America, Madame Devereaux."

The last image that passed before her eyes was of her looking down at cigarettes in Sigerson's soot-covered hand.

CHAPTER FOURTEEN

The wait for someone to relieve Sigerson of his latest charge was not as long as the man had dreaded. Shortly after the clock struck midnight, there was an urgent banging on the door. It was Jean-Luc Masset.

"I am searching for Madame Devereaux," he announced as Sigerson opened the door. "Do you know of her whereabouts?"

"I do," replied the researcher, indicating the parlor.

Masset barely glanced at Sigerson as he pushed by to reach Elizabeth. He was shocked to find her bloodied, bruised, and unconscious on the sofa.

"My God, man! What has happened to her?"

"She was attacked on the road," Sigerson replied. "I found her just outside my door. She needs medical attention quickly."

"Clearly!" cried Masset. "Why is she lying here rather than with the doctor?"

"I could hardly transport her in this condition in my cart," said Sigerson, glaring at Masset. "I would question the wisdom of moving her even in your carriage."

Masset's face softened a bit. "My apologies, Sigerson," he mumbled. "I have been sick with worry these past hours. With good reason, as you can see."

"Apologies not necessary," replied Sigerson, waving his hand in dismissal. "Still, she should not be moved until a physician can examine her. With you here to stay with her, I will head into the village and bring the doctor back. She will be safe with you."

Sigerson could see the questions in Masset's eyes, could see the man's need to know more about what happened and why, about the dangers Elizabeth faced—and what explanation he himself could offer. Sigerson was not about to comply.

⚜

Once again, Sigerson found himself rattling toward the village in search of medical assistance for an unwelcome guest in his home. This time, however, the patient was in urgent need and there were no side stops. He headed straight toward the pub he knew Dr. Moulin visited—all too frequently, in Sigerson's opinion.

Laughter and song burst from inside l'Hotel de Ville pub's oaken doors as Sigerson pushed his way through. Wrestling with the crowd, he finally spotted the young medical man at his table, surrounded by dark-haired, doe-eyed girls who seemed entranced by his every gesture.

"Pardon, Doctor," Sigerson interrupted, speaking directly into the man's ear to be heard. "I must ask you, once again, to accompany me to my cottage. This evening it is a seriously injured Madame Devereaux who needs your attention."

Dr. Moulin looked up at the Norwegian with heavy, bloodshot eyes. "Good heavens, Sigerson! You do collect them!" He laughed heartily as he pushed himself away from the table. "I'm sorry, ladies. But once again, duty calls."

A chorus of whimpers and moans came from the physician's adoring audience. "But Doctor," whined one particularly disappointed young lady, "you've only just returned to us. Can this duty, also, not wait?"

"I am afraid not, Angelique," Moulin replied, draining the last of his pint. "It is merely the burden of my calling. My expertise is needed and off I must go!"

Sigerson took one arm of the stumbling physician, who used the other to wave a flamboyant farewell to his ladies. The men fought their way toward the door of the pub and Moulin included the entire house in his *adieu*.

"Until my return!"

"Thankfully, Madame Devereaux will not require surgery," Sigerson said as they climbed into his cart. "Proper bandaging and something for her pain should suffice."

"Don't judge me so harshly, Sigerson!" Moulin said with a laugh. "The women here are so friendly, no? Surely, you have found this to be true?"

Sigerson shrugged his shoulders.

"Come, come now, Monsieur!" cried Moulin. "I have seen the alluring Monique Picard set her cap for you. Yes, indeed. And no man can escape that feline's claws!"

He laughed long and hard as Sigerson shrugged again.

"Just as well if you have kept your distance," the doctor continued as his driver remained silent. "Her husband has returned—and with a vengeance."

Finally, Sigerson turned to look at him.

"Yes, yes, Monsieur!" Moulin giggled, pleased to have captured the researcher's interest. "*En garde:* the husband has returned! I understand half the village watched as he thrashed Monique about the square a few days ago. As the story goes, he then hurled her into his carriage, slammed the door and stormed off down the road. The footman got her home. Ha! He must have been boiling mad and beaten her even more soundly when he arrived home himself. His man, Pierre, dragged me out of the pub not an hour ago to get bandages and alcohol…and not for the first time this week, I can tell you that!"

Sigerson's eyes grew wide. "What?!"

"I know, I know," Moulin rambled on. "It just doesn't seem right to beat a woman, even a tramp like Monique Masset. At least not enough to draw blood, that is."

Sigerson shook his head and muttered under his breath.

"Don't worry, man!" the doctor reassured him. "She may be out of commission for a bit, but it's hard to keep an old girl like her down, eh?" After a moment he burst into drunken laughter. "Or is it? I wouldn't know! She hasn't been my way yet!"

Sigerson snapped the reins and urged his horse to move faster. Partly in hope that the cool night breeze might clear the doctor's head before they reached his patient, but mostly to hasten the end of this bizarre ride and besotted conversation.

CHAPTER FIFTEEN

Two days later, the village was still humming with the news of Elizabeth Devereaux's attack. Shock and worry for her recovery, even fear of becoming victims themselves, dominated most conversations. But not all.

"The woman is a menace."

Jon Gregoire towered over Jacques Olivier, his height and girth filling the messenger's doorway. He glared threateningly, holding his hat as though expecting to use it as a weapon.

"The woman is harmless." Olivier pulled on his ragged coat and maneuvered around the corpulent man. "She merely wants to know where her husband's papers are. Surely, she has a right to them."

"Surely," Gregoire said. "When I'm finished."

That day will never come, thought Olivier with an involuntary smirk. "You've only raised suspicions"—*of what a fool you are*—"by taking all the man's materials from the library."

Gregoire seized Olivier's arm and shoved him into his waiting horse. "I'm willing to keep you on at the school, but I'll not tolerate your insolence. You'll spend the rest of your miserable life picking rotten grapes from the dirt if you cross me."

Olivier let the matter drop. "Of course, Monsieur."

"The packet I gave you contains two letters for you to deliver," said Gregoire, finally getting to the point of his visit. "The first shouldn't be too difficult for you; it's just down the road to that Norwegian. The second is to Paris."

"Paris?!"

"Yes, Paris. You know the place?" Gregoire asked with a sneer.

"Yes, I know the place," Olivier retorted. "*And* I know they have telegram offices there."

Gregoire looked about to thrash his new messenger, but took a deep, exasperated breath instead. "Devereaux met with some important people in Paris before he died. As his successor, I shall open communications with them by introducing myself—via my personal messenger. Are you that man or not?"

"If paid well, I am that man," Olivier replied.

"You will be paid well and live to enjoy it," Gregoire said. "Again, I warn you not to find yourself opposing me."

"Of course, Monsieur." Olivier looked down at the letters and studied the writing. As stated, the first was to Sigerson. The second was addressed incompletely. "Octave Chanute, Le Grand Hotel du Louvre? The man is in residence there?"

"He was a few weeks ago, when Devereaux arranged to see him," said Gregoire offhandedly. He shrugged his shoulders. "Your business is to find out from there how to make your delivery."

"I'll visit your offices this afternoon for a purse to finance the task, of course," said Olivier. "Tracking down tourists and conventioneers can be costly."

Without another word Olivier turned his back on his guest, climbed onto his horse and kicked him into a gallop, heading toward the vineyards. He was perfectly happy to spend days, even weeks, in Paris asking around about some tourist long headed for home. But he would be certain not to cross the stupid yet influential Jon Gregoire. He'd seen what happened to those who did. The critically injured Madame Devereaux, attacked so soon after leaving his cottage the night before last, came to mind. He cringed. Had *she* crossed Gregoire?

He hoped to God not.

ॐ

Elizabeth lay once again in Nicole Masset's bed, still unconscious, still unaware that she had been rescued at last from Sigerson's sitting room. But her sleep was not a restful one.

Dreams crashed through her tender brain cells, frightening scenes in which she tried with all her might to scream for someone to help. Running from a fire that aimed to consume her, tasting the smoke it spat out after destroying all she owned and loved. Faces appeared all around her, but no one seemed to hear her, or to care. Blank faces, bored faces, neither alarmed nor concerned for her plight. There was only cold darkness ahead, but she ran toward it nonetheless—darkness being a preferable option to the lethal light and heat of the raging flames. And to the tormenting indifference of the onlookers.

Unable to break through her dreams to waking, Elizabeth couldn't know the Masset family, except the now-dutiful Madame Picard, stood round-the-clock vigil, waiting for her to come back to them. Even in his intoxicated state, Dr. Moulin could confirm that Elizabeth had lost a dangerous amount of blood. This loss, combined with her concussed brain, made her condition serious. Only time would tell if she could survive her injuries, he told them.

"Mama, I'm so afraid for her," whispered Annette, who had come in to light the lamp as evening fell. "She's so quiet and still and white. Is she dying?"

Marie Masset hugged her daughter tightly. "Elizabeth has been badly hurt, my sweet one. She needs to rest and try to mend. We can only sit by and wait."

"Is she dying?" Annette repeated.

"I cannot answer you," her mother replied at last. "There are things we simply cannot know. Our job is to pray for her, that God's love and healing will bring her back to us."

Annette sat on the stool at her mother's feet and resumed the watch in silence.

"Who would do this?" she whispered angrily after some time. "Who would want to hurt Elizabeth? Who could be so cruel as to leave her in this condition? It's almost too much to bear, what she's suffered these past weeks." Annette paused, looking up at her mother intently. "Could she have done something to bring it all on? Is God punishing her?"

"You surely ask the difficult questions," Marie answered as the lamplight flickered. "And the impertinent ones." She smiled faintly as her daughter bowed her head, looking abashed.

"I'm sorry, Mama," said Annette. "I merely wonder…"

"We all wonder when something as senseless as this brutal attack on Elizabeth occurs. When it follows the string of horrors she has lived through, we can't help but look for reasons. I'm afraid we are seldom satisfied in such instances, sweet one. Our faith must carry all of us through, and it will. It must." Marie sighed. "Too often there are no answers for our questions. Don't you think she also wonders why?"

"Of course she does," Annette replied, nodding her head. "We can pray she gets strong soon so she can find her own answers."

Marie chuckled silently. "Don't let your father hear such prayers!" she whispered.

❧

As Elizabeth fought specters in her dreams and her caretakers tried to make sense of her plight, drunken patrons fought out their own frustrations in the dim light of l'Hotel de Ville pub's common room. Music played, wine and ale flowed, the occasional glass shattered—a good night's worth of entertainment by most standards.

Stephan Picard slipped onto one of the gouged benches for a pint of ale and to celebrate hard-won progress in negotiating terms for a new client's shipping contract. Although watching the local villagers act out a day of hard labor and disappointment in life was not his idea of a stimulating pastime, it was a welcome respite from the fretting Monique. So much a respite, he ordered the barmaid to bring him another pint when the first was gone.

"You look familiar," Renée said demurely as she slopped the overflowing mug onto the table. "I see you here often."

"Every night this week," said Picard, flashing a brilliant smile. He was careful to be as congenial as possible to every one of every station about the village. No need to allow his low regard for the locals to betray that he was from Alsace. Even here in the provinces—especially in the provinces, perhaps—there was an irritating suspicion of the Alsatian. He saw the questions in the villagers' eyes: Had he remained loyal to France after the war that sacrificed Alsace-Lorraine to Germany? Or was he an accommodator to the conquerors? One couldn't be offended by such ignorance; it was merely inconvenient. As for himself, his loyalties were firmly with the businesses that would best line his pocketbook.

Under what country's flag he conducted that business mattered little. "And it's been a gift to watch you at work on each of those nights."

Renée flushed with pleasure. "Thank you, Monsieur," she said with a quick curtsy and skittered away. The flustered girl missed the sous her patron had left on the table for her. He replaced them in his waistcoat.

As he set to work on his fresh pint of ale, Picard became aware of a shadow falling across the table. He looked up to see Jon Gregoire eyeing the empty space at the end of his bench. He waved his arm in invitation, hoping the enormous academic wouldn't upset the pew with his girth. Gregoire jammed himself in behind the table.

"Good of you," he mumbled.

"Not at all."

They sat in silence for some time, watching the raucous villagers at play.

"Quite an evening they're having, no?" said Gregoire at last.

"Indeed."

Gregoire mumbled under his breath. Picard glanced briefly toward his companion then quickly looked away, hoping he wouldn't try to initiate conversation. His hope was in vain.

"Small wonder competent help is hard to come by…" Gregoire gestured toward the crowd.

Picard chuckled softly. "Yes, I understand your distress," he said, unable to resist the temptation to bait him and risk the conversation he wished to avoid. "You've quite a task ahead."

"What do you know of my task?"

"Only that with Devereaux gone, you are…exposed, in the eye of the storm! You must take the institute forward, no?"

"I must take the institute forward, yes," said Gregoire. "Not that it is any concern of yours…or anyone else's!"

Picard laughed outright and slapped his companion on the back. "At ease, at ease, Gregoire!" he said, and took a long quaff of his ale. "It is indeed no concern of mine. I merely say: taking up Devereaux's work will be a challenge."

"Drivel."

Picard chuckled quietly again but said nothing.

More time passed. Renée sailed by and Gregoire signaled her to bring two more pints. As their refills were plunked down before them, Picard's eyes popped open wide. Luc Masset had just entered the pub.

"My evening is done." He lifted the stein in thanks to Gregoire and began to slide toward his end of the bench.

Gregoire looked up and watched Masset. Luc seemed to be fighting his way through the crowd to their table, but suddenly veered off and was gone. He hadn't seen them.

"Just taking a break from nursing Madame Devereaux, perhaps," Gregoire speculated.

Picard looked at him with a puzzled expression.

"The Widow Devereaux," Gregoire explained. "I heard she was attacked…two, three nights ago, I believe. Concussion, blood loss. I am certain she was taken to the Massets' home to recuperate."

Picard's expression turned to one of horror. "Good heavens! I met with her briefly just before departing for London…I had no idea!"

"Apparently, she was riding from the Olivier cottage and was pulled from her horse, beaten, slashed. A dreadful scene."

"What a terrible shame." Picard shook his head as he drained his mug. "She's a stubborn woman who knows she shouldn't ride alone at night. She's fortunate to have escaped with her life!"

"For some women, it can be just as dangerous at home, no?" Gregoire locked eyes with Picard and downed the last of his ale as well. "Enjoy the rest of your evening, perhaps tending to those things that *do* concern you…?" He extracted himself from behind the table and began making his escape through the boisterous revelers.

Stephan Picard opened his mouth to respond but thought better of it. No need to taunt that flabby bear. What Jon Gregoire lacked in intellect was more than compensated for by the deep and numerous tendrils he manipulated throughout the village. Picard would not risk attracting the man's malicious attention, interference that might very well get in the way of conducting his business. There was a great deal of coal in the hills of northeastern France and western Germany; wine, as well. A great deal of money was to be made transporting it all to where it was so urgently needed. With Montpellier experiencing a drastic insufficiency of the coal and an insatiable longing for a drinkable vintage, Picard was here to do what was necessary—as inconspicuously as village-related dramas would allow—to be sure he was the man to get the valuable goods transported to the region.

And as for what went on in his home and why, it was definitely no one's concern but his own.

CHAPTER SIXTEEN

Elizabeth struggled to a sitting position and prepared for the nausea and lightheadedness that accompanied the slightest movement. For the first time in several days, she managed to sit up without queasiness and with relatively little pain. Today, perhaps, she might be able to venture from the house.

"It is you and me, alone, Madame!" said Luc, seeing her eyelids flutter. He sat at her bedside and began to prepare the breakfast tray he had brought from the kitchen. "The Masset ladies have flown the nest for an overnight to Nîmes, entrusting you to my care. Clear evidence of your improving health. You have proven them all wrong, my dear. The drunken Moulin would have you dead and buried by now. We all underestimated that strong pioneer blood in you!"

Elizabeth smiled, glad to hear the women had taken a break from her bedside. Every conscious moment, it seemed, she was aware of their presence, their anxious faces and soothing voices. They had never left her alone.

"I feel quite fit this morning," she claimed in a hoarse voice, "and am considering a walk. I long for the sun and fresh air."

"They would both do wonders for your body and soul," Luc replied. "I'm pleased you feel strong enough."

Elizabeth pushed back the downy quilt and swung her legs over the side of the bed. Luc lent his arm and guided her to the nearby armchair.

"Halfway to the door already," she said breathlessly.

"With such progress, you'll be on the front steps before noon," Luc teased. "Do think about coming to the school with me later today. Although the walk would be too much, you will surely enjoy getting out of the house for more than a few minutes. We'll take the carriage."

Elizabeth took the dish of fresh grapes and berries from his outstretched hands. No, this won't do, she thought as she put a grape in her mouth and her stomach jumped. Perhaps a croissant. She took the bread and nibbled on it. Better…

"This lack of appetite is not encouraging, Madame," Luc chided, looking at the fruit and barely nibbled-upon croissant she passed back to him. "You are not permitting me to do my job."

"Some more *café* might help," she suggested. "I'll come down for it."

"No, you will not." Luc helped her, not to the door, but back to her bed. "Rest here until you feel ready to get dressed. You surely can't go to the school in my dressing gown. And with Yvette also gone with the ladies, you'll have no one to assist."

Elizabeth felt wonderfully, unexpectedly pleased to return to bed. Holding herself in a sitting position to munch on the croissant had worn her out. Her hopes for a trip down to the carriage and then to the school were not great.

By the time Luc was ready to head off to the school later that day, however, Elizabeth had managed to not only dress herself, but make her way downstairs to the parlor as well.

"Wonderful!" Luc cried when he saw her perched on the settee. "The gown Marie chose from the dressmaker's radiates on you! I will be honored to escort such a lovely…"—he eased her out of the seat—"…and fragile creature as yourself."

"Fragile!" Elizabeth laughed as she pulled down on the lace-trimmed sleeves of her burgundy silk gown and situated the hat off her swollen forehead. "That is one word that has never been applied to me!"

"Yet another dimension to describe the indescribable," cooed Luc. "Come! Your carriage awaits!"

Elizabeth said little during the pair's drive down the rue de l'Université. Her body suffered the shakes and jolts the road sent through it as the carriage wheels caught each hole and rut, while her mind attempted to piece together the scattered events of the previous days. While she vividly recalled her visit to the Olivier cottage, the rest of the evening, including the attack itself, were hazy. Especially troubling was her neighbor, Sigerson. Luc told her he had saved her life. Why, then, was she still so frightened of him?

At least Luc hadn't scolded her as she deserved. Just as a father welcoming home the child he thought lost forever, Luc had greeted her with moist eyes when she finally awoke from her ghostly nightmares. Elizabeth slipped her gloved hand into his as he sat beside her in the coach. She knew he would always be there for her.

"My appointment should take but an hour," Luc said as they reached the school's front courtyard and exited the carriage. "Will you sit out here and enjoy the day?"

"I shall do just that, Monsieur," she replied, arranging herself on the sunniest stone bench. "It will surely take at least that long to recover my strength for the return ride. Do take your time."

As Luc headed into the building, Elizabeth looked about her and marveled at the sizable crowd enjoying the warm, sunny day outside the school. Some women sauntered along their way in beautiful walking outfits, complete with parasols; others scooted by in simple dresses as they collected or delivered laundry or completed errands for their mistresses. Men were out and about as well: gentlemen escorting the ladies, students burdened with books and papers, farmers peddling their wares. Elizabeth thought she recognized a face or two through the slight blur that still clouded her vision; she wondered anxiously if they had heard of her attack. Happily, none approached her, as she felt simply unable to carry on even the most mundane exchange. She began to relax, realizing at last that the high-collared gown and broad-brimmed hat she wore covered up most of her injuries. She felt quite invisible.

As time wore on, however, her precious invisibility vanished, and the figure of Monique Picard drifted before her. Elizabeth tried but could not focus clearly on the gentleman who accompanied her.

"Elizabeth," sneered Monique. "I am shocked to find you still about Montpellier. With poor Philippe mourned and buried, I assumed you would be headed somewhere you might belong. If there is such a place."

"Why, I have been in exactly such a place," Elizabeth replied, casually bringing her hand to her throbbing head as though to block the sun. "The Masset family has made me most welcome in their home."

Monique rolled her eyes and turned to her companion. "Oh, Stephan, Papa has always been such a fool for the strays."

Of course, Stephan! thought Elizabeth, befuddled as ever to imagine the seemingly mismatched pair together.

"*Excusez-moi*, Stephan," she said, starting to rise from her bench. "I am simply without patience for the games today. Please forgive my moving on."

"Please forgive us, Elizabeth," Picard said, looking disdainfully at Monique. "On many fronts…"

"Thank you, Monsieur," she said with a rueful smile. "Unfortunate, yes, that the woman continues to be an irritation to us both?"

Picard let out a sonorous laugh that delighted her. Although Monique tossed her head and turned her back on them to continue her walk, her husband remained at Elizabeth's side.

"May I also express my relief to see you out and looking so well," he said. "I was horrified to hear of your attack. Are you truly strong enough be here on your own?"

"I am…but I am not alone." She indicated the carriage. "I've come along with Luc on his trip to the school. We will be returning shortly." With that, Elizabeth began to walk toward the building, trying somewhat unsuccessfully to avoid faltering as she turned. "It has been a pleasure."

Picard's brow furrowed. "Elizabeth," he said, reaching out to steady her. "You seem so shaky. May I escort you to Masset's offices?"

"You are too kind, Stephan!" Elizabeth said, charmed as ever by Picard's solicitousness. "This brief outing is meant to build up my strength. Taking your arm will cheat me of the opportunity. Luc is not far. But thank you."

With a quick bow of his head, Picard acknowledged her wishes and stepped over to the door to hold it open for her. "As always," he said, "it's been a delight to see you." A warm glow shone in his brown eyes, perhaps along with a hint of regret at being dismissed? "Best wishes for your continued recovery."

Elizabeth returned his warm smile with one of her own, nodded her thanks, and made her way into the building.

Once inside, her thoughts returned to how odd it was for the gentlemanly Stephan to tolerate a shrew like Monique in his life. Was it merely resentment that his wife had preyed upon her husband that made Elizabeth feel a fond rapport with him? She tried to think back to their "sip" at the hotel before she was attacked. What else about him piqued her interest? She always enjoyed his tales of adventure, traveling the world bringing goods to areas that needed them—not the least of them wine, she thought with a smile. He was from Germany, of course. Well, yes, she supposed, but Alsatian, truly. French by birth.

Now, something about Germany bounced around in her head, trying to peek through the fog.

Germany. German.

There was something else. Something she wanted to do. Elizabeth leaned up against the cool brick walls of the corridor and clenched her head, frustrated at her inability to grasp the meaning of a fleeting thought: *Brincker was German.*

Brincker?

An image of the Oliviers' parlor flew before her eyes, and she with tea in her hand. Yes! Elizabeth suddenly recalled wanting to visit Monsieur Brincker, who studied the German language and had helped Philippe in his work. A wave of triumph washed over her as if she had solved the most difficult puzzle after hours of thought. How long had she been outside before Monique ruined her afternoon? It hadn't seemed long. Surely Luc wouldn't be finished with his business so soon. Here was the perfect opportunity to call upon Brincker, while she waited for Luc.

Wandering without guidance through the tall, dark hallways, she came upon room after room of empty desks and chairs, signaling the declining finances of the school, and the country itself, which were decimating opportunities to further education and improve livelihoods. Hearing only the swishing of her own skirts and the tapping of her boot heels, she was about to surrender the task as hopeless. As she rounded a bend, however, a young student appeared at the far end of the corridor. He turned as she called to him.

"I am looking for Monsieur Brincker," she explained. "Would you know where to find him?"

"I do not believe Brincker is at the school today, Madame," the student answered politely. "However, his office is on the second floor, right beside this staircase. Do try there."

The student, it turned out, was mistaken about Brincker's absence. After Elizabeth slowly, wearily climbed the stairs, clutching the railing for support, she could see through the office's open door that a gentleman did indeed sit at the desk inside. She knocked gently on the door and was called to enter.

"Monsieur Brincker?"

"I am Brincker." The man who scrutinized her was about her age, perhaps a little younger. She could see that the documents he had been looking at on his desk were written in German. She had found the right man.

"I am Elizabeth Devereaux, the Professeur's wife," said Elizabeth. "Monsieur Olivier tells me you worked with my husband on certain aspects of his research. I thought you might be of help with some research of my own."

Monsieur Brincker narrowed his eyes and leaned back in his chair, arms folded obstinately. "Please, take a seat."

Elizabeth gratefully complied. "I am looking for some papers of my husband's relating to a correspondence with Otto Lilienthal. I understand you provided the translation of that correspondence."

Brincker stared at her. "My work with Professeur Devereaux was of a confidential nature, Madame. If your husband chose not to take you into that confidence, I am afraid I must respect those wishes."

The open window and the breeze that came through it offered no relief to the stuffiness of the room. Elizabeth could feel the nausea returning, could see the black specks beginning to fly around her field of vision. She swallowed her pride and decided to try taking him into her own confidence.

"Of course, I completely understand your reluctance to share what you know, Monsieur. However, I am in a very difficult situation. You may be aware that our villa was broken into a few days after my husband died; the following evening, it was burned to the ground. About a week ago, I myself was brutally attacked." At this point, she lifted her chin and slowly turned to the side to better display the bandages around her throat and on her forehead beneath the bonnet. Deciding that passing out before the man would be overly dramatic, she took a deep breath to clear her head. "It is my belief that these incidents were attempts to obtain, from me, information you might possess."

A splendid story, she thought with an inward smile.

Monsieur Brincker narrowed his eyes once more. "Who was involved in these episodes?"

"I do not know, Monsieur," Elizabeth replied, ever so patiently. "But I have come to suspect these people might be interested in Philippe's correspondence with Herr Lilienthal. With your help, perhaps I can obtain the answer. Will you help me?"

"Have you consulted the police?"

"I have," she lied. "They have been of little assistance."

Brincker sighed deeply and leaned farther back in his chair. "No doubt," he said at last. "The local prefecture could never know who might want what I possess."

Elizabeth's heart began to pound. Could she have stumbled onto the answer here, with Brincker? She gripped the arms of her chair in silence, hoping she could hold on for a few moments longer. Deep breaths gained her what little air was available in the room.

"What do you know of Otto Lilienthal?" he asked.

"He makes the huge kites," she replied. Beads of sweat began to form on her forehead. "The gliders."

"Precisely. Do you know the ultimate purpose of those gliders?"

Elizabeth stared at him blankly, all thoughts of her discomfort gone. She knew Lilienthal *rode* in the tremendous kites, but that was hardly a practical use for the glider. She shook her head no.

"He is testing the principles of aerodynamics."

"I see," Elizabeth replied, not seeing at all. But several thoughts swirled around her foggy brain, telling her she *did* see: the article about the kite, a correspondence with Lilienthal, the German's attempts to fly. To fly!

"Lilienthal is trying to build a flying machine. Philippe was trying to help."

"Yes, Madame."

Elizabeth sat back in her chair, her eyes wide with amazement. "Oh, my!" she exclaimed. "What an amazing, exciting undertaking. If only…"

What a privilege it would have been to be involved in such an endeavor. Had Philippe meant for her to be involved? Was *this* the project with "global implications"? She must know more.

"Why would someone be so desperate to obtain such a correspondence?" she asked Brincker. "What information do those letters contain?"

"That the communiqués themselves are of value, I am certain," he said quietly. "Why they are so is another matter. I do not pretend to be capable of unraveling the mysteries of the charts and diagrams that passed between the two men. I merely interpreted the words."

Elizabeth pursed her lips, deep in thought. "I suppose any information about work on a flying machine would be valuable," she mused. "But the world over knows of Lilienthal's experiments. They are not secret."

Brincker shrugged his shoulders.

"Unless Lilienthal was getting close to being successful? Close to achieving flight?" Elizabeth speculated.

"No, Madame," said Brincker, chuckling. "Lilienthal has been having great difficulties. The man spends more time in hospital than in gliders. In fact, it was only days after Professeur Devereaux was killed that the German's latest letter broke a six-month silence due to his injuries." A toss of his head indicated a stack of papers on the table behind him.

"He doesn't yet know Philippe is dead."

"No, Madame." Brincker looked wistfully out the window. "And Herr Lilienthal will be devastated when the news reaches him, poor fellow." He turned back to face her. "Professeur had promised some help, contributed by someone in America, with the problems in glider maneuverability. This last letter was merely repeated pleas for that assistance."

This could be *the project Philippe had promised,* mused Elizabeth, trying to understand the implications of what Brincker was telling her. But questions and doubts stymied her ability to organize her thoughts. However far-flung her husband's ideas and interests were, there was always some tie, some connection to the earth, to life…the soil, plants, growth, human health. Why would the skies have caught his attention?

"Was there anything else of interest, anything unique, in that most-recent letter, Monsieur?" Elizabeth's heart was racing. How mortifying it would be when she fainted. If only she could get this man to tell her something useful before she did.

"Well…" The man's jaw slackened, his eyes widened. "He did say his silence was the combined result of a hospital stay and the unexpected need to travel to Berlin to advise the Kaiser of his progress."

"The Kaiser!" whispered Elizabeth. "Did he ever mention Wilhelm's interest before this?"

Brincker shook his head.

"Well…" Elizabeth worked to focus her thoughts. "The Kaiser wanted to be apprised of the endeavor…" she began, fighting waves of nausea. "Did Lilienthal ever mention government support of his efforts?"

Brincker shook his head, smirking. "No, Madame. Despite intense lobbying, there's been no interest from the Kaiser in the least. Until now… Perhaps, despite all the difficulties, he believes Herr Lilienthal to be on the cusp of a real breakthrough."

"But, if Lilienthal has been making slow but steady progress for years," Elizabeth said, "what is different now?"

Brincker looked out the window again, considering her question. Elizabeth had given up all hope of retaining consciousness for another moment when he spoke.

"His correspondence with Professeur Devereaux."

Elizabeth shook her head. "Why ever would a request for help attract the attention of the Kaiser?" Whatever Brincker's answer, she was determined to get Philippe's papers from him, and she knew her time was running out.

Brincker smirked yet again. "Germans do not share."

A memory flashed through Elizabeth's mind: *"...a scientific, diplomatic undertaking to benefit the world!"* Philippe had said.

Was Philippe planning to help Lilienthal gain international support for his effort to fly in exchange for sharing the advances he'd already achieved? If the Kaiser suspected this plan, he might very well insist the inventor keep his findings to himself. To what end?

"So, Kaiser Wilhelm has decided Lilienthal should not be so open about the results of his work," she said, rising. The room spun furiously. "What an advantage a country could have in Europe—in the world—with the sole ability to fly. Merely getting to the skies first would be an inestimable asset, both economically and militarily."

"Those documents could be dangerous to the person possessing them," said Brincker thoughtfully.

"Give them to me, Monsieur." Elizabeth held her arms toward the papers he had indicated earlier on the table behind him. "I will take responsibility. The French authorities must be notified. You cannot risk your personal safety and the security of the school. Please."

Brincker hesitated. *Not out of concern for my safety,* Elizabeth guessed, *but for your obligation to Philippe.* She imagined he would be quite happy to put any personal risk on her.

"Brincker." Elizabeth leaned closer to the desk that separated them as the world around her continued to whirl. "Professeur Devereaux is dead. Your duty to him is finished. I am already deeply involved in this matter. Please give me the papers so I can get them to the proper authorities."

Brincker dumped the pile onto the desk. "Your problem now."

"Yes," said Elizabeth as she gathered the portfolio into her arms. "My problem, indeed."

Chapter Seventeen

Winding her way back through the corridors to the school's entrance, very much swaying now, Elizabeth considered the problem she had just fought to acquire. Of course Jon Gregoire would pursue such valuable material, if he knew it existed—but she was certain, now, that she faced a much larger, more formidable foe. Forces of the Kaiser had accosted her over the contents of these papers. Surely, being first in flight would give a considerable military advantage to any country; Germany would hardly let the opportunity pass. Suddenly, the blood in her veins went cold, the thought of Sigerson thrusting itself into the forefront of her mind. The enigmatic Englishman with disguises in his room, here posing as a Norwegian?

Neither could Great Britain miss such an opportunity.

After three wrong turns, Elizabeth found her way out of the musty school building. Limping into the garden courtyard, she found her bench and collapsed onto it. She dumped the papers in her lap and her head in her hands. With deep, sumptuous breaths, fresh, cool air filled her lungs. After some time, convinced at last she wouldn't faint, she lifted her head from her hands and looked around her.

She was alone.

The sun was sinking fast. The crowd had disappeared. Luc's carriage, too, was gone. Elizabeth tried to piece together what had happened. The incessant pounding in her head and the dull ache in her body made thinking it through all the more difficult. Why would Luc leave her? How had the sun set so low in the sky while she was inside the school? Had it been so much later than she thought?

Realizing she must navigate the darkening Montpellier streets alone, panic overcame her confusion. Elizabeth hugged Brincker's portfolio to herself as she got up from the bench and stumbled down rue de l'Université. Every corner seemed to conceal someone who would hurt her, every face a menace. The foolhardiness of her decision to take these damnable papers became apparent. Barely able to continue walking, she would be completely unable to defend herself against another attack.

Leaning against a tree to keep from toppling to the ground, Elizabeth paused to gather her strength. Up ahead, she could at last see the Masset house, only a few hundred meters away; Luc's carriage stood outside it. Elizabeth steeled herself for the final steps of her journey. There, at the house, she would be safe. Tighter and tighter she held the papers as she stumbled forward, willing them to become invisible. Just a few more steps and she would be with Luc. He would tell her what to do. He would know.

Finally, finally she reached the steps. As she climbed them, looking up at the windows, Elizabeth sensed something wrong. Why was the house so dark? Where was the welcoming lamp that should be burning for her? For Marie and the girls?

Troubled, she reached for the door lever. In a flash a hand came out from the shadows and grasped hers. She tried to scream but another hand covered her mouth. With all the energy she could muster, Elizabeth twisted around to face yet another attacker.

Sigerson. As her body surrendered and sank to the steps, her spirit fought back. She screamed through his fingers with all her might.

"Quiet, if you value your life!" hissed her captor, seizing the portfolio and dragging her down the stone steps and toward his horse and cart.

Sigerson's trap rumbled down the rue de l'Université, turned onto rue de la Log and continued weaving its way south and out of the village, its riders jostled about in strained silence. Elizabeth rested her head in her hands but suffered the bumps more painfully than when upright. Excruciating pangs shot up her spine and through her head. Whatever Sigerson's plans for her, they would surely be tame compared to the torture inflicted by his cart.

Elizabeth thought to scold herself for so meekly surrendering both her papers and her freedom, but knew in her heart she was no physical match for this man. Now, eyeing him with a sidelong glance, she attempted to determine his intent. Sigerson had her papers; if they were his objective, why take her, too? If he were concerned with leaving behind a witness, he could have killed her and been off without a trace. What value was she to him alive?

"Why have you abducted me?"

Sigerson did not respond.

"I demand you tell me where we are headed!" The pain in her head throbbed greater with each word. It was some moments before he spoke.

"To my cottage," he replied at last.

Elizabeth knew little more than before. *"Why?"*

Another lengthy silence ensued. She had all but given up hope of obtaining any information from the man when he pulled his horse to a halt. They had reached the clearing near her fire-ravaged home. The road to Sigerson's cottage lay before them to the right.

"You will be safe there."

Sigerson had turned to face Elizabeth and looked at her intently, waiting for her reply.

"And *you* will see to my safety?" She tenderly touched the shoulder he had wrenched so violently on the Massets' steps, searing in pain now along with her head. As fatigue overtook her, Elizabeth found it suddenly difficult to continue caring—about this man's motives and even for her own safety.

"If you so choose," he replied. "You are not being abducted. You are at liberty to go your own way at any time."

"Why was I not given this choice at the Massets'?"

"The option was not available to you there."

"I do not see that one is available to me here!" Elizabeth angrily twisted forward in her seat and replaced her head in her hands, resolving to vomit on Sigerson's boots if the need arose.

Sigerson snapped the reins, and they were off once again.

Before long, the pair sat opposite the cottage's cold black fireplace. A small lamp burning near the coal scuttle provided the only light Sigerson would allow. Indeed, the researcher behaved very much like one concerned for his guest's safety: hurrying her inside, closing the draperies, searching the rooms. When he was satisfied no one lurked about, the man flung himself into the armchair opposite Elizabeth's. Digging out a handful of cigarettes from his coat, he chose one, lit it, deeply inhaled, and closed his eyes.

"I am afraid I must interrupt your moment of relaxation to demand an explanation, Monsieur."

"And I am afraid I must comply." Sigerson stood and began pacing about the sitting room, peering at his guest through the smoke. Elizabeth sat quietly, anxiously watching him. Up and back, up and back.

"I could not allow you to enter the Masset home," he said at last, "because a man waited there to kill you."

Elizabeth's eyes widened in astonishment, then narrowed in disbelief.

"How could you know this?"

"He was breaking into the house as I happened by."

"Foolish man." Elizabeth was not convinced.

"I was on foot," Sigerson said slowly. "He could not have heard my approach, yet I could hear him working in the rear of the building."

"And how did you come to be lurking about the Masset home to notice him?"

"Again, I happened by."

"Hmm." As she prepared to express her skepticism yet again, Elizabeth recalled her sense of foreboding as she climbed the steps. Something was wrong about the windows. "There was no light," she murmured. The drapes hadn't been drawn, yet the house was dark. There should have been a candle in the window. Suddenly, her puzzled look was replaced with one of terror.

"Luc! What of Luc?" His empty carriage had been outside the house. "What of Luc Masset?"

Sigerson took the deepest breath.

"I was not in time to prevent his murder."

Elizabeth stared at him blankly, rejecting the meaning of his words. Luc left the school, she reasoned, thinking she had gone already. He had probably only just gotten there and hadn't had time to light the lamp. She was certain he sat there now, worrying about her yet again.

"No," she declared, rising.

"Yes," Sigerson said softly.

Elizabeth looked at him as he stood near the fireplace, fingering his watch chain. His pained expression told her he spoke sincerely. The man before her was nothing like the petulant, indifferent Sigerson she was coming to know. Now, he stood before her, looking troubled, unsure—and the panic began to rise within her. She squeezed her pounding head between her hands, attempting to shut out his words.

"You lie!" she cried.

"Madame." Sigerson reached out to sit her once again, but she seized him first.

"Please!" she gasped. "Please tell me it is not true." She sank to her knees. "Please…"

After some moments, Sigerson knelt beside Elizabeth, looking on as she sobbed. Finally, he awkwardly put his arm about her, and she buried her head in his shoulder.

"I am so sorry," he whispered. "I could do nothing more than see to his killer's own end. I am truly, truly sorry."

It was to be a long night for them both.

Chapter Eighteen

When he thought she had no more tears left in her, Sigerson saw Elizabeth to the sofa and once again retrieved his dressing gown to warm a guest in need.

Hours more passed, however, before she whimpered herself into a fitful sleep; even then, she cried out time and again for Luc Masset. Throughout it all, the researcher hovered silently nearby. Although unsure what the woman needed, he was surprised to find himself prepared to do whatever she asked.

Well after midnight, Elizabeth seemed to lapse into a deep, even breathing that evidenced true sleep, and Sigerson finally left her side. Taking the portfolio containing Jean-Philippe Devereaux's correspondence, he tucked it under his arm and headed upstairs to his bedroom. Once there, he spread the papers out on the bed and began to study each page in painstaking detail.

The first few pages were lightweight paper filled with a scraggly script, folded inside a finer sheet of a higher-quality weave. Lilienthal's correspondence consisted primarily of scribbles and scratches on scrap paper, he realized. The finer paper, of the school's stores, contained Brincker's translation of the German into French. *A student, for certain, given the atrocities committed to both languages*, thought Sigerson. He shook his head in dismay and focused his attention on the French, consulting the original German as necessary.

As he had expected, Sigerson found few surprises among the letters between the men. He saw Devereaux's restless brilliance on full display, coming to understand how the two men had met while the Professeur was in Germany seeking information about the handling of the cholera outbreak there and searching for evidence of food- or soil-borne transmission. It seemed Lilienthal had been a patient at the hospital in Berlin—not for the disease, but for injuries sustained in his misadventures in testing the gliders. Having decided that the outbreak in Germany was not a threat to France, Devereaux became absorbed by his new friend's attempts to reach the skies. The glider-builder was inspired by the Professeur's questioning and encouraged by the worldly academic's assertion that he might know people who could offer ideas more valuable than his own. Their friendship survived Devereaux's departure via the lively correspondence that ensued.

Lilienthal's latest additions to the correspondence were pages of frustrated pleas for the mechanical help Devereaux had apparently suggested might be available. Few diagrams or charts were included in the papers; the images Sigerson did find were mere sketches, less decipherable even than the script. Finally, he arrived at the latest communication from Germany, posted just weeks before, perhaps even after Devereaux's accident.

Greatest apologies…unavoidable delays…the Kaiser's summonses. It was a panicked Lilienthal who wrote this last time, sending along the most detailed drawings of all. The German's language seemed almost coded, with frequent references to his recent hospital stay—a stay he implied was not related to his glider mishaps. While Brincker did not capture the deepest emotions of the words in his translation, Sigerson heard very clearly the despondent resignation couched in the original German: an almost last-resort bequest of his letters to an enigmatic "OCT." To Sigerson, Lilienthal sounded nothing less than a man who believed his days were numbered.

Standing up straight and tall, Sigerson stretched his back out after more than an hour poring over the letters. Nodding his head confidently, he began gathering the pages and returning them to their folders. He had seen enough.

Downstairs once again, Sigerson resumed his watch.

ҩఀ

Morning was approaching when Elizabeth sat up abruptly from the sofa and looked at Sigerson with glassy eyes.

"Luc?" she asked.

Sigerson only looked away, seeming unable to say the words again. She fell back onto the sofa and groaned softly in response.

Philippe dead; then Lucien. Now Luc. Luc Masset, who had been the one pillar in her life here in Montpellier, even more so in her heart. If not Philippe, she was certain Luc and Lucien were dead because of her: her selfish insistence on digging up her husband's work, her need to make her mark, to emerge from the shadows. To matter. None of it mattered now.

"Monsieur," she said after some moments, "it appears that once again, I owe you my life."

"Not at all."

"Hmm," she replied, a bitter grimace on her lips. "Then perhaps I might at last deplete your supply of sherry. I would owe you a new bottle."

"That could be arranged," Sigerson said, rising. "While I doubt alcohol is best for one recovering from concussion, the sherry certainly appeals to me." Once the liquid was poured, they raised their glasses and drank.

"You think I drink to excess," she accused him as he filled her glass again. "Luc does also." A single tear rolled down her cheek. She glanced up with swollen eyes and managed a faint smile. "Never fear. I am too weak to resume my weeping."

"Weep as you will, Madame," he replied. "As for any overindulgences on your part, I am no one to judge."

"You smoke incessantly," she confirmed. "No harm in that, I'm sure." A long pause. "My father smoked a great deal. The aroma of tobacco has always been a great comfort to me." At this memory, she rested her head on the royal blue dressing gown Sigerson had used to cover her and breathed in deeply. Another stray tear crept down her face. "No harm in that."

Another long silence followed.

"I have become convinced," Sigerson said at last, "that another of my habits is more destructive than the tobacco." Elizabeth cocked her head, all attention. Was this perplexing stranger suddenly to confide in her? "For many years I lived in the shadow of a powerful drug. It was nearly my undoing. I have worked to wean myself of its vise these past three years. A bitter battle that I am afraid is not over."

"Cocaine?" she asked.

Sigerson nodded as he tamped out his cigarette.

"A dear friend lost his life to the drug," Elizabeth said. She couldn't imagine this man before her being so vulnerable as to succumb to addiction; wondered who had been there for him in his recovery. "It is no mean feat to break its spell. You have my admiration."

"Hardly," he replied. "It is no admirable thing to place one's own life in such peril."

Elizabeth nodded. "I am familiar with placing one's life in peril…and the lives of others." She gazed at the lamp's flame. "Luc begged me to give up my search. And now he is dead, and Lucien too, because of me."

"Because of you…?"

"I haven't the strength to enumerate the mistakes that have led me to this moment." She looked at her host, studying his face carefully for some time: the piercing gray eyes, the studious expression. Again, she needed to know more about this man. "Perhaps you will choose to share more confidences of your own?"

"I have no secrets that would interest you, Madame."

"The reason you pose as a Norwegian interests me."

He shrugged his shoulders slightly.

"You are an Englishman," she persisted.

"I am."

"You hide from someone."

"I do."

"The authorities in England?"

Sigerson shrugged his shoulders again. "The details of my quandary have no bearing upon your own."

"What do you know of my quandary?"

"Someone is trying to kill you for the papers you hold."

"How can I be sure that someone is not you?"

He shook his head. "You cannot."

Elizabeth raised her eyebrows and pursed her lips in grudging acknowledgment. Sigerson placed his fingertips together and, sinking deeply into his chair, closed his eyes.

"Of course, if I needed to kill you for those papers, you would have been dead long ago," he murmured.

"Of course." Elizabeth waved her hand dismissively. "And now you needn't trouble yourself. Those papers, paid for with lives more precious than my own, are yours. You've had your time with them, and now you know all."

"Not all," he replied, peering at her with narrowed eyes. "Do tell me what you can about your situation."

"*Now* you propose to help me?"

"Events have conspired against me. I have little choice."

"It appears that I too have little choice," said Elizabeth, sitting up straighter on the sofa.

For the next hour, Elizabeth recounted the most harrowing tale she had ever told: of the break-in, Gregoire, the fire, Olivier, the attack, the German student, even the flying machine. Suspicions about Philippe being murdered, she kept to herself. She didn't understand this man, his motives, his intentions; couldn't purge the thought that he was involved in it all somehow; couldn't bring herself to trust him completely.

All the while Sigerson listened intently, eyes closed, interrupting twice for clarification. When she was finished, he asked, "Had you been able to get to Masset, what would you have done?"

"I hoped he would tell me what to do." Elizabeth's eyes welled up. She listlessly brushed the tears away.

"Would you accept that advice from me?"

"I would listen."

Sigerson offered a faint smile. "I ask nothing more."

By the time Sigerson had collected the Devereaux-Lilienthal correspondence from upstairs and arranged the documents on the floor at Elizabeth's feet, she had composed herself to the point of feigning interest in his presentation. If the daggers piercing the back of her eyes from deep inside her head would only ease a bit, she might even be able to process and understand what he was trying to tell her.

"A collaboration?" Elizabeth brought her hand to her head, in confusion more than pain. "What could Philippe have possibly contributed to a collaboration aimed at creating a flying machine?" She shook her head. "Yes, his interests meandered…but always relating, somehow, to the earth. Not the skies. While he may have been fascinated by Lilienthal's pursuits, what ever could he have expected to bring to such an effort?"

"You, Madame."

Sigerson had gotten up from amongst the papers on the floor and was preparing his pipe. Elizabeth looked up at him with a furrowed brow as he continued. "I believe he intended to bring *you* to the effort."

She sighed, exasperated. "Ah, yes," she said, rubbing her red and swollen eyes. "My own passion for uncovering the mysteries of…aerodynamics? What an asset I would be…"

"Not to the subject matter, I suspect," Sigerson mused, "but to the collaboration itself."

Elizabeth recalled being in Brincker's office, thinking that this collaboration might be their project, the global initiative Philippe had suggested. Somehow, none of it seemed likely now. She shook her head.

"I have nothing to add to such an effort," she said forlornly, curling herself up and resting her head on the arm of the sofa. *Or to care,* she thought. Who else would be hurt, murdered even, with further attempts to uncover motives for and participants in this unrelenting nightmare? Hadn't she done enough damage? But for Sigerson seeming to be somewhat outside the law himself, he might be hauling her off to the police.

"I have been in Montpellier only a short time," said Sigerson. "But I have heard much about your efforts to bring attention to the growing catastrophe of the village's unclean drinking water. Your ability to persuade people of influence is widely admired throughout the village."

"Brought attention, yes," she replied. "Not answers. Not clean water. Attention doesn't make the water clean. But when Philippe lost interest, I had no voice, no way to push on."

"The attention made the problem known, and now it cannot be ignored. It isn't ignored. Steps are being taken, in homes if not by the prefect at present. You lit the torch."

Elizabeth sullenly shrugged her uninjured shoulder. *Was there more sherry to be had?* she wondered.

"Further," Sigerson went on, "despite your husband's judgment that the cholera outbreak in Germany was not a risk to France, the agencies you brought together to devise a response still exist. With their awareness raised, their readiness becomes an important weapon when the epidemic does ultimately spread."

"Another job left unfinished," said Elizabeth, now more regretful than harsh. True, although she hadn't brought any of these projects to a conclusion, important advancements had been made. Yes, people became aware of the problems; progress would continue. Perhaps she hadn't utterly failed for not having kept it moving forward herself. Could Philippe have been right? Had he been such a visionary, so wise and insightful, that even a stranger like Sigerson saw what she would not: That their job was to dream, propose, begin; then, move on to address another need where they could make a greater impact? That true satisfaction could be realized in the initiation, even without being part of the successful conclusion?

"You may fail to see, Madame," said Sigerson, as though reading her thoughts. "Your husband, however, seemed to have a clear vision for your integral involvement." He bent to the floor and picked up a sheet and handed it to her. "This is his last letter to Germany, here in the French which Brincker translated into German and posted to Lilienthal just prior to the ill-fated trip to Paris. He offers hope for a source of guidance on glider manipulation."

Elizabeth raised herself on her elbow and tried to read the script. Her eyes were unable to focus, her swollen brain unwilling to engage. She handed the page back to Sigerson.

"Not clear to me," she said, resting her head back onto the couch's arm. Enough riddles! Sigerson had Philippe's papers. Why was he tormenting her, forcing her to wade through yet another of the quagmires her husband attracted to himself? "I see simply an example of the scattered paths my husband followed, a reminder of his inability to fully commit to anything." She sighed heavily. "Or anyone."

"It appears your husband's intent was merely to help an acquaintance he'd made in Germany," said Sigerson. "He was not interested in refining the gliders himself. He was trying to connect Lilienthal with people who *were* interested and able to do so. People in America."

America? Again, elements suggesting that this initiative was indeed the project Philippe had promised. Had he imagined they would bring Lilienthal's records to the United States? But to whom? Her head began to swim with the exertion of thought.

"I am afraid I come up short counting friends who are willing and able to tinker with kites," said Elizabeth, burying her head into the dressing gown again. How long must this conversation continue? Surely, dawn would be breaking soon. Did this man never sleep?

"Have you an acquaintance with the initials O.C.T.?" Sigerson asked her.

She shook her head and tried to shrug her shoulders, but searing pain jolted her to a sitting position, her head back in her hands.

"If only you had found it necessary to kill me for the papers, I would be released from this torture!"

"Someone in America, perhaps," Sigerson persisted.

Elizabeth looked up at her host, despite herself. "The Thomases," she said, scrunching her nose in thought. "The director of the Chicago Orchestra, Theodore Thomas; his wife is Olivia." She smiled. "Olivia Clair. She could certainly host a lovely gala for this initiative, this collaboration. They would have me perform, of course, as I did at the dinners honoring generous benefactors of the orchestra." Then she smirked, trying to find a comfortable position to lay her head. "Ah! The entertainer. My contribution becomes clear."

At once, Elizabeth was transported back to America and the elaborate affairs she attended—and headlined. However she resented her role, she recalled relishing the warm and welcoming spotlight, performing for the wealthy donors to Chicago's crown jewel of culture. She groaned as she imagined herself skulking back there in defeat, returning to reclaim her position as a draw to the rich and famous, in attempts to relieve them of some of their wealth.

Could she mine her memories and revive the positives? Elizabeth thought back to her final performance in Chicago at a dinner party at the Thomases' home. How proud she had been to introduce her new husband to her colleagues and benefactors. And how in awe of her Philippe he had been as she introduced him to icons of American society. Elizabeth almost smiled as she remembered how her husband, in his boyish enthusiasm, would not leave the side of...

"Octave Chanute!" she cried. "Chanute! The engineer. He builds railroad bridges and the like, not gliders." She recalled how she had dismissed Luc's suggestion that Chanute might be able to tell them what was on her husband's mind. "But Luc said that Philippe was planning to see him in Paris. O-C-T. Octave. It must be Chanute!"

CHAPTER NINETEEN

Having finally—painfully—extricated from Elizabeth Devereaux the last piece of information he needed, Sigerson was prepared to bring an end to this encroachment on what had been an otherwise peaceful and anonymous existence. Later that morning, after feeding and grooming his horse, he hitched the animal to his cart and turned it toward the village. Some provisions for the cupboard, a few necessities for his guest, and a hearty meal for his own belly would set them all on the path toward a quick and successful resolution. He hoped.

Sigerson stepped into the millinery shop and pulled the door shut behind him, tinkling the miniature bells the proprietor hung in the jamb to alert her to new customers. He breathed in the lilac scent from the plants that filled the windowsills. Spring felt even closer today, here in the village, than it did near his cottage on the outskirts.

"*Bonjour,* Monsieur," said the elderly shopkeeper, popping from behind the dressmaker's mannequin that held court from its pedestal at the back of the room. She plucked two pins from between her lips and jabbed them into the cushion at her wrist. "How may I help you today? Perhaps you retrieve a parcel for your lady?"

"*Bonjour,* Madame Doucette. No, I have no packages waiting. However, I do need to replace items lost with my sister's luggage as she traveled from Paris. I am hoping you could provide some pieces for her to wear until the bags are recovered."

Madame Doucette took in her would-be customer's rumpled jacket and canvas trousers, scrunching up her weather-worn face into even deeper crevasses.

"And you come to me?" she asked, looking puzzled. "Get whatever you need from the San Michel Church basement. Return them in good condition and the nuns will give you a good meal, perhaps enough to share."

Sigerson smiled with what little charm he could summon. "Please do not judge my sister and her needs by my own appearance, Madame. Clothes from the Benefit Hall—and I myself—would be most unwelcome were I to take your advice."

At this admonition, he pulled a leather billfold from his pocket and opened it to reveal the francs inside. "And I am prepared to finance her finer tastes."

"I see," replied the old woman, although her skeptical look remained. She picked up her chalk and a scrap of cloth from the table. "Describe her to me—the woman and her… tastes."

Sigerson then proceeded to describe Elizabeth in minute detail, from her height, weight, waist and shoulder measurements to her auburn hair and sky-blue eyes. "Something in blue would be preferable. Nothing fussy. A simple walking outfit and hat, perhaps. She rides, astride. And all the accoutrements, of course."

"Of course," repeated Madame Doucette, continuing to write. At last, she looked up at her customer, still a bit wary.

"I have several garments I can alter to suffice, but it will take the afternoon. You will pay me before I begin."

She turned the cloth she was writing on around so Sigerson could read her tally. He nodded agreement to the number and pulled out the amount and then half again in francs.

"I assume you would also be able to procure other necessities my sister might require for her daily routine?"

"Of course, Monsieur," Madame Doucette replied, taking the francs. "Your items will be ready before supper."

"Thank you, Madame," said Sigerson, closing the door behind him. As the bells chimed his departure, he did not hear the shopkeeper's parting words.

"Sister," she scoffed. "Pfft…"

Sigerson reached up into the back of his cart and retrieved his leather bag. Flinging it over his shoulder, he made his way down rue Justine toward the Café Bleu. The week's news sheets were bound to be in, he thought. Perusing the pages and partaking in a hearty meal would certainly pass the time required for Madame Doucette to prepare his parcel. More importantly, Bleu was a central gathering place for the more sociable characters of the village—and those most knowledgeable about their neighbors' business. Truly, aside from the inn's pub, it was the best place to acquire the latest of scuttlebutt.

The heavy oaken door creaked loudly as Sigerson pushed his way into the café. He attracted little attention, he was pleased to note, as most of the midday patrons had vacated for home or the stables or the vineyards. A few groups remained, however, so he chose the large, empty main table of stone slab with rough-hewn pine legs. Once settled, his mouth began to water as he took in the heavenly aroma of the *pot-au-feu* wafting from the hearth. At his request, the server girl rushed off to gather the wine and baguette he'd requested and to determine the owner's willingness to stoke the fire for more stew.

Before Sigerson could arrange his newspapers or tuck into the bread and cheese and carafe of burgundy that were placed before him, he found himself awash in the swirl of tales recounting Luc Masset's tragic passing.

"I heard Marie herself found him," said a grizzled, graying man at the next table. "Blood everywhere. The assassin had escaped only moments before. Marie might have been a victim as well. She *and* her daughters!"

"Nonsense!" exclaimed another from the bar. "Authorities took over the scene hours before the women were home. And the killer was found dead in the back alley with a broken neck. Masset shoved him out the window with a last dying effort!"

"There were TWO killers!" claimed the servant girl, as she slopped two pints of ale down on another table. "The one pushed the other out the window after the deed to cover his own identity so the police would believe they'd found the culprit and think the murder solved!"

"Solved?!" said the older man at the table next to Sigerson's. "Not so! They haven't even identified that dead man in the alley!"

"Says you!" came word from the bar. "It wasn't the murderer at all. It was a household servant, the daughter's coachman, or some such. He tried to save Masset…"

Suddenly, dead silence fell over the room. The door had swung wide and the next patron through the door was none other than the dead man's son-in-law, Stephan Picard. He looked about and chose a seat at the large main table, across from Sigerson.

"Carry on!" Picard shouted to the group. "Don't be somber on my account. Carry on!"

Sigerson pushed the carafe of burgundy across to Picard as the other patrons quietly continued their own separate conversations. "And the *pot-au-feu*," Picard called to the girl. Now, at least, the oven would be stoked for two bowls of stew.

"My condolences on the loss of your wife's father," Sigerson said to Picard. "Tough business. He was a good man."

Picard nodded his thanks for both wine and sentiment. "Yes, a good man. Didn't keep to his own affairs, I suppose."

Sigerson looked up from his bread board with a wrinkled brow. "Masset?" He cocked his head. "Not the type to wander much beyond his academic orbit, by my thinking."

"Is that so?" mumbled Picard, pouring himself some wine. "You rarely hear of a man with his nose in a book getting slashed to death in his parlor…"

Sigerson eyed his table companion for a moment. "Hmm," he replied, then returned to reading his news sheets.

The two men sat in silence until the pots of stew were placed in front of them and then gave the food their undivided attention. The other patrons also turned to their own conversations and meals. More patrons came and went. The afternoon wore on.

After some time, finished with his meal, Sigerson looked up from the news sheets. "You have a financial interest in transportation…?" he began.

Picard looked at his dining partner for a moment before responding. "Yes. Railroading, currently."

Sigerson nodded. "Passenger? Material?"

"Both. Any. All." Picard frowned. "You have an interest of your own?"

"My research at the university involves coal tar. I hear it is in scarce supply. Any hope of the school connecting with better sources via the rails?"

"I have been in conversations with the school," Picard replied, turning his attention back to his meal. "Transporting coal from the northeast is expensive. I am hopeful, but negotiations have been slow."

"Hmm. Perhaps private investments in improving and expanding the railroads would bring some relief," suggested Sigerson.

"Public investments in alternatives, I believe, are destined to have a much greater impact."

"Indeed!" said Sigerson. "Motor?"

Picard shrugged. "Sure. Why not?"

Sigerson nodded again, smiling thoughtfully. He returned to his newspapers.

Shortly thereafter, the servant girl began pulling out the candles and gas lamps for the supper guests who would be arriving soon. Before it was time to light them, however, the door creaked once more and two local police officers entered the café: the tall and broad LeFevre and the squat, mustachioed Dupont. They proceeded to the bar and ordered their libations. Then, LeFevre turned to address the room.

"Listen here!" he began. "We need information on what happened at the Massets' home yesterday. The killer is dead, of course." A barely audible titter of skepticism went through the group. "But there may have been an accomplice. Madame Devereaux is missing, suspected to be a kidnapping victim."

"What? Oh! No!" The café's patrons were all attention now, many rising from their tables and approaching the officers with questions. Sigerson and Picard also got up, but both moved toward the door.

"Please! Remain in your seats! We will question *everyone* about their whereabouts yesterday. Where, who with, why. No one leaves until our interrogation is complete!"

At this, the room erupted in shouts and protests. Villagers pushed around each other—some to argue with the policemen, others to leave.

"That's my cue," grumbled Sigerson, who was already in the doorframe.

"Yours and mine both," responded Picard, following him across the threshold and into the late afternoon light.

Sigerson began to turn toward the right to head back to Madame Doucette, and to his horse and cart hitched outside her shop. When he saw Picard move left, however, he adjusted course and fell into step with his newfound friend.

"So…" said Sigerson, "Elizabeth Devereaux, kidnapped? Good heavens!"

Picard shook his head angrily. "Monstrous!" he said. "Such a sparkling breath of fresh air, that woman. She certainly deserves better than the grief she's found here in Montpellier."

"Yes," said Sigerson, locking eyes with Picard. "She has indeed suffered a great deal—in many ways."

"Village life is not at all for the fragile," replied Picard, quickening his pace. "Pardon my racing off. Arrangements must be made…"

With that, he nearly trotted to break away from his interrogator. Sigerson gladly slowed his gait until Picard was far enough ahead to not see him hook around and head in the opposite direction toward the dress shop.

༄

As Sigerson traveled into the village to manage chores and procure food, clothing, and information, Elizabeth managed herself into a fitful slumber. After what seemed like an eternity of days and unspeakable horrors, she found herself so overwhelmed by pain, grief, and fatigue she was unable to function at even the most basic level. Feeling for the pistol buried within the folds of her skirt, she willingly surrendered consciousness, without fear or interest in what danger lurked or what harm might result.

Much later in the day—nearly dusk—Elizabeth finally stirred and eased her aching body and pounding head to a sitting position on the couch. Where was Sigerson? Her host...or her captor? Why was she here? Was she safe? She didn't feel safe, and with a pain in her chest that took her breath away, realized Luc would not ride in to her rescue this time.

It all came back, and the tears threatened once again. Such loss for some ridiculous plan—one she had hoped would be her opportunity to make her mark on the world, to contribute, to matter.

Managing to swing her legs to the side and place her feet on the floor, she wiped her nose on the arm of the dressing gown Sigerson had surrendered to her now for the third time. Rumpled and stained with her tears, it no longer surrounded her in the deep, musky tobacco smell she loved. But it did cover the mess she'd made of the beautiful burgundy silk walking outfit Marie Masset had loaned her...was it only yesterday? Marie! Good god, Marie! Before Elizabeth could think of how to get to Marie, the devastating reality hit: She had no comfort to offer the woman and her daughters. Indeed, how could she even face them? To atone for putting Luc at mortal risk?

"Make them pay," she said aloud.

It was all she could offer. She had nothing else left. No plans, no desire, no reason to go on. At least not for herself. Sigerson seemed to have some motive for confronting the murderers, and she seemed to be of some value to him. While her usefulness held out, there was hope she could engage his help in her own efforts: to avenge Luc's death.

She rested back on the sofa once again to wait. Once Sigerson returned, she resolved, they would plan.

CHAPTER TWENTY

Before Elizabeth could ruminate further about the Masset women and how she needed to avenge Luc, the door crashed open and Sigerson wedged his tall frame through the narrow front door, stumbling under the burden of his parcels. She could make out the faint aroma of fresh bread and her stomach responded with an interested rumble.

"A pity you didn't take advantage of the sun, Madame." Sigerson emptied his arms carelessly, sending the parcels bouncing onto the parlor floor. A lid came off one of the boxes and a deep blue silk gown spilled out onto the carpet. "Spring has truly arrived."

Elizabeth's eyes widened as she glanced down at the beautiful dress—its gold buttons, velvet collar, and cuffs.

"How did you guess I stayed inside?" she asked, reaching down from the couch to pick up the dress.

"I don't guess. Your boots remain by the fire and the well in the sofa has deepened significantly from the afternoon you spent in it."

"Hmm… You have an impeccable eye, Monsieur," she said, examining the royal blue dress in minute detail. "I hardly feel worthy of such a gift."

"Consider it a self-indulgence on my part, then." Sigerson gestured in dismay at her rumpled walking outfit covered by his grimy robe. Picking up the bag smelling like supper from the pile, he headed to the hearth.

Elizabeth flushed, first touched by his thoughtfulness and the care he'd clearly taken on her behalf, then in embarrassment of her filthy, disheveled appearance that had forced his hand. She pulled herself from the couch—acknowledging with a grimace the pain remained with her—and headed toward the table near the hearth where Sigerson was re-laying the fire.

He looked up and saw her leaning against the wall: hair disheveled, eyes swollen, skin pale. She knew she looked like the scraggly ragamuffins who roamed the village, begging a piece of bread. Indeed, her objective at that moment was precisely the same.

"May I trouble you for something from the heavenly smelling sack, Monsieur?" she asked. "I suspect something to eat will ease my lightheadedness…"

"Of course, Madame," he replied, fanning the embers in the fireplace. "A few short moments and I can offer tea to accompany it."

She looked at Sigerson, part in the hope he would tell her more of his outing, part hoping he would not. How were the Masset women coping? Did they blame her somehow?

Elizabeth sat herself on the bench at the table and watched him work the fire. She took a deep breath, gathering her courage.

"I must know about the Massets."

It was some moments before he responded. "The women prepare to say goodbye to a beloved husband and father," he began, putting a pot of water on the growing flames. He looked up at her. "And worry deeply about a missing friend."

"I have been no friend to that family."

"You are certainly no friend to yourself."

"No, I suppose not," agreed Elizabeth, picking from the crusty loaf of sourdough Sigerson had just pulled apart. The promised tea was on its way to the table as well. "It is no gift to be your own harshest critic."

"A harsh critic, indeed," said Sigerson, pouring the steaming tea. "Too harsh to recognize her own successes?"

"Yes, yes," Elizabeth replied with a heavy sigh. "The drinking water, the cholera…"

"The sounding board for an extraordinarily brilliant man?" Elizabeth glanced up from her cup. "Whose logical and structured mind offered the perfect foil to her husband's sweeping intellectual pursuits?"

Elizabeth looked into Sigerson's eyes and was taken aback by what she saw there: regard; respect, even. It took her breath away.

"Yes," she said softly, peering down into her teacup. Thoughts jumbled in her head. Yes, she *had* helped Philippe in his work—to such an extent that even a stranger could see it. Why hadn't she?

The answer came to her with devastating clarity: So much had been missed, buried by her relentless demands that Philippe pay for his indiscretions. All she could see in her husband's eyes was betrayal. Would she have seen more if she hadn't been so blinded by anger and hurt, if she had put her frustration aside to look for more? Would she have seen love and respect in those beautiful blue eyes of Philippe Devereaux's?

An opportunity lost forever, Elizabeth thought. But just now, seeing the look of respect in Sigerson's eyes touched something in her heart and she felt hope.

"I am glad you agree, Madame," said Sigerson as he pulled a wedge of cheese and a small piece of cured mutton from a second bag. "You have a great deal to offer the world…even beyond the keyboard. And certainly beyond subjecting yourself to another's lead."

"Yes, the keyboard," said Elizabeth, recalling how enrapt he had been as she played at the inn. She dismissed the thought. "Now, however, I wish only to find the people who did these awful things to us. My only goal."

"Very well," said Sigerson, sitting himself down at the table across from her with his own tea. "We have a scheme to plan."

"Indeed."

Sigerson reached for a match to relight his pipe.

"Ah, the pipe," said Elizabeth. "You have one in mind."

"You must go into the village and make it known that you have the papers and where they can be found."

Elizabeth stared at him, expressionless. He was giving her an opportunity to act, to take the lead. With a trembling hand, she reached out for another piece of the bread, but her stomach lurched with the fear that was overtaking her. She picked up her case of cigarettes instead. After lighting one with a taper, she smoked in silence, softly exhaling into the air and adding to the clouds above her head. Finally, she looked at him.

"No."

"We have no other option. They don't know you are here with me. We must go to them."

"You go to them."

Sigerson shook his head. "Brincker, and I suspect our culprits, know you have the papers," he said. "There is no reason for me to have these documents…unless I killed you for them. If I am arrested for your murder, I will be of little assistance when someone eventually does come to collect the material."

"Well, then," said Elizabeth after some time. So, this was how she was to continue to be of use to him. "I am to make it known that I have the correspondence between Philippe and Lilienthal and reveal that I am here with you. If we are correct that the murderers want the papers, they will come to us, and we will apprehend them."

"Yes."

Elizabeth eyed him through her cigarette smoke. "And your thoughts on the details of such a scheme…?"

Sigerson pushed himself from the table and began to pace the room, hands behind his back.

"Who among your acquaintances is most skillful in spreading talk about the village?" he asked. "That person would be the best choice for revealing yourself."

"And when I am seen? What am I to say when the police come to question me about my disappearance? Perhaps to investigate my potential role in Luc's attack?"

"The police!" Sigerson exclaimed. "Truly? Their hands are full interrogating the villagers in search of a course of action. In the unfathomable possibility they stumble upon word of you and your whereabouts, I'm confident I would be able to…deter them." He chuckled, shaking his head. "The police! Nevertheless, we won't have you strut about the pub telling your story. I suggest a message delivered to someone you know, requesting a private meeting. You should not be seen by anyone else."

"And I would tell this person I have been kidnapped by the evil Norwegian for papers I hold," Elizabeth said with a frown, "and that I've escaped for the moment to get help?"

"Of course not," murmured Sigerson, deep in thought. "Once free you would hardly choose to return if you believed you were in danger."

She sat and he paced, both in silence, thinking of an effective scenario.

"Perhaps…I am in love with you," said Elizabeth. She nodded as Sigerson frowned. "Yes. I have taken up with you and want us to leave Montpellier…but I suspect you desire the papers more than you desire me. I want someone to come take them and leave us be."

"And to whom would you tell this tale?" Sigerson asked, still scowling. "Someone who might believe you, someone who would not go to the police, someone who would talk enough to get the news to those we need to have it."

Elizabeth thought. Who would be foolish enough to believe such a story, yet meddlesome enough to care?

"Jon Gregoire."

"The academician? The man who replaced your husband at the Institute of Botany?"

Elizabeth nodded.

"Certainly, the man does speak freely on matters that don't concern him, but…" Sigerson began. Then, his eyes narrowed. "You think *he* has an interest in this correspondence?"

"Whatever I think of the man, I know he's a hateful one," Elizabeth replied. "But he does get about town, and he spends plenty of time at the pub. After downing a few pints, he would never keep silent about having seen me. Whether or not he wants the papers for his own purposes, he would certainly take advantage of the opportunity to tell my story and discredit me, with or without bringing up the reason we had met. The whole village would know of my appearance. He is the ideal candidate."

What did it matter if she thought Gregoire wanted her papers? Having decided to perform Sigerson's task, why be overly cautious? If she were to risk her life and liberty by exposing herself, there was no reason to take a chance on their ruse not working, of not getting the message to the right people. Throw the harpoon right at the whale himself.

She knew Gregoire was fully capable of conspiring with the Germans if it were to further his own ends. If he had uncovered any of Philippe's connections and thought he could profit from them, it was no great fantasy to consider him having sold out to the Kaiser.

Sigerson sat down and gazed toward the window for several minutes, silent. "I'll need a pipe or two to consider it," he said at last, rising from the table. "We couldn't send the message until morning, in any case. Get some rest."

Elizabeth thought of the previous hours she'd spent, fighting her demons in a fitful sleep. She followed him into the parlor and watched as he sat down in his chair and prepared yet another pipe.

"What needs consideration?" she asked.

"I know little of this man Gregoire," he said. "I don't know what his stake is in this material, and I don't believe he would accept such an implausible story."

"That I am in love with you?" How easily the words spilled out.

Sigerson responded by tossing his match onto the grate, closing his eyes, and inhaling deeply. "Please rest, Madame," he said.

Clearly, the conversation was over. Elizabeth was dismissed.

"You would be wise to consider, Monsieur," she said, glowering at him, "that what *you* may judge an 'implausible story' is the very lifeblood upon which Montpellier thrives. You may discount its believability. I assure you, the villagers will not."

She marched into the "music" room in the back of the house and slammed the door for effect. Curling up on the sofa there, she welcomed being alone among the beautiful, silent instruments. Here, at least, she was able to sense a measure of peace settle over her, even as the rage seethed beneath the surface.

Elizabeth rested her head on the tufted arm but lasted there only moments. Thoughts of being discounted, yet again, by someone she had no choice but to rely upon, battered her brain. Anger competed with confusion over Sigerson's claimed motives for helping her, his making her feel capable and respected with one breath, then dismissing her attempts to participate with the next. Other than to expose herself and put herself at risk, of course. Darkest thoughts of all, however, were those that tempted her to abandon hope. What benefit would result from finding the murderers, seeing them brought to justice? For identifying a body she suspected was not her husband, enabling the killers to work unimpeded, she could very well be right there in the dock with them. Philippe, Lucien, and Luc were gone forever. And all so she could act as courier for Lilienthal and connect him with Octave Chanute? Preposterous.

Finally, she moved to the mantle and found matches to light the candles there and her heart warmed a bit to the glow they created. She took in the room. So small, so safe. The bare floorboards creaked as she shifted her weight and stepped over to the worn piano, which somehow managed to reflect the flickering light. She sat down at the keyboard and ran her palm silently along the smooth, cool ivory. A melancholy etude ran through her mind, but her hands stiffened before her fingers could make contact with the keys. No. Elizabeth pushed the bench back and, after puffing the candles out, returned to the sofa to sulk until sleep overtook her once more. She would not be Sigerson's entertainment tonight.

After some time, with great satisfaction, she heard what she imagined was a heavy sigh of disappointment on the other side of the music room door and listened as Sigerson made his reluctant way up the stairs to finish the "pipe or two" in his bedroom.

Despite Sigerson's two-pipe consideration of alternatives to Elizabeth's scenario for spreading the word about their possessing the coveted papers, no approach any less absurd than hers had come to light. And so it was that Madame Devereaux and her host Sigerson were forced to put her "implausible" scenario into action.

Still irritated by the previous evening's conclusion, Elizabeth awoke even more determined to do whatever necessary to ensure their plan's success. After several frosty exchanges to arrange the logistics, Sigerson was free to escape his miffed conspirator and head back into the village to arrange for a message to be delivered to Jon Gregoire. Several hours later he returned driving a horse and carriage for their task, as well as news of having secured a meeting with their adversary that very evening outside l'Peyrou.

Elizabeth took over Sigerson's bedroom to at last shed her soiled walking outfit, clean up as best she could, and step into the charming gown Madame Doucette had prepared for her. She marveled at the woman's work and how precisely the garments fit her form. Irritation at Sigerson eased as she admitted it was because of his efforts that the beautiful clothes were hers to wear, and she found it difficult not to relish the dazzled look in his eyes when she emerged at the top of the stairs. Indeed, as Elizabeth descended, dressed in the striking blue gown, eyes bright, cheeks rosy, the transformation startled Sigerson out of his seat to greet her.

"Madame! Your radiance cannot help but pull a full confession from your suspected villain's lips!"

"I would congratulate you on your own work as well."

Sigerson, dressed as an elderly driver and groom—
cropped pants, jacket, and low-fitting hat—gave a curt bow.
He circled the room, with a limp and stooping shoulders to
complete the effect. *Apparently, the makeup and disguises are
still in his wardrobe*, Elizabeth thought uneasily.

"I can hardly present as myself this evening, Madame."
He chuckled silently. "Gregoire might be convinced of your
lovesick tale. That I would assist in your betrayal? No."

"Well, then. Fetch my carriage, coachman. My party
awaits!"

Once outside, Sigerson helped Elizabeth up into the
coach. She settled herself onto the rich, tufted leather
seats and moved the curtain aside. She could see nothing
in the darkness. But as her driver whipped the horses into
motion, she felt them turning into a direction opposite the
village. Her heartbeat quickened. Why distrust Sigerson
now, she thought, trying to calm herself. He'd had many
opportunities to turn on her over the past week, if that
were his intent. Rather, he had been a source of support
and direction.

Still, his motivation for providing that support was still
unclear.

As the carriage rumbled along, Elizabeth tried to force
thoughts of Sigerson and his dubious intent from her mind
and focus on the work ahead. She understood the first step
was to identify who was trying to keep Philippe's work
from her—and would be willing to kill in the process. Was
Gregoire clever enough, or cruel enough, to be one of them?
He needn't be clever to follow orders, Elizabeth reasoned,
especially if he had captured the attention of the Kaiser.
He was cruel enough, of course, and must be convinced to
come after the papers.

While she had every confidence of being up to the task at hand, Elizabeth was terrified of the aftermath. Once Gregoire was caught in the act, what would happen to her? Would the fact that his ambition may have led to Luc's and Lucien's murders, perhaps even Philippe's, exonerate her for making a false identification at the morgue? Of disappearing after Luc's murder? Even of collaborating with her kidnapper? Would Sigerson's mystifying influence, such that enabled him to "deter" the police, keep her from arrest? Not in the least, she was certain. Despite it all, she knew, even if miraculously free of consequences, nothing could remove the regret from her own heart.

But was it that regret, even the guilt, that gave her the courage to confront Gregoire? Perhaps because this adventure would expose her to discovery, and the punishment she deserved would be the thing to cleanse her soul? Surely, the act of paying for her deeds would be a decided improvement over hiding like a coward to avoid the price.

Endless minutes later, Elizabeth was able to see out the window that Sigerson had taken her into Montpellier from the north, entering close to l'Peyrou itself. She gave the slightest sigh of relief that her suspicions of him were, at least at this point, unwarranted. Relief, too, realizing they would not pass the Masset home and see into the windows, leading her to further imagine the pain and heartache that engulfed the women inside. There would be plenty of time for seeing them and their pain firsthand once this ordeal was completed. That, too, would be part of her price to pay.

L'Peyrou came into view on the left side of the carriage. The gates were still opened, gaslights lit the arch, but Sigerson pulled the vehicle up along the stone curb that lined the front gardens. Peeking through the curtains, Elizabeth was amazed for a moment to see an elderly man precariously stumble down from the driver's bench. What a metamor-phosis! She watched as Sigerson in disguise doddered to the horse and held on to it for support as he began to brush down the animal after its trip. She could even hear him muttering, seemingly in argument with himself. After what seemed like forever, the clock struck 10.

Only now 10 o'clock! she thought, the panic welling up. *I'll surely die if I must wait another minute!*

But her life was to be spared as a sharp tap came on the carriage door. Elizabeth pushed it open and admitted Jon Gregoire, dressed in evening clothes and reeking of alcohol. The coach rocked heavily back and forth as the large man climbed in and took the seat opposite the woman who had summoned him.

"I've postponed an important engagement for this non-sense. It'd better be worth my time." After inspecting the well-appointed carriage, Gregoire finally set eyes on Eliza-beth, looking up and down her body, her blue silk gown, her red lips and pink, glowing cheeks. "You look well for some-one who's been missing and feared dead. Perhaps the investi-gation of your 'kidnapping' should take another direction?"

"Monsieur, are you interested in knowing the reason I've asked to meet you? Or would you rather speculate aimlessly on your own?"

"Oh, yes, Madame," he replied with a sneer. "I am very interested in your version of the past week's events."

"My version is this," Elizabeth began, quelling the temp-tation to engage the man in a verbal sparring match. "I've obtained the documents of a correspondence between my husband and some influential people in the academic com-munity. I can't be sure"—Elizabeth swallowed hard—"but I believe the information to be quite valuable. On my way to Luc Masset's the night he was…attacked, the Norwegian

Sigerson accosted me and brought me and my papers to his cottage. Someone must find those papers and use them as my husband meant them to be used. Sigerson cannot be allowed to take this correspondence out of the country. He watches my every move; I am unable to even look for the material without raising his suspicions. I need help. I thought of you."

"Why me?" Gregoire minutely examined his fingernails.

Elizabeth shifted in her seat. "Of anyone at the school, I assume you would be most aware of Philippe's work and would be able to continue it." Gregoire let out a loud snort. "You have been collecting his work yourself, correct?"

"To keep it away from you, goes the story about the school," he snapped. "You have made my life difficult, Madame, telling people I have absconded with your husband's precious research. Now, you wish to hand over more of it? Something valuable? Why should I believe any of what you say? Your past behavior and your current story are most suspect."

"I understand your reluctance to trust me," she said quickly. "And I regret that I have no proof to support my sincerity. The game I played was a dangerous one; too many desperate people want the information I possess. I am out of my depths, and now I feel an obligation to see that the material is used as my husband wished. I must get it away from Sigerson because I am convinced he means to take it to Norway for that government's use. Luc Masset is unable to help me." Elizabeth's eyes began to fill, not an act at all. "He was the man I would have trusted most. Will you be the man to help me now? Or not?" She brushed the tears angrily from her cheeks.

Gregoire squinted at her through the folds of fat around his eyes. "You *claim* to have been kidnapped by the man who may very well have slaughtered your Masset. He has taken your documents. Why come to me for help?" he asked with a nasty snarl. "If you're truly concerned about retrieving the material from Sigerson, let's both go to the police right now. We'll have the papers by midnight. France and your husband's reputation will be saved."

Elizabeth couldn't help but let a look of horror creep to her face. Not the police!

"No!"

She regretted the outburst as soon as the word left her mouth. Her chest felt tight, her breaths came short, the carriage walls closed in on her. *Stupid, stupid woman!* she chided herself. Twisting her gloves in her hands, Elizabeth looked down at her lap, avoiding Gregoire's probing stare. He said nothing for what seemed an eternity. The clock struck the half hour. Silence roared in Elizabeth's ears so loudly she wanted to cover them and scream. How could she have become so unstrung? Thoughts of what to say next, of how to fix the blunder, clamored in her head.

Suddenly, Gregoire spoke, sounding amazed. "You're protecting him!" he cried. "You want to get the papers away without implicating the man. You've fallen for that befuddled researcher!"

Elizabeth looked up, as astonished as he. *No*, she thought. He couldn't possibly have concocted this ludicrous story on his own… Averting her eyes, she felt the color of excitement rise in her cheeks.

"You *are* protecting him!" Gregoire slapped his wide knee with a vicious laugh. "You silly little fool!" He wriggled himself forward on the seat and struggled to his feet; the carriage dipped precariously to the right. "I don't need your damn papers—I've already connected with your 'influential people.' Even if I knew nothing of the matter, I wouldn't lift a finger to help you, Madame Devereaux. You've been nothing but trouble to me—and to yourself as well. Now, let the Norwegian deal with you and your troublemaking!"

Elizabeth could hear Gregoire's lurid laughter as he slammed the door shut and stumbled away. Had she enough distance from him, she'd have joined in. The idiot had convinced *himself* of their story. And as for not needing her papers? Rubbish! Hadn't he been aware of Philippe's published work? Yet he still cleared it all from the shelves. There was no possible scenario where Gregoire would leave the correspondence with Sigerson. A plan to obtain them would be hatching any moment now, especially if Gregoire's "important engagement" was at the pub. She banged on the roof.

"Home, sir!" she called cheerily to the groom, who was attempting, with great difficulty, to climb up to the driver's perch.

The elderly groom, whom she knew would also be anxious to return and hear every word of the conversation repeated, whipped the horses in a hurry to oblige her.

CHAPTER TWENTY-ONE

Elizabeth's hopes for a quick attempt on the papers were not justified. After the first anxious days when each of them both feared and sought a confrontation, a distressed pall fell over the cottage. She, agitated by every creak in the floorboards, expected the police to arrive at any moment to demand answers for her absence, for abandoning Luc to his attacker, for conspiring with her abductor, for lying about her husband's body. While he, keeping to his routine of heading into town for the news sheets and provisions, was driven to a sullen distraction over the stalemate, becoming even more irritable and withdrawn as time passed and no one approached.

On the fourth morning since her meeting with Gregoire, after futilely attempting to contain her mounting trepidation, Elizabeth emerged from the music room dressed in the khaki jodhpurs and crisp white blouse Madame Doucette had altered for her. She found Sigerson in the parlor, wrapped in his red dressing gown and drawing thoughtfully on his pipe as he read the news sheets. A vaguely familiar tin box rested near the chair by his feet. He glanced up at Elizabeth with such unexpected warmth in his eyes, her heart skipped a beat.

"Something to calm your nerves...?" he said, glancing down at the box.

She studied the box on the floor. The lid was deeply dented and charred; the latch was gone, but it still closed tightly. Suddenly, her eyes grew wide with delight.

"Why, it's *my* dispatch box!" she cried, falling to the floor and poking desperately around the edges of the crushed lid for a way to pull it open. "My music! You've rescued it from the ashes!"

Sigerson took the box from her, found a grip on the corner, and pulled it apart. Sheets of music fell to the floor. "During a detour by your burned-out home I came upon the box and this." He withdrew an old book from a bag at his side and handed it to her. "There was little else worth taking."

She clutched the book to her breast as a child would a treasured doll. "*The Origin of Tree Worship,*" Elizabeth read lovingly.

"Riveting…" Sigerson commented dryly.

"My music and my books are so precious to me," said Elizabeth dreamily. She smiled suddenly at the thought of a soot-covered Sigerson, serving her sherry the night of the fire. "You saved them."

"I retrieved them, yes," he replied. "I stowed the box… out of sight, out of mind. I regret not returning it sooner."

"The piano." Elizabeth looked toward the music room and her fingers itched. "You play?"

Sigerson shook his head. "I prefer the strings. Violin."

"The violin!" Elizabeth exclaimed in wonder and excitement. She took her tin box into the music room. "The piece you rescued…it is a duet…"

"So I came to notice," said Sigerson, rising and following her.

"I have never heard it performed." She pulled out the bench and sat herself at the keyboard. As she executed repeated glissandos, a soothing peace came over her, enveloping body and soul. How childish of her to have refused to play it before now. "So beautiful."

"You bring it to life," he replied softly. "Please, indulge yourself."

Elizabeth indulged herself at the piano, indeed, filling the cottage with the sounds of Chopin and Liszt, pieces only recently received from the publisher and committed to memory. Forgetting the fire, Lucien, murderous thieves, Luc, Philippe, and her attackers, she was in her own world—knowing and feeling only the music in her heart and the ivory and ebony on her fingertips. She indulged Sigerson as well. He sat down quietly on the sofa beside the piano and listened with the closed eyes and whimsical smile of a man who'd admired this musician before.

After more than an hour, Elizabeth finally rested her hands and looked around to find Sigerson still enrapt. She slid off the bench and picked up the violin from the floor.

"Will *you* indulge us?" she asked, handing the instrument to him.

"Another time, perhaps," he replied gruffly. "Thank you for your sublime performance. You are indeed a most gifted musician." He rose from the sofa and made his way toward the door.

Elizabeth reached into the tin box and pulled out her composition. "I've never heard it performed," she said again wistfully. "Could you possibly join me…if only in the theme?"

Sigerson let a faint smile creep to his lips. After some thought, he finally took the instrument from her and carefully, lovingly tucked it under his chin. Taking bow in hand, he waited for her to begin.

Elizabeth sat down once again at the keyboard and felt a gentle tingle as she became aware of Sigerson standing close behind her, his warm breath on her neck as he leaned closer to read the music. After a moment, she began the piece, bringing the notes on the pages to life.

Sprightly, light, trickling up and down the scales. As always when surrendering herself to the keyboard, she was off to another place; a place where she was happy and free. Not a location, but a corner of her very being where all was well, and she was innocent of any selfishness or wrongdoing.

Then, reality entered the score as Sigerson joined in with the suddenly mournful sigh of the strings. Eyes closed, he seemed to move with the bow, becoming the sounds he produced. He, too, appeared to have left the room, gone to a place that was melancholy and somber. Piano and violin intertwined their music, at once resisting and supporting the other's part. The positive, optimistic keys fighting to remain so, but always pursued by the gloomy and foreboding strings.

As the final notes died away, each musician's spirit came back into the room to join the other. Elizabeth sat motionless, afraid even a creak of the bench might break the fragile bond the music had formed between her and her accompanist—the passionate violinist the composition was written for. Facing the window, his arms at his sides, Sigerson stood silently, still clutching the violin and bow, seeming to also want the magic of the performance to continue.

After some moments, Elizabeth slid quietly from the piano bench and moved behind him, softly touching his hand. Sigerson turned and looked at her with dreamy eyes—the eyes of the man who had so fascinated her at the inn.

"You've played it before," she said. The image of him caressing her face with cool, soft hands suddenly materialized before her eyes.

Sigerson looked down at their fingers interlaced around the violin's neck. He took a deep breath, slowly exhaled. "Yes, I have." He moved away from her and looked about for the instrument's case. The dreamy artist was gone. "Since about the age of six."

She smirked. "I refer to the duet."

"If I've taken a liberty, please accept my apologies," said Sigerson with a slight smile. "The music, even on paper, was so beautiful and pure...I couldn't help but experience it." He paused for a moment. "I was deeply moved by the piece."

"I was deeply moved by your performance of it." Elizabeth followed him and took his arm gently, turning him to face her. "Such a gift—I feel as though you've burrowed into my heart and played what you found there."

"You flatter me, Madame," he said, his eyes seeming to seek escape from her grasp. "I played the notes you set down. I know nothing of what's in your heart."

"*Au contraire*, Monsieur. I believe you do."

Sigerson managed to make his way to the mantle and fumbled with the humidor, preparing to fill his pipe. "Affairs of the heart are not my *forté.*" Tamping the tobacco into the bowl of the pipe, he settled himself on the sofa and struck a match. "I focus my energies on the practical pursuits of the intellect."

"Your performance contradicts you. Each time you drew your bow across the strings you described the emptiness, the loneliness I feel inside—and the hope I cherish of someday filling the void. You know the feeling, too, don't you?" She looked at him accusingly. "You are as lonely and empty inside as I."

"I am an accomplished musician," Sigerson replied, raising his chin in defiance, yet avoiding her gaze. "I performed the duet as you composed it. The magic of the piece is your own. As for loneliness? You say you are lonely; I am merely alone. There is a difference."

"Yes," said Elizabeth with a wry smile. "The difference is that I confront what's in my heart, however impractical a pursuit it may be."

Sigerson shrugged his shoulders and sank deeper into the cushions, drawing heavily on his pipe and glancing toward the piano. *Willing* her toward the piano? Resolved to continue the conversation, however, Elizabeth settled herself on the sofa beside him. She took his hand in hers and her heart pounded in response to his stunned expression.

"You have been a true compass through this nightmare," she began hesitantly. "For reasons I don't understand, you came to my aid and somehow pointed me toward the right course of action. Even now, you seem to act as my protector while we wait for this confrontation." Her brow furrowed in bewilderment. "It cannot be out of obligation alone that you act. The clothes, my book, my music… You seem to care about me, my happiness. I can't imagine a truer friend."

"I am honored to be considered a friend." Sigerson closed his eyes and tried to reclaim his hand. Elizabeth would not surrender it.

"More than a friend, perhaps?" she murmured. "You give me something I've felt denied for so long: respect. My music, my ideas—your very presence here makes me feel valued." She paused, gathering her courage. "I am confused and sad to have developed such feelings for you…knowing you feel nothing in return."

Sigerson's eyes popped open and he sat forward, reclaiming his hand at last.

"Madame," he said shaking his head. "Your feelings for me are not…"

"Do not speak for me."

He set his pipe down and turned to face her. "You are grateful for my assistance. Do not confuse gratitude with something else, something you might feel is missing from your life. You'll not find what you're looking for in someone else—and certainly not in me. There can be nothing more."

"You are in love with someone else."

Sigerson chuckled. "Yet another intriguing scenario."

Elizabeth was surprised by a cautious sense of relief. "Who is the woman in the picture on your mantle?"

"That you found while inspecting my house as I sought help for your maid?" Sigerson's face was unreadable.

"Precisely the one."

"That portrait represents defeat to me," he said, staring out the window. "She was an adversary who bested me in an intellectual battle, not in a matter of the heart at all. I keep it with me for humility." Another shrug of his shoulders. "Sometimes it works."

"No," Elizabeth said, shaking her head. "Your expression softens as you speak of her, even now."

A frown overshadowed his face. "The reality is, I've nothing to give you."

"You've already given me more than you can know," she whispered, leaning even closer and brushing his ear with her lips. An uncharacteristic flush came to his cheeks. "My music touched the heart you claim doesn't exist. Why couldn't I?"

Slowly, unbelievably, she saw Sigerson transform before her—the fierce gray eyes softened, the lines in his penetrating face smoothed, his firm lips parted. Before reason could stop her, Elizabeth turned his face toward hers. There was a glimmer in his eyes, she imagined, perhaps of hope that someone might prove his careful self-evaluation wrong? She inched up and met his lips with her own. He didn't resist.

For a thrilling moment she felt his arms suddenly around her, his lips passionately returning her kiss. This man with nothing to offer moved his fingers sensuously through her hair and released the pin that held the remains of her chignon. She sighed with pleasure as his lips found her neck, gently explored her throat, brushed her bared shoulder.

Then, just as suddenly, he was grasping her arms, pulling her from him.

"I am not in love with you."

Elizabeth gasped, startled. Recovering, she smiled wistfully.

"How utterly gallant," she said, shaking her head. "The truth is, I've heard the words before: *I love you.* They held little meaning for the man who spoke them, they've come to mean little to me now. Withhold the sentiments from me if you wish. I don't need or want them from you or anyone else."

She touched her cheek to his and whispered softly. "Make love to me, Sigerson. It's what I do want from you…"

He pulled her away from him yet again.

"This is *not* what you want." He stood up and snatched a cigarette from the mantle and stalked about in search of a match, the smoldering pipe forgotten.

Elizabeth eyed him from the sofa, attempting to reconcile the man pacing erratically before her with the one who had just held her in his arms. Frustration overwhelmed her. "I decide!" she cried bitterly. "I decide what it is I want."

"If I am what you want, you have decided poorly," said Sigerson as he flung his unlit cigarette into the fireplace. "I am not the man you believe me to be!"

In the next instant, Elizabeth found herself alone as Sigerson stormed from the room.

Much later that evening, Elizabeth stood at the foot of the stairs, looking up with concern at Sigerson's bedroom door. No sound came from above, just as had been the case for most of the day.

Immediately following his dramatic rejection of her advances, she had positioned herself near the hearth, stoking the fire and brewing tea. She even warmed the remains of the mutton for what she hoped might be their midday meal—if only he would come down for it. The thought sickened her, however. How could she face him? What a fool she'd been! A pathetic, lonely woman, throwing herself at the first man to… What had Sigerson done to cause a spark in her battered, hardened heart? Why was she so moved to offer herself to this man? It was only too clear to her now: Because she had already given herself to him, had joined in the most intimate way she knew, through her music. The rationale failed to justify her behavior, of course. She put her head down on the long table and groaned.

Then, for a short time, the stomping of floorboards and screeching of drawers being pushed and pulled had emanated from the second floor, and it panicked her. Was he packing, preparing to leave? No, the deafening silence returned. As the afternoon wore on, Elizabeth ached to climb the stairs and set things right; to have him join her in the parlor and read the news sheets together, to go back to the way they were—as if the morning had never happened. But she couldn't bring herself to act, couldn't bear to have him reject her again. Finally, with nothing else left, she turned to the piano.

Making her way through an animated concertina distracted her mind for a bit from her inner turmoil. But she just went through the motions, her performance technical and rote. Her heart demanded melancholy; pensive, at least.

Beethoven's *Moonlight* felt better, and Chopin's *Nocturnes* let the desolation and overwhelming loneliness pour out through her fingers and into the keys. After the third Nocturne, Elizabeth's hands took control and she moved on to her own duet. Not halfway through the theme, however, her hands—and her heart—became too heavy to continue. The joy was gone, the piano shrill and sickeningly sweet. The absence of the violin created an enormous hole inside her, caused a pain so overpowering, she couldn't bear it. After having Sigerson on the strings at her side, the piano alone wasn't enough.

Elizabeth banged her hands down on the keyboard, angry, frustrated, and confused. Sigerson had united with her in this most precious, cherished place—a gift so much more sacred than any physical bond. She wanted to share that bond again, and more. Yet he wanted none of it.

An overwhelming sense of loss descended, one so deep it emptied her of everything: her desires, her hopes, her spirit. Elizabeth pushed back from the piano and stepped over to the fireplace and reached down into the brown clay urn beside it. She pulled out her derringer and then proceeded to curl up on the sofa. What matter if she spent the rest of her life here, waiting? What if the documents were taken now? Elizabeth sighed. Feeling such indifference, she couldn't even imagine summoning the will to pull the trigger if anyone came for the papers. None of it seemed of consequence. She tucked the pistol deep into the hip pouch of her jodhpurs.

She could no longer feel the music.

After hour upon hour of silence from above, the empty darkness of her heart stirred slightly with concern. Finally, with midnight approaching, desolation lost out to anxiety.

Taking a deep breath and lighting a candle, she started the climb to Sigerson's bedroom. At the top of the steps she found the door closed tightly. Elizabeth knocked gently at first, then firmly. Nothing.

"Monsieur," she whispered.

There was no reply.

"Sigerson?"

Not even the sound of movement came from within. Elizabeth's heart began to pound. Something was very wrong.

"Sigerson," she called. "I'm worried. May I come in?"

She pushed open the door, not waiting for the answer she knew wasn't coming. Inside, the room was so dark it took some time for her eyes to adjust, even with the candle. The bed was empty.

"Sigerson?" Elizabeth wondered how he could have left the cottage without passing her. Then she saw he hadn't. The chair near the window held a huddled mass of dressing gown. Sigerson's head protruded from the pile, hanging over the arm at an unnatural angle.

"Sigerson!"

Rushing into the room, Elizabeth put the candle on the nightstand and knelt by his side, easing his head onto a pillow. His skin was cold and damp, beads of perspiration dotted his brow. She could barely hear him breathing.

"Sigerson! Can you hear me?" she called into his ear. Elizabeth tapped his cheek, and he began to stir. "What is it? What's happened?"

He murmured something she couldn't understand. Elizabeth glanced about the room for the water pitcher. Instead, she found the cause of his condition. On the sideboard was a rubber tourniquet, the type used by physicians to expose a vein. Beside it was a glass vial, such as might hold a solution of cocaine.

"Oh, no." Elizabeth's hand flew to her mouth. Had her unwelcome advances driven him to the seclusion of his room and the dream world of the narcotic?

"What do you want?" Sigerson mumbled, squinting at her in the dim candlelight.

"I am so sorry," she stammered, reaching out to him as he struggled to a sitting position. "Forgive me."

A mixture of confusion and frustration showed on his face. He dropped his head into his hands and groaned. "You are persistent, Madame."

Elizabeth took a deep breath as uncertainty, then anger, welled up inside her—an almost welcome response, given the stifling numbness of the previous hours. "You've been locked up here all day without a sound," she said. "I was concerned for your well-being. Do not think I came here to continue our discussion of this morning. I have humiliated myself enough for one day." She stomped toward the door.

Sigerson eased himself over to his bed and collapsed into it. "Fortunate," he whispered weakly. "Most fortunate."

His tone made her stop and turn. She didn't recognize it; it did not sound like the man who had guided her through the horrors of the past weeks. Studying Sigerson, curled up amongst the tangled linens, she stepped back toward the bed.

"Why the cocaine?" she asked. "You've fought so long and hard against it. Can my feelings for you be so offensive they turn you back to the drug?"

"Nothing turns me toward or away from anything but my wretched self," came the muffled reply.

Elizabeth recognized all too well the deadness in his voice, a deadness she felt so acutely at this moment as well. And hadn't she shared those same sentiments with him, such a short time ago, a dark time when this man had remained by her side. Slowly, she moved closer to him and finally sat on the edge of the bed.

"I see." Despite herself, Elizabeth reached out and smoothed his damp, rumpled hair. "Wretched."

Sigerson coiled away, turning his back toward her like a child avoiding an intrusive parent. Silence enveloped the room for some moments.

"You insult me," Elizabeth said at last, trying to arrange the covers over his shivering body. "I would have preferred to replace the need, rather than drive you toward it."

Burrowing deeper into the covers, Sigerson mumbled more unintelligible words. The sound of those words was so desolate and mournful, they moved Elizabeth to take his hand from under the pillow.

"Sleep," she whispered, knowing he wouldn't hear. "I'll be here."

Still keeping his face in the pillow, Sigerson closed his fingers around Elizabeth's. She climbed onto the bed and curled up close to him, preparing for a long night waiting for the drug's effects to wane.

Chapter Twenty-Two

Her vigil ended sooner and much more abruptly than Elizabeth expected. With Sigerson clutching her hand, she had tried to drift off to sleep herself, but was kept alert by his occasional stirrings. Her back ached from maintaining her silent watch, trying not to move so she wouldn't disturb him. Throughout the night, Sigerson would frequently call out suddenly, turn his back to her, and resume his uneasy sleep.

Such a deeply troubled man, Elizabeth thought, trying once again to cover him with the blanket. What tormented life had molded such a guarded, stoic man, yet one so vulnerable to addiction? She knew nothing of his past, his hopes for the future. He was a dark, empty cavern to her. The slightest bit of himself was revealed as he played the violin, yet he snatched it back so forcefully when she sought more.

It was then she knew this vigil wasn't at all an attempt to extract more from him. No, it was merely because of her deep need to help a friend that she sat, scrunched up on his bed, hoping to ease him through the difficult period ahead of him. He was there for her when she needed him; he needed her now. That was enough.

So it was that the ever-so-slight scratching that came at the window early into the morning hours reached

Elizabeth's wakeful ears immediately. Slinking like a cat preparing to pounce on her mouse, she eased herself away from Sigerson and lowered herself from the bed. The scratching continued.

Certain this intrusion was the attempt to acquire her papers, Elizabeth felt with relief the weight of the derringer in her pocket. The scratching became a soft, intermittent clicking; the window was being forced open. Elizabeth slipped quietly around the bed and moved near the window so the draperies blocked her from the trespasser's view. Let him enter, she instructed herself, then hold the gun on him until she could get help, or Sigerson came to, or… She would worry about the next step when the time came to take it.

At last, the window slid quietly up and an inky figure stepped soundlessly into the room. Sigerson stirred suddenly; the black figure froze. Elizabeth held her breath, hoping the researcher would come around to offer assistance, but it was not to be. He mumbled, then resumed his sleep. The figure floated toward the bed and pulled a gun from the folds of a great overcoat, the metal glinting in the moonlight. Raising his arms, the intruder trained the weapon on the bundle of blankets as he started to make his way around the bed, headed for the door.

Fumbling with her own gun, Elizabeth decided that Sigerson's life couldn't be trusted to her aim. She grasped the barrel and raised it over her head. With all her might, she brought the butt down hard, feeling it make contact with a thud. The intruder's gun dropped to the floor; the black figure followed. Elizabeth picked her way over the form and kicked the firearm toward the bed, out of reach. She trained her own pistol on the man and poked at the black folds with the toe of her boot. The figure moaned.

"Get up!" she ordered.

The intruder pulled himself to his hands and knees, still moaning. Elizabeth reached down and pulled the hood back from his face to reveal…Monique Masset.

"Monique!" cried Elizabeth. Monique looked up at her in pain and disgust. Anger replaced the disbelief on Elizabeth's face.

"What have you done?" she cried.

"I am hardly in a position to answer you from the floor."

"Get up!" Elizabeth pointed her gun toward the armchair.

After struggling to her feet, Monique stumbled over to the seat and rubbed her head with her hands. "Who would have expected the chaste Widow Devereaux to spend the entire night in her lover's bedroom?" She glanced at the sleeping Sigerson and smirked. "You appear to be more skillful than your reputation would have you, Elizabeth. Your paramour seems quite satisfied—he hasn't moved an inch throughout our little scuffle."

She was rewarded with a hard slap to the face.

"What are you doing here?"

"I am breaking into this cottage."

"Why?!"

"This bookworm has seduced you into surrendering very important papers," Monique replied. "I am here to relieve him of them."

"What need have you of those papers?"

"Nothing you would understand."

"You insolent witch!" cried Elizabeth. "I have nothing to lose now. Answer me or I will kill you as the armed intruder you are. I would welcome the opportunity to send you to your father. Perhaps you might earn his forgiveness."

The arrogant attitude faded as Monique's mouth dropped open. "My father?"

"Can you not know? The previous attempt to get the correspondence left your father dead." Elizabeth's eyes narrowed, she cocked her pistol. "Truly…I don't care about your answers; they make no difference to me. I know all I need to, now. You can explain to your father."

"No!" Monique cried. "He was to be unharmed. They wouldn't have hurt him."

"They?"

"Stephan," Monique replied, her voice trembling. "And Pierre. They merely came to get Philippe's documents. There was no reason to hurt Papa."

Stephan. Hearing his name took Elizabeth's breath away. *But of course.* Monique would have little reason—or capacity—to conceive, plan, and execute such a scheme herself. She felt a new, deeper level of betrayal descend upon her. It was not camaraderie, a shared sense of being wronged, that brought Stephan to her side. Or even, as she sometimes imagined, an unspoken desire. It was deceit, a coldhearted attempt to acquire information about her husband and his work. She tried to focus again on Monique.

"Yet there was reason to hurt Lucien, and me, and now Sigerson?"

"They only did what was necessary." Monique's frightened eyes glistened as she appeared to struggle with rationalizing the horror she knew might very well have occurred. "Those papers have value far greater than anything you could understand."

"A value great enough to warrant murder?"

"Stephan is my husband," Monique offered in explanation. "He is a businessman with valuable contacts in Germany. His successes in efficiently transporting goods across the continent caught the attention of the Kaiser. Wilhelm commissioned Stephan to explore novel approaches to improving the methods of transportation. He was directed to monitor Otto Lilienthal's work, to see that faster progress on the flying machine was made and would ultimately result in aerial transportation of people, goods…weapons. Soon."

"Yes, yes, the Kaiser wanted to be apprised of Lilienthal's work," Elizabeth said impatiently. "Why come for Philippe?"

Monique glanced quickly at Elizabeth, seemingly surprised that she knew of the Kaiser's interest. "During Lilienthal's most recent stay at the clinic, Stephan…gained access to his files and found messages from Philippe. He was shocked to realize Lilienthal was sharing his work with France. When he read of the important information Philippe had to pass along regarding the effort—important information that never reached Germany—Stephan had no choice but to retrieve the correspondence."

"How convenient for him to have a whore wife to assist in the endeavor," said Elizabeth. "But then, you still haven't done the job, have you?" Her voice increased in volume. "Despite leaving a trail of blood and death in your wake—including your own father's—*you still haven't got the papers*!"

Monique jumped up from the sofa and rushed at Elizabeth, grabbing her pistol. The sound of scuffling and glass breaking filled the room as the nightstand toppled. They were still struggling moments later when the gun discharged. Both women fell to the ground as terrified screams filled the air.

"Ladies!" croaked a voice above them.

Sigerson's voice shocked the women into quiet. They turned their flushed, scratched faces up to see him swaying over them, one hand holding Monique's pistol. His free hand clutched his upper arm, blood trickling from beneath.

"Sigerson!" Elizabeth struggled to disengage herself from Monique. "You're hurt!"

"A scratch," he replied. "It provided enough of a jolt, however, to make me aware of a brawl in my bedroom. Elizabeth." Sigerson extended an arm to help Elizabeth to standing and handed her Monique's gun. "Madame Picard"—he indicated the armchair— "if you would be so kind."

Monique gathered herself up and sat down, rubbing her head once again as Elizabeth quickly retrieved her own gun from the floor and returned it to her hip pouch.

"Madame Devereaux may have no interest in your story," said Sigerson. "But I myself am overwhelmed with curiosity." He stumbled a bit as he moved toward the armchair and fell into it. "I'm sure you have no objection to answering a few of my questions?"

"Why should I satisfy your curiosity?"

"Two reasons," he replied, awkwardly lighting a cigarette. "One, you have some time before the police return with your husband. Two, I can help you avoid the gallows, because you were not directly responsible for the deaths that occurred."

"Stephan…"

"…is outside, waiting for you to gain entrance," said Sigerson, blowing smoke into the air. "No?"

"Yes." Monique fell back in the chair, defeated. "He was just doing his duty. No one was supposed to get hurt."

"Unfathomable!" Elizabeth murmured. She took a step forward, bringing the pistol up to train on Monique. As Monique took a breath to speak, they heard a banging on the door downstairs, followed by the scuffle of people entering.

"Up here, le Villard!" Sigerson called.

Suddenly, a disheveled Stephan Picard filled the doorway, his hands cuffed before him. A tall burly man with gray hair and dressed in a Paris officer's uniform pushed him into the room.

"Monsieur!" the policeman cried upon seeing Sigerson. "What…"

"Inspector le Villard," interrupted Sigerson abruptly, "may I present Madame Elizabeth Devereaux and Madame Monique Picard. Ladies, Inspector Francois le Villard of the Paris Sûreté."

"Enchanté," said the Inspector with a curt bow. He turned immediately back to Sigerson and pulled a telegram from his pocket. "Sigerson? What is all this about?"

"Sigerson," the bleary-eyed researcher replied, tapping his chest. "Monsieur Picard can share what he knows of the situation."

"I've told them all they need to know, Stephan," interrupted Monique. "Do not say another word."

"Would you be so loyal to your father's butcher?" cried Elizabeth, glancing disdainfully toward Stephan Picard. "I would expect even someone as cold as you to have some remorse."

"Your story is simply untrue," returned Monique, but her voice was quiet and uncertain. "Stephan?"

"I did not attack Luc," he replied. "I was not the one."

Monique's face dropped, her head fell into her hands.

"You wouldn't want your hands dirtied with the physical attacks, of course," mused Sigerson. "No matter. Your accomplice did not himself survive his savagery. I imagine he was also responsible for killing the Devereaux stable boy and for the attack on Madame Devereaux in the woods. You did accompany him on the original break-in, correct? You believed the Professeur's correspondence to be in the house and meant to find it yourself."

With his wife and counsel weeping mournfully on the armchair, the Alsatian had no one to silence him. "Yes. It happened as you say. I meant for no one to be killed;

auxiliary consequences, all." He then matter-of-factly ticked off the incidents of terror he had perpetrated or directed. "The stable hand tried to stop us from searching the study again. I mightn't have set the house afire if he hadn't made it necessary for Pierre to kill him. The attack on Elizabeth was intended only as a scare tactic. She was much too curious and clever. She needed to be kept from the search." Picard turned to Elizabeth. "I am truly, deeply sorry," he said.

Elizabeth's hand stole to her throat and the vicious gash that, but for Sigerson, would have cost her life. A scare tactic? "Bastard!"

"I admit it was your very persistence that put me on the path to Brincker," continued Picard, unruffled. "When I realized you were getting the documents from him, I had Pierre wait for you at Masset's. When Luc came home, early and alone, Pierre must have panicked."

Monique's sobs became wails. "How could you have let this happen?" she choked out. "And to have kept it from me? My mother…!"

"You haven't exactly made yourself available these past weeks to discuss such news, now, have you, Monique?" said Stephan.

"Bastard!"

Over the din, Sigerson asked Picard, "What did you hope Devereaux's notes would tell you?"

"Lilienthal's progress has been slow," said Picard. "The Kaiser, in his…anxiety, some would say, demands he complete his work, quickly." He sat down on the edge of the bed and rattled the cuffs on his wrists. "Are these necessary?"

Sigerson glanced at le Villard and inclined his head toward Picard. The cuffs were removed.

"These are dangerous times in Germany and Wilhelm is increasingly erratic," Picard continued. "Truly, Otto is not safe, certainly not since choosing to share his data. It should be seen as much a favor to him as to bolster my own standing and finances that I worked to fetch the material and bring it back to Germany. Of course, learning that Devereaux had valuable information that would help Lilienthal's success? A boon indeed! I wasn't about to leave without it."

"The documents relating to the work on the flying machine are in the drawer behind you," said Sigerson. "Be my guest. See what you can learn."

Elizabeth gasped. "You would give this monster what he wants?!"

"Monsieur Picard will be able to make little use of any information he gleans from the papers, given his next destination," Sigerson replied, stubbing out his cigarette and rising. "Further, I am quite confident he will not recognize the 'valuable information' once he finds it."

Picard sneered at Sigerson as he hurried to take the portfolio from the cabinet and shuffle through the pages. As predicted, the man grunted and scoffed at the notes as he made his way through the pile. "There is nothing here that was not in Otto Lilienthal's work, except perhaps some messages from the Americans." He nearly spat out the last word.

Sigerson was pacing about the room, cradling his wounded arm, head on his chest. He turned to face Picard. "Do you understand what the engineer Chanute has written?" His voice was high-pitched and slow, as though addressing a child.

"Do not speak down to me, Sigerson. I see merely some attempt to involve themselves in the years of work done in Germany. They had hoped a Frenchman would give them *entrée*. Hah!"

"Their comments regarding Lilienthal's attempt to control his gliders—they suggest nothing to you?"

"The world knows Lilienthal controls his crafts by shifting body weight. Chanute offers no insight."

"He suggests the key to controlling one's direction in flight lies in the craft's *design*," said Sigerson slowly, patiently.

Picard scowled, although with less arrogance than before. "I see no markings to the charts or the diagrams," he replied warily.

"It is clear from the correspondence between Devereaux and Lilienthal that they had indeed been focusing their efforts to control the craft on the pilot's movements," said Sigerson, as though lecturing a class of first-year students. "In all those papers, the only document that offers a unique approach, the only one that might contain 'valuable information' the two men had not considered, was the suggestion made by Chanute that the answer might lie elsewhere." He looked at the Alsatian in disdain. "Read the letter to America again, Picard. See that Devereaux was removing himself from the project, trying to connect Lilienthal with Chanute and the International Congress of Aerial Navigation so *they* could collaborate. Your bloody search for information to put Germany into the skies has merely uncovered the plans these men had to make this initiative an international effort to benefit the world. The Professeur, armed with an agreement from the university in Paris, was on his way to propose that the school here sponsor such a collaboration the evening you drove him off the Arneau Bridge."

"You killed Philippe as well," said Elizabeth dully, "by attempting to drive a coach carrying your own wife off the bridge. Has your evil no limits?"

"We only planned to stop him and take the trunk containing his papers," explained Picard. "The accident was just the first in a series of unfortunate events. Once we took over his coach and found he'd stored the papers elsewhere…it was almost our undoing. It took weeks to determine where the material was—and not in enough time to get to it before you did, Madame."

Able to hear no more, Elizabeth pushed past Sigerson and flew down the stairs. Making her way through the dim light of the new day, she crossed the parlor and entered the music room. She felt her way to the sofa she'd languished in all the previous day and buried her face in the cushions.

How could she have thought that confronting the monsters responsible for all these tragedies would end her own heartache? No punishment, hers or anyone else's, would bring back Philippe and Lucien and Luc. But she had hoped when the solution was found, the murderers apprehended, all would become clear, and she would see how and why all this horror had to be. But none of it needed to happen… So much death, all just a series of blunders.

A few moments later, Elizabeth became aware of the group now gathering by the front door. There seemed to be some confusion over an unexpected guest. She strained her ears to hear the exchange between le Villard and his deputy and whomever had come to the door. The name Gregoire floated in to her. *Gregoire?* Thoughts of the sinister academician had been obliterated from her mind once she discovered Monique under the black hood. Could her suspicions of him have been so entirely unwarranted? Perhaps not, given his presence now.

With her curiosity waning, however, Elizabeth felt no desire to join the group at the door, no need to delve any further into this tragedy. Waiting here, curled on the sofa, inhaling the scent of tobacco, she would wait until they decided her fate. Gregoire would have to suffer his own. When she heard Sigerson send him on his way, having no business being on the premises, she buried her head farther into the pillows, feeling an even deeper sense of defeat. How wrong she had been…even about Gregoire!

Finally, le Villard announced he was prepared to escort the Picards to the village jail for confinement. More mumbling; more protests. Sigerson, it seemed, needed more information from the prisoners, however.

"One more question," Elizabeth heard his voice booming as the front door creaked open. "Where is Professeur Devereaux now?"

CHAPTER TWENTY-THREE

Elizabeth sat bolt upright and strained her ears to hear more.

The body she had buried was *truly* not her husband's—and Sigerson knew! Yet he'd never questioned her. And now he thought Monique and Stephan knew where the body was? No longer able to hear more of the conversation, Elizabeth was compelled to join the group at the door. She saw puzzled amazement on the faces of the Picards, obviously shocked by the researcher's question.

Sigerson glanced quickly at Elizabeth, then back at le Villard's prisoners.

"Professeur Devereaux survived the fall from the bridge. Where is he now?"

With her head spinning, Elizabeth sat down heavily on the staircase. Philippe, alive? The dead man she identified at the morgue had been presented as Jean-Philippe Devereaux to hide that her husband still lived? The protests that resulted from Sigerson's accusation were lost on her.

"Philippe Devereaux was buried weeks ago, Monsieur," said Picard. "How could you believe he still lives?"

"How could you believe things will go better for you by keeping his whereabouts secret?" asked Sigerson. "There will be one less murder to your credit."

"He's right, Stephan," Monique interrupted, then turned to Sigerson. "Go to Philippe and help him. He is in a small hut on the northern bank of the Lez, five kilometers upriver from the bridge itself." She looked away. "He is badly hurt."

"Philippe...alive?! And you kept him from me? From medical assistance?!" Elizabeth, revived and enraged by yet another horror revealed, rushed at Monique to strike her again. Sigerson's strong arm restrained her.

"We could not allow him to be found," Monique explained to Sigerson, turning herself away from Elizabeth. "Stephan arranged for the other body—a man found beaten and drowned, washed up on the riverbank—to be identified as Philippe so Elizabeth would stop meddling and leave France. Before the officials arrived to take the corpse, Pierre and Stephan found Philippe. Alive. We panicked."

"*You* panicked, Monique," corrected her husband. "What a mess he was when we found him! Again, we were merely trying to locate his valise, which we assumed had gone off the bridge with him since the papers were not in the carriage. Finding Devereaux himself was quite a snag. Dragging him ashore and finding him alive, Pierre dug him out of his clothes and attempted to revive him. He would have died soon enough without Pierre's help."

"You would have preferred such an outcome," snapped his wife, "because I share a love with him you and I could never have."

Picard smirked. "No, my preference would have been that he hadn't regained consciousness, then recognized us and become aware of our plans," he said indifferently. Then, to Sigerson: "With Devereaux alive, knowing we had a part in his accident, we had to...contain him until nature took its course. Where Pierre was staying provided the perfect venue. We emptied the dead man's pockets of anything that would identify him. Given how he faintly resembled Devereaux—despite the poor condition of the body—we were confident he would pass as Philippe. We expected this development to send his wife home to the United States, leaving us free to obtain Philippe's correspondence. "You are doggedly persistent, Madame," he said to Elizabeth with admiration in his voice. But then the tone turned to steel. "Of course, we still had the living Professeur to deal with. Monique so generously took up residence at his bedside to nurse him."

Monique glanced at Elizabeth spitefully. "Once he recovered, I could have compelled him to join us, to understand what we had done and why."

Elizabeth broke free from Sigerson's grasp and grabbed Monique by the shoulders. "*You* should have gone off that bridge!" she cried, pushing her through the door and out onto the brick walkway.

Inspector le Villard separated the women as Sigerson led Stephan to the police carriage. Once the Picards were properly secured, le Villard promised to send medics to tend to Philippe at the location Monique had described. Elizabeth looked up at Sigerson.

"I must go to him." She moved toward the house, then toward the road. Finally, she halted before Sigerson. "Take me to him."

As Elizabeth stared blankly ahead of her, Sigerson darted inside, came back out with a kerchief tied around his arm, and hitched his horse to the cart. Oblivious to the crisp breeze that moved her hair across her face, and to Sigerson as he guided her up onto the bench, she thought of her husband, alive all this time, suffering in an abandoned hut. Then, jolted as the horse leapt from the snapping reins, she at last addressed her driver accusingly.

"You knew."

"I suspected."

"How?"

Breathing deeply, Sigerson spoke carefully.

"I had plans of my own to meet with your husband when he returned from Paris, so I took particular interest when news of his accident spread. My curiosity brought me to the scene of the mishap. After looking around the bridge and its surrounds a bit, I knew the body that was recovered could not have been his. For kilometers, the bank was undisturbed; no body had been recovered as the young man 'on holiday' had testified. A few remarks you made when discussing your experience at the mortuary—as well as your farewell at the cemetery—supported my suspicion. I investigated farther down the river and found evidence of a shredded leather garment. Someone had been pulled from the water; his coat was cut away. Hardly something to be done for a corpse. He was loaded into a vehicle and removed from the scene. I strongly suspected that man to be your husband."

"We could have gotten to him sooner!"

"I couldn't determine where they took him, or even in which direction they'd headed. We needed to catch the *who* to tell us the *where*."

Elizabeth shook her head. Tears of frustration and self-reproach filled her eyes. She should have known, she should have been able to help him before now. All these weeks! Here, at last: an unthinkable punishment for claiming the poor man in the mortuary was Philippe. She stared stonily before her as the cart made its way north around the outskirts of town toward the Lez. If, after all this time, no body had been found, mightn't the police have concluded he could be alive? Mightn't they have continued the search, found him, rescued him from his captors and his pain?

But officially, the body had been found, the case closed. And Philippe was held a wounded captive in a remote part of the river valley. All the while, she, his wife, put lives at risk trying to fathom what his plans had been, how he had intended to make things right for her, to atone for what he had caused her to suffer. She had thought only of herself and of making her mark on the world. Yes, she had even offered herself to another man, a man she suspected of being involved in Philippe's and Lucien's murders. She had proclaimed her love for him. While she felt her heart set free, playing a duet with a stranger, her husband—the man she had vowed to honor and obey—lay dying in a riverside hut. Now she would face the damage she'd done, see how egregious were her crimes.

Philippe was *alive*.

Self-hatred overflowed her heart. But where was the joy? Could the loathing she felt for herself have edged out the thrill of anticipation and hope? The elation of finding her husband alive? Elizabeth brought her hands to her face and dug her nails into her scalp. Why couldn't she feel the exhilaration? Tears of frustration and confusion seeped out through her fingers. This miracle second chance at mending her marriage was a gift. A gift she didn't deserve. She felt a sudden wave of disgust envelop her. She didn't deserve to have Philippe back. She'd given her heart to another man.

Elizabeth looked at her driver. Ashamed, she mourned the lost opportunity to win this strange man—something Sigerson had made clear would never be. She hated the glimmer of hope that nevertheless sparked inside her.

"Was this why…?" Elizabeth choked on the words. "Because my husband was alive…?"

Sigerson stared at the road ahead without indicating he'd heard her. She cringed. Who but a beast would have these unforgivable thoughts—that perhaps Sigerson had not rejected her, only her circumstances, when he suspected her husband was alive, gravely wounded?

The remainder of the ride was long, uncomfortable, and silent. Elizabeth's intermittent tears were quiet ones, while Sigerson focused his full attention on navigating the cart. After hours, it seemed, they pulled up to the hut housing Professeur Devereaux. Both riders sat motionless, staring at the structure.

"I was leaving him," she said, more to herself than to Sigerson. "The day of the accident, I was on my way to Paris when the news reached me. I felt numbness then, I feel confusion now. I have only the deepest remorse that I was never free to speak or act or feel as I have done…nor free now to act as I wish to do. *I* am the monster!"

Sigerson climbed down from the cart and circled around to her side. He stood vigil as she wiped her eyes with his kerchief and smoothed her disheveled hair. She looked into Sigerson's eyes as he helped her down from the bench; they were cold and unfeeling. It was not difficult to see he had the same loathing for her as she did herself.

The steps from the cart to the hut were the longest, most difficult she had ever taken. The glaring sun stung her eyes, her ankles turned on the caked mud as she left the man she'd fallen in love with to help the man she'd married. Reaching the hut door, she took a deep breath, grasped the handle, and pushed.

Inside the dank hut, a musty, sickly odor hit her nostrils. As her eyes adjusted to the room, dimly lit by the morning sunlight, she saw a cot in one corner. Elizabeth could barely make out the huddled form of a man lying upon it.

"Philippe?" she whispered. A faint moan came from the bed. Elizabeth moved closer. It was her husband. She stepped quickly over the packed earth floor and knelt by his side, gently taking his hand in hers. "Philippe, I'm here to take you home. You are safe now."

His eyelids fluttered open. "Elizabeth?" He could barely utter her name; then, a tear rolled down his scraped and swollen cheek. Her heart ached for him, seeing his tears, his broken body. She tenderly stroked his black hair, matted with blood and sweat, certain it could be the only part of him not in searing pain. He took in an agonizing breath. "Don't leave me."

"We'll leave together," she said, trying to smile through her own tears. "Medics are on their way to take you to hospital. You are safe now."

"Sigerson," he gasped.

Elizabeth looked at him, puzzled. "Sigerson…?"

Philippe tried to nod his head. "They told me that you…" He took a feeble breath. "And he…"

Elizabeth paused. What had they told him?

"I don't understand," she whispered. "Rest. Help is on the way."

"Don't leave me," he said again. Another painful, wheezing breath. "They told me about you…" He paused to collect his breath. Then, "He cannot love you as I do…"

Elizabeth's heart stopped cold. They had told him about her…and Sigerson? Monique and Stephan had found it necessary to torment their nearly dead prisoner with fabricated tales of his wife's infidelity? She could certainly see Monique taking such a stance. Elizabeth regretted yet again Sigerson's preventing her from ripping the woman's throat out back at the cottage.

"It's untrue," she said soothingly. But the pain and confusion she had felt in the cart resurfaced. Ashamed to admit it still, she had desperately wanted her and Sigerson to be lovers, but he wouldn't have her. Damn Monique and Stephan for their cruelty. "It's simply untrue."

Philippe clutched at his wife's hand. "I love you," he said. "Don't leave me. I'll make you forget him…"

Elizabeth softly kissed his bandaged forehead as he drifted once more into unconsciousness. "It's simply untrue," she whispered.

When Elizabeth exited the hut, she could see Sigerson basking in the warm southern breezes. Sitting crossed legged under an olive tree and finishing a cigarette, he tossed stones far into the river. So intent upon the trajectory of the rocks and the ripples they made in the water, he didn't notice Elizabeth until she sat down close beside him and placed her hand on his.

"His injuries are horrific," she said, looking deeply into Sigerson's frosty gray eyes, looking for something to ease this moment. Didn't he feel the loss she felt? Could he truly have nothing in his heart for her? His eyes revealed nothing. A deep nothingness that crushed her.

"The medics are not far off. I hear their carriage."

"He needs me." Yes. And that was why she would stay, what gave her marriage a chance. Philippe needed her now. Sigerson clearly did not.

"My observation is that he always has," Sigerson replied, rising, and heading to tend his horse.

"Yet I need you," she whispered.

CHAPTER TWENTY-FOUR

Yes. Philippe needed her.

Looking down at her husband in his hospital bed, broken and bloodied despite the medics' attention, Elizabeth wondered what she could possibly do for the man. What could she offer that would help him survive the horrors of the past weeks? To overcome the trauma to both body and soul? And selfishly, to overcome her own doubt that being here for him could be enough for her.

The broken bones, the concussed brain, the torn flesh… So much damage! The sight of him lying so helplessly beneath the rumpled sheets and bandages broke her heart. Beyond cleaning and dressing the wounds and putting him in fresh bed linens, the surgeons themselves seemed to have few answers. *Little better than the Picards "letting nature take its course,"* thought Elizabeth, dabbing the sweat from Philippe's brow with a cool cloth. Until he gained his strength, there could be no attempts to reset improperly knit bones, no exploration of hidden injuries that might hinder his recovery. If the physicians couldn't help him, how could she? Worse: how to address the violation he'd suffered at the hands of Stephan and Monique. Could he even comprehend what they'd done to him and why?

Elizabeth tried to tamp down the anger she felt toward Monique, not only keeping Philippe from proper medical care, but torturing him with her lies and attempting to drive yet more nails into the coffin of her marriage. At least the woman was paying dearly for her cruelty. Elizabeth, too, had her penance to serve: to concentrate on Philippe and his recovery. Still, what she could contribute was unclear. Philippe himself answered her.

"Please," he murmured, eyes pinched closed in apparent pain, "please don't leave me."

Here again, at the dreaded coda, Elizabeth thought as she dabbed his forehead. After the unspeakable terror of the past weeks, here they were again: she dissatisfied, wanting something she couldn't identify; he pleading for another chance to be what he thought she wanted. Could this time be different? Had Sigerson been right, that she was expecting to find her happiness by reaching out for something—someone — that didn't exist? Was there hope she herself might find value in what she had to offer, rather than lay blame for her dissatisfactions in life at the feet of the men who failed to find it for her? Apparently, the Fates had given her another opportunity to try.

"I am here, Philippe," she said, resting her hand lightly on his chest, avoiding the straps that secured his ribs. He gave a gentle sigh and slipped back into unconsciousness.

"Elizabeth!"

Hours later, the effects of the opiates waning, Philippe awoke and cried out for his wife. Still keeping vigil at his bedside, she leaned over and placed the cool, wet cloth on his forehead, then took his hand.

"I am here, Philippe."

"More than I deserve," he said, turning his head slightly and peering at her with squinted, misty eyes. "My angel…" Silence for some time, then, "To be here now…the cad that

I've been…the mess that I am…" A longer silence followed, and she thought he had fallen back asleep. He hadn't. "I cannot fault you for finding another."

Elizabeth sighed heavily and patted his hand absently. "Oh, Philippe," she said softly. "Our troubles are no one's doing but our own. You know this."

Clearly, the pain was sharpening his thinking and keeping him from rest. She needed to occupy those thoughts—and not with attempts to work out their differences. Seemingly an impossible feat in the best of circumstances, unfathomable now; and surely the stress would be detrimental to his still very fragile chances at recovery.

"Tell me of your visit with Octave," said Elizabeth. She even smiled as Philippe's eyes popped open wide, then closed as a sheepish pout came to his lips. "Yes, Professeur. I know you saw Chanute in Paris. Does he send me his love?"

"Of course he does," Philippe replied softly. "He adores you. I adore you…" He tried to grasp her hand tighter but winced at the effort.

"Does he also agree to help your friend in Berlin with his kites?"

Philippe's lips quivered in an attempt to smile, and he squeezed her hand firmly, despite the pain. "Yes, my clever girl!" he whispered. "Yes!"

"And we are to bring Lilienthal's papers to Octave for collaboration with other American…aeronauts?"

Philippe nodded slowly, but Elizabeth was surprised to see his lips pout once more.

"It is all that can be done," he murmured, his frown deepening. "To make that smallest of connections. Yet even that is beyond me now." He looked up at his wife. "I will not see America again. We needn't the physicians' word to know there is little hope of me seeing beyond these four walls." He closed his eyes; a tear escaped and traced its way down his cheek. "I am so very, very sorry…" Elizabeth tried to hush him, but he continued. "For us… For Otto…"

"For Otto?" she asked. Philippe nodded once.

"He is not safe in Berlin," he mumbled, sleep overcoming him as the fatigue and pain showed on his face. "And I am powerless to help."

∾

Late the following afternoon, Elizabeth drove Cheval hard from the hospital all the way through the outskirts of the village and on to Sigerson's cottage. Still wearing the riding boots and pants she had donned two days before, she was able to comfortably manage the rougher trails safely and efficiently, and in excellent time. With Philippe so gravely injured, driven out of his mind with pain, she needed Sigerson's help getting the Lilienthal documents to Chanute… and in devising a plan to help the German. She didn't care what he thought of her, how he felt about her. He simply had to help her—and they had to act soon.

Sigerson seemed to have other plans.

When the cottage came into view, she spotted in the waning sunlight a rich carriage pulled by a pair of sleek black horses, waiting at the front door. The coachman was loading a bag, a trunk, and a box onto the roof. Elizabeth slid off Cheval and stepped inside the house, just in time to see Sigerson himself descending the stairs, dressed in the fine gentleman's tweed she had discovered rummaging through his armoire on her first visit here. How comfortable he appeared in this attire, Elizabeth thought. His previous life had not been a poor one.

"I'm not a moment too soon," she said, attempting indifference. Emotions swirled around her head, fogging her brain and piercing her heart: disappointment, panic, grief. "I might have missed your departure."

"No," Sigerson replied. "I could not have left without seeing you." He took an uncertain deep breath, quite unlike the aloof man who had left her on the steps of the hospital two days before. "I assume you and your husband could make use of this cottage? With your villa no more, you will need someplace to call home."

"You are not coming back."

"No," he said, heading toward the door. "I am going home."

Elizabeth's jaw dropped. "To London!"

Sigerson smiled. "Yes, to London."

Elizabeth smiled too, wanly, as she dropped down to sit on the stairs. She pressed her lips together to keep them from quivering. "But I need you," she said quietly. "Here."

"Elizabeth…" Sigerson lowered his eyes and shook his head. "No."

"Yes," she said firmly, standing up again to her full height and facing him, eye to eye. "I need your help. In Philippe's delirium, he confirmed his arrangement for Octave Chanute to bring Lilienthal's work to his recently formed International Congress on Aerial Navigation. In the two years since its formation, the group has made significant progress in gathering the best minds in the field. They are now even considering the work of Pierre Mouillard of Lyons. Details of Lilienthal's progress will be an important contribution to the consortium. And yet, his actual participation as they move forward will be even more important. You must help me get his papers to America so the work can begin."

Sigerson raised his eyebrows and nodded. Again, Elizabeth saw a look of respect in his eyes, even if just a flash. Her heart soared.

"Yes, Mouillard. Of course he is to be involved," he said, looking off into the distance. Then, focusing on Elizabeth, "You needn't my help or anyone else's to get Lilienthal's papers to Chanute. You booked passage to America before. You can do it again."

"But Lilienthal himself!" Elizabeth insisted.

"No doubt Lilienthal is in danger," said Sigerson. He paused for a moment, deep in thought. "Regrettably, there is little to be done for him…at least at this moment. Your only move is to rid yourself of those documents. Picard will not be the only one to come for them. If the Kaiser's…anxiety continues, there will be more. Soon, I suspect."

"Who *are* you?" she cried, her head spinning with each new declaration. He raised his hands and shook his head. Her exasperation complete, she tried a different tack. "Why the urgent departure? Why now? Is this, too, a truth that must remain unspoken?!"

Sigerson took another deep, unsteady breath. "My life for the past three years has not been worth living," he said. "It's time for me to go home, to again be the man I was forced to bury."

Elizabeth was taken aback by his words, so startlingly revealing. She so longed to know about that man and why he needed to be buried. And what was the life Sigerson returned to after so many years? The questions were all on her tongue, but she needed him to tell her, needed him to want her to know. Whatever those answers were, however, they wouldn't change the past, the future, or the devastation she felt at this moment.

"I wish you luck," she said instead, and turned away from him. Her heart ached and her head pounded as she stubbornly held back the tears. Sigerson stepped toward her and turned her back around, taking her hands in both of his.

"I have a confession to make," he said, not meeting her eyes. "Two, in fact. I make them selfishly, I am afraid. They will not be easy for you to hear."

Elizabeth cocked her head to the side, wondering what he could possibly need to confess to her. He had been an unrelenting guide through the darkness of the past month. Despite the hard-fought distance he kept, he'd somehow managed to show her a glimpse of what she might want from life, had even given her the courage to seek it out. She did not want to be his confessor. She wanted the painful anticipation of his leaving to end.

"First, your trust in me was misplaced," he began. "I, also, sought your husband's papers." He continued as her eyes widened and her jaw slackened. "Throughout my adventures as Sigerson, I have been, at times, in the service of the British government. The Foreign Office knew of Picard's attempt to keep Lilienthal's work from the International Congress. I was asked to be sure he was not successful. So, I, too, waited at Luc Masset's, planning to bring you back here to determine what you had found at the school. I only regret that I wasn't there in time to prevent Pierre's savagery."

"Then your work was done," she accused, her heart racing. "Why did you permit me to remain here with you? Why did you care about capturing Stephan?"

"I could hardly leave you to the fate of Masset," he replied, distantly. "Nor could I allow this murderer to go unpunished."

"I see," said Elizabeth quietly. *None of this matters, nothing about this man matters*, she repeated to herself. She had her husband's recovery to manage, their marriage to mend. Revealing himself as yet another man trying to take something from her wasn't painful. The truth would help her let him go. "And your second confession?"

This second revelation appeared more difficult for him to admit than the first. "My duplicity extends beyond an interest in your husband's work," he said, looking away from her yet again. "I was unforgivably intrigued by something else of his."

Elizabeth shook her head. "I do not understand."

Sigerson forced himself to look into her eyes. He clutched painfully at her hands.

"You."

Elizabeth stared at him blankly, unable to utter a word or even form a thought.

"I... You...opened my eyes. And my heart," said Sigerson.

She thought of days before and his anger at her advances; a man so disturbed by her behavior; a woman unaware that her husband might still be alive. The cocaine made perfect sense: an attempt to escape her without explaining, without raising her hopes that her husband might return to her. But this admission? Now?

"Utterly inconceivable!" she cried, pulling her hands from him.

"From the moment I evaded a hurled beaker in the laboratory, I was curiously enamored," he said, shaking his head in wonder. "But my...situation required me to steel my heart. Here, after the duet, I said what I thought would turn you away, make you reconsider a step I could only dream about. I didn't want to admit that it was too late for me, that my heart was already yours."

"Naturally, you would protect yourself against such a calamity."

"It is difficult enough an exercise now, I assure you." Sigerson searched through his pockets but found them empty, except for a broken cigarette. He crumpled it in his hand and took a deep breath. "You asked if I resisted you because I suspected your husband was alive. Humbling to find I am not so noble. I merely sought to protect myself, knowing I must leave someday. Perhaps to run from discovery, perhaps to at last return home. Indeed, that day has come already, requiring me to again become a man who would never have allowed any of this to happen."

Elizabeth shook her head in confusion and frustration. Had he opened his heart to her two days ago, she would have welcomed the words lovingly, ecstatically. Her choices today might have been different. Now his words angered her. She didn't want to believe them.

"What purpose does this confession serve?" she managed to choke out. "Why do you torment me?"

"I must leave Sigerson behind," he replied. "His thoughts, his words. I have already been unburdened of his heart."

"Yet I am left here with my own heart to nurse while you retrieve the untouched heart of the Englishman..."

"He has no heart," Sigerson interrupted. "The work he does, the life he leads, does not accommodate the feelings a heart must suffer. He is not a man to be in love, and surely not a man to be loved by another."

"And yet I do," Elizabeth said softly.

Sigerson shook his head. "You know nothing of the man I truly am. Your feelings are for the person who merely existed here in hiding, living in fear of discovery. Sigerson is not a person at all. *I was here to acquire your husband's papers!* Doesn't that tell you something of my true character? Cold, logical." He smiled suddenly. "A calculating machine, a brain without a heart... That picture was drawn by my closest friend."

"Why return to such a bleak, passionless life?"

"The fact that I do supports my assertion," Sigerson replied. "My work is my passion—and without it I am no one, a Sigerson. The life you describe as 'bleak' is one I anxiously waited to reclaim...until I was drawn to help you.

When I realized my Alsatian competitor had taken a more deadly approach to winning our contest, I did my best to keep you safe. It wasn't until too late that I realized you represented deeper waters than he."

"So, your feelings for me are so hateful, you return to a former life to confront what you hid from for years."

Sigerson let a slight smile creep to his lips. "Not so hateful," he said, brushing a lock of hair from her cheek and smoothing it into place. "But it has had a rending effect upon my spirit. My heart wishes nothing more than to remain with you, a Sigerson, and idle away the rest of my days. Yet today, in the wake of such a realization, I become aware of developments that make this the time to return home—and I cannot help but go. I must accept that my soul will never be content without the work which I have prepared for and have done all my life."

"You are wise to know to satisfy your soul," she said quietly, with a begrudging nod. "Yet, I so deeply regret, as you leave, to know so little…about you, about your work, your life. I would cherish your trust, even as a friend."

Sigerson looked at her intently. Did she see hesitancy in his eyes? Doubt?

"It would be unwise for me to tell you about myself," he replied at last. "Unwise for either of us. The less you know of me the better, the safer you will be."

Unwise.

Elizabeth sighed sadly. "Your driver becomes impatient."

"Yes, it is time." Sigerson picked up the one remaining bag as Elizabeth stepped quickly into the parlor. She returned with a book in her hand.

"I would be pleased if you accepted this volume as a souvenir of our…adventure," she said to him. "I know the title intrigued you."

"I shall treasure it," Sigerson replied, smiling as he looked at the spine. *"The Origin of Tree Worship."* He tucked it into an inside pocket of his overcoat.

There was an awkward silence between them. Finally, Elizabeth held her arms out to him, and he gratefully fell into her embrace. For some moments, they stood holding each other quietly, as if willing time to stand still as well. Elizabeth could feel the heavy weight of his body clinging to hers, his breath in her hair heavy and erratic.

"Such a price…" he murmured at last. Elizabeth wanted to assure him that such a price needn't be paid, that they could be happy together, here or any place in the world. If only she could believe it herself. She had an obligation she meant to fulfill, and Sigerson spoke the truth when he said she knew nothing of the man he truly was. Sad words, but true.

"Your soul may govern your decisions today," she said, pulling back from him and looking into his eyes. "But once awakened, a heart as true as yours will not slumber for long. You will find love. I am certain of it."

With a slight shrug of his shoulders he became the remote and distant man she remembered from the laboratory. Today, however, there was a more bitter edge to the fierce look in his eyes. *"Au revoir*, Elizabeth."

"Yes," she said, brightening. She stood on tiptoe and kissed him gently on the lips, but the softness was gone. He did not return the kiss. *"Au revoir, mon amour."*

Elizabeth watched as he walked away. He climbed into the gleaming coach, closed the door, and signaled the driver to leave. He never looked back, now—unknown to her—on his way to reclaim a life he had begrudgingly surrendered years ago on a remote mountain pass in the Swiss Alps.

As the carriage made its way toward the village, Sigerson nestled himself into the luxurious leather seats and lit his cherished cherrywood pipe. Three years had passed since his last ride in such comfort. After endless weeks steering a dog-cart through the unforgiving cobblestoned streets of Montpellier, his senses reveled in his surroundings: the mahogany smell of the carriage's interior mixing with his tobacco; the gentle rock and sway of the ride; the almost distant clopping of the horses' hooves. He tried to think about home, about the people there, about the work he had left behind. He wanted to think about anything but what he left behind here. But a phrase kept playing in his head.

"Parting is such sweet sorrow," he said aloud.

For the first time in his life, Sigerson truly felt some understanding of the line. The sorrow upon leaving her, undeniably marked by a tight heaviness in his chest, was all too apparent. The sweetness of this parting, however, was missing. The coach was halfway through town before he realized why he couldn't feel it: the sweetness came with an anticipation of tomorrow—a tomorrow he and the intriguing, blue-eyed Elizabeth Devereaux could not have.

That conundrum resolved, Sigerson sat back and relit his pipe. Despite popular belief, he never really cared for Shakespeare.

CHAPTER TWENTY-FIVE

Weeks later, when the physicians had done what little they could for Philippe Devereaux—far too little, in his wife's opinion—they released him from hospital and sent him home with their greatest hopes and best wishes. As for guidance, direction, and advice, however, they were at a loss.

Settled at last in the university cottage vacated by Sigerson, the Devereauxs made the effort to heal, body and soul, and tried to reimagine their future together. Having committed herself to her husband's recovery and to their marriage, Elizabeth immersed herself in the role of wife and caregiver. Philippe himself was less committed to the struggles ahead.

"Don't waste your time." Philippe gritted his teeth in pain and turned his head toward the wall, away from his wife, as she tried to readjust the cushions under his splinted right leg.

With skull, both legs, an arm, a shoulder, and several ribs broken in his fall from the Arneau Bridge, Philippe was unable to take a breath without pain. Deep scrapes and gashes, received as he was dragged down the River Lez, complicated movement further. With help from Claude, still recovering from his own injuries, and the burly, resourceful Jacques Olivier, his former messenger and now neighbor,

Elizabeth was able to reposition Philippe twice throughout the day, as advised. For all else, she found herself very much on her own, managing the lengthy recuperation process ahead of them. As had quickly become her habit, she ignored her husband's gloomy moods and focused on tending to his injuries. Redressing wounds that were slow to heal, tightening straps and rods that kept broken bones in place as they reknit themselves, Elizabeth worked to nurture him and his recovery as best she could. In constant pain and overwhelmed by despair, Philippe listlessly participated to the limited degree he was able.

She looked hopefully at the clock, grateful that within an hour or two Marie, Annette, and Nicole Masset would arrive for their midday visit. Each day since Philippe's release they had come: to share gifts of food and time, and to share the pain of their common grief; to help each other cope with the horror they had all experienced—and couldn't yet claim to have survived. Elizabeth lived from noon to noon each day, knowing she couldn't endure without these caring, loving women to help her. While her husband's physical injuries were serious and required much attention, she felt capable of her caregiving role. It was the couple's emotional state that was foundering, and she felt simply unable to salvage it.

"Please sit, Philippe," said Elizabeth. "Marie and the girls are due. You know how they fret when you lie so still."

"Neither should they waste their time."

"And yet we do," said Elizabeth, sitting on the edge of the couch in the parlor where he lay and holding out her hands to him. "Please."

Philippe surrendered his own hands to her, grimacing with the effort. She gently pulled him to sitting and tucked a cushion behind his back and eased him onto it.

"Bravo," she said with an attempt to smile. "Four days in a row."

Philippe didn't return her smile, looking back at her with misty eyes.

"I cannot continue," he murmured. "I am hopeless, of no value to you or anyone else. Just leave me…as *they* did. It's nothing less than I deserve."

"They," said Elizabeth with narrowed eyes and harsh tone, "are heartless, savage murderers. May they suffer in kind. You survived their cruelty for a reason—and I intend to see that you fulfill that purpose."

"Yes, I survived," Philippe admitted scornfully. "To spend the days and weeks coming to truly understand the pain I cause those around me. To experience powerlessness and being at someone else's whim, their mercy. To realize how I went about my life taking what I wanted without regard to the implications, the consequences to those I loved. Worst of all, to you." His eyes brimmed over, and he turned his head away from her again. "Perhaps, by going to my grave with the regret that crushes me, I will not burn in hell as I so desperately deserve…"

Elizabeth's heart ached to hear the desolation in her husband's voice and the hopelessness in his words. She wanted to comfort him, reassure him that all was not lost for him, or for them. But she had been where he was now, knew too well the impenetrable wall that built up around such convictions. Mere adages and hackneyed words of good cheer would not break through. She thought back to her own dark hours of the past two months, the worst of them spent in this very room. How had she broken free? Not without help. Sigerson's voice echoed in her ears, his wise words giving her strength, even still.

"A sounding board for an extraordinarily brilliant mind" was how he had unexpectedly described her role in Philippe's

life and career. *"…the perfect foil to her husband's sweeping intellect."*

Empty reassurances hadn't helped her see the situation clearly that day. It was Sigerson's insightful observations and willingness to share them that brought clarity and hope to her heart. Philippe needed the same.

"The Philippe Devereaux who swept me off my feet and carried me a world away from home would hardly settle merely for escaping eternal damnation," she said softly with a smile, wiping his tears and brushing a lock of black hair from his sweat-soaked brow. "When that man saw an error in his methods, he threw himself into setting them right. I simply cannot believe your work, your life, is truly finished."

"My ability to accomplish anything more is surely finished," he replied, grimacing once more as he reached for her hand. "My condition…"

"Your condition improves every day, Philippe. You know this as well as I." Elizabeth's voice was firm, even as she gently leaned forward to brush her cheek against his hand. "Your melancholy is driven by something other than a slow recovery from the trauma you've suffered. Please. You needn't have your thoughts neatly packaged for me. What rumbles around inside your head, and your heart, causing such pain? Tell me."

Philippe sighed. "The full understanding of how little I've accomplished in my life," he said softly, avoiding her gaze. "The pain I caused you, the opportunities I squandered. And knowing I've no agency to correct any of it. In my recklessness I've failed everyone, and my time to make amends has run out."

"There is still time," said Elizabeth, turning his head to face her. "We have your documents. We can get them to Octave."

Philippe closed his eyes and gave a nearly imperceptible shake of his head. "At this point, the correspondence with Lilienthal is nearly as useless to the effort as I have been," he whispered. "It is merely a record of the work Otto has done and the value he would bring to any collaboration on reaching the skies. It is the man himself we need to connect with Chanute. The work he has yet to accomplish will be critical to an international effort."

"But the university in Paris," Elizabeth began. "They agreed to partner with the school here…"

"There *was* an agreement." Philippe interrupted her with angry words through gritted teeth, surprising her with the strength he mustered to utter them. "An agreement to partner with *me*…on a collaboration that would connect Lilienthal with Chanute and his International Congress. But the problem is, you see…since that pact was made…I have been *dead*!" He twisted himself to slam his unbroken arm against the wall in frustration.

"Philippe!" Elizabeth reached for her husband. He turned his head away from her once more as she tried to settle him again. "Is the role of the university in Paris so vital to this collaboration that we cannot proceed without it? Will it provide the influence necessary? The finances required?"

"Yes," he replied weakly. "Yes, exactly."

Then, for the next hour, Elizabeth extracted from her husband, one painstaking word or phrase at a time, the details of the plans he had made for them, the plans for which she had risked—and lost—so much. She learned about the Paris institutions that would connect the Devereauxs with the academic and political experts to represent France in the collaboration, and make available the funds to bring the parties together—including Octave Chanute and Otto Lilienthal. The school in Montpellier would provide the people, resources, and facilities to serve as the alliance's hub.

"Then…bringing the papers to America, to Octave, was not truly the aim of this project?" Elizabeth asked, blue eyes innocently wide, but with a slight smile playing on her lips. For the first time in days, Philippe smiled, too. A sheepish smile, but a smile all the same.

"Oh no, my love," he said with the slightest pout of his lips. "Our aim was to be off to America, I assure you! But it was only a step, a first step. There was so much more to be done…" Again, he closed his eyes and turned his face toward the wall. "So much… Too much, too exhausting to even contemplate…"

Elizabeth gently kissed her husband's forehead and pulled the coverlet over his shoulders. She stepped lightly to the window, hoping to find some distraction for herself as he drifted off to sleep. Something to take her mind off the thoughts and ideas swirling around her head and insisting on organizing themselves into a plan. Philippe had served his critical role, she mused: securing support from the University of Paris. Now, the school in Montpellier would surely relish the opportunity to honor a favorite son, thought lost, by providing the support he had planned to request the day of his accident. All that remained was to include Octave Chanute and his International Congress of Aerial Navigation. Philippe might think all was lost. Elizabeth did not.

Before long, she heard the Masset carriage rounding the bend and rumbling into view. Her heart ached as she watched Marie and her daughters descend from the familiar carriage. How gut-wrenching, still, to realize Luc would not step down with them.

"How is our patient today?" asked Marie as she stepped into the parlor. Nicole and Annette edged their way around her and headed toward the sofa, stopping short when they saw Philippe asleep.

"Come by the hearth," whispered Elizabeth, indicating the kitchen table. She sat down on the bench closest to the fire and poured the *café* she'd prepared in expectation of their visit. "He has finally nodded off. It seems to get more and more difficult each day for him to stay positive, to fight to get well. I'm so worried for him, for us."

Marie slid along the bench to put her arm around her friend. "We've been given such a gift," she said, "to have him back with us. He needs us to help him see it as a gift, too. Life is so precious…"

At her mother's words, little Nicole lost her struggle to be cheerful and burst into tears.

"Elizabeth…" came a murmur from the sofa. "What is it? Are you there?"

As Elizabeth circled the table to take the sobbing Nicole in her arms, Marie and Annette stepped into the parlor to greet Philippe.

"I'm sorry, Elizabeth," said Nicole through her tears. "But I miss Papa so. Mama said we aren't to burden you… but I am always so, so sad. Nothing will ever be the same, nothing will ever be happy again!"

"I know it feels that way, little one," said Elizabeth, putting a biscuit before the girl to go with her warm brew. "I feel it too. And for a while, it will be so. But we will work together to bring about happy times again. A different happy, but surely better than today."

Nicole wiped her eyes as her mother returned to the table. "I'm sorry, Mama," she said forlornly. Marie smiled sadly and patted her head.

"You have been a very brave girl, Nicole," said her mother. "Now… Philippe is asking for you. I think he could use some of your courage today."

"I certainly could," said Elizabeth as Nicole went into the parlor, seeming pleased to be of help. "He and I are both at a loss. I don't know how to proceed, how to pull us from this quicksand beneath our feet."

"The best we can do is to establish ourselves on this patch of ground we find ourselves," said Marie, reaching for the pot and pouring more *café*. "However shaky it may be. Until we become stable and strong here, we won't be able to successfully move forward to the next."

"Why *this* patch of ground?" asked Elizabeth dully, shrugging her shoulders. "Luc and Lucien taken from us; Philippe, an empty shell, wishing for death himself. This is not what I wanted…the unending horror, the unspeakable loss."

"What *did* you want, Elizabeth?" Marie asked quietly.

Elizabeth sipped from her *café,* hoping to swallow the lump rising in her throat. Marie—her dark, penetrating eyes wide—drank from her own cup in silence, waiting.

Yes, Elizabeth thought, both she and Marie knew it was her need for some grand purpose in life that had brought about the devastating grief they were living now. She owed this woman some explanation—an acknowledgement, at least—of her contribution to their suffering today. Although it was Stephan and Monique who masterminded the treacherous scheme, Elizabeth had involved Luc and put him at risk. Marie deserved to hear her admit as much.

"I wanted to make my mark on the world, didn't I?" said Elizabeth, managing to meet Marie's eyes. "To justify my value and validate my right to participate in something great, something that mattered. And here we are."

"Yes, here we are," said Marie. "And have you made your mark?"

"Certainly not for the good," Elizabeth replied softly. "We've lost Luc and Lucien. I've lost my home. I remain saddled with papers that ruthless people want kept secret. I watch my husband's spirit slip slowly away day by day, his mind unwilling to even consider fulfilling his plans in America. I could go on."

"It would seem, then, that your work is not done."

"Oh, Marie…I have done such damage…"

"Perhaps so," Marie replied. She put her cup down and looked deeply into Elizabeth's puffy, bloodshot eyes. "More reason to take steps to repair the damage done."

Marie's gaze unnerved her. "Impossible."

"You can," said Marie. "You must. You owe it to us—to honor Luc and Lucien; to save Philippe. You owe it to me… and to yourself."

Elizabeth could only shake her head as Marie continued.

"That day you came to us, to say goodbye? You were running away, no?" Elizabeth lowered her head in assent; a tear straggled down her cheek. "You are adept at running away, my dear. But where are you headed? Where do you want to *go*? To find adventure? Your muse? Another man who will provide the meaningful role you seek?"

"There is no one out there I can look to."

"Exactly right!" said Marie, grabbing Elizabeth's hand. "You need only look to yourself…and to that man in the parlor. That imperfect man who somehow inspired you to join him in his life, and in his causes! Now, after all that's come to pass, you say he has a plan he feels unable to carry out and you claim not to know how you can help him?"

Elizabeth took a breath to speak, but Marie cut her off.

"On that afternoon—a lifetime ago—you didn't know what was ahead for you in America, didn't know where your running would lead. Well, possibly, now you do. You need to find out for yourself what role you are meant to play. Perhaps help give all this horror meaning. You owe it to us all."

As Elizabeth looked into Marie's eyes, her heart began pounding with an excitement and a sense of conviction she thought long lost. "*Now* is the time to go to America," she said. "I am to carry out Philippe's proposal."

"Yes," whispered Marie, pulling Elizabeth to her and holding her tightly. "We will be here for Philippe until you return to us."

Chapter Twenty-Six

Paris!

After years living in France, Elizabeth finally found herself in its capital city. And it was everything she had dreamed it would be. While Philippe complained about the crowds, about the services, about the lack or overabundance of everything, he'd only generated a sense of mystery and wonder in his wife about the city. Never willing to take her there, never willing to go at all except to conduct business, the Professeur had left his wife dreaming and wanting.

On this splendid day, she sat at a café table on the Champs d'Elysee with her brother, John, his wife, Emma, and their little girl, Louisa, on holiday. The bright sunshine warmed them on this brisk autumn afternoon. Here, she was reveling in being Elizabeth Wellington Devereaux: confident in herself and her abilities, excited at the progress already made on her mission, and anticipation of its next stage in America. Best of all, feeling a new sense of peace with herself, of understanding and love for Philippe, and satisfaction in her soul as she worked to further an international collaboration to reach the skies.

"Will you continue on with us to London?" her sister-in-law asked. "I've never been before, and I just know it will be a thrill. Please consider joining us."

Elizabeth thought back on all the "thrills" she had endured over the previous months and the work that lay ahead of her. Of course, the University of Paris had been an amazing adventure—so much more sophisticated and worldly than the provincial school in Montpellier. She almost felt welcome there. The scholars and agents Philippe had arranged for her to meet were not overtly gracious; however, they seemed willing to cooperate and give her what she needed to complete the package for Chanute, which would facilitate including Lilienthal's work in the Congress's efforts. Discouraging, however, was the lack of hope expressed that actually working with Lilienthal—or even contacting him—could ever be a reality. Whether or not Otto's situation was as dire as Philippe had implied, there seemed to be no course of action that anyone in France was willing to risk; Germany was to be appeased at all costs. It seemed her only option was to continue on to America, consult with Chanute, and see what support could be raised there.

Now, heading to America was her only goal. There, she planned to invoke the "Devereaux Doctrine": Introduce the initiative, generate enthusiasm, enlist support, then hand the workaday chores of implementation off to others. Throughout it all, Montpellier and her recovering husband would be far, far away. She looked forward to the day when she could return, hoping to find the seeds of a new life she'd sown sprouted and thriving. Only time would tell.

"No, I think not, Emma," Elizabeth replied absently.

John reached across the table and covered her hand with his. "You are still grieving for friends, we know," he said softly. Then, in a firmer voice, "I must imagine you still grieve for your husband and his behavior."

"Marie Masset is a strong woman," Elizabeth began. Her voice was distant as she gingerly approached this topic that threatened her calm, self-controlled demeanor. "She will bring her family through this tragedy, and my family as well. As for my husband…" She smiled. "Philippe is a good man, John—and a *changed* man. We have come through the tragedies of the past months strong. He loves me and cares for me—and I for him. I truly know this now. Much of our troubles have been my own doing. One day soon I hope to return to him a happier person than I've allowed myself to be. I've been unfair to both of us in this marriage. It's only right that I find my own happiness. He will be well cared for while I'm gone."

John Wellington grunted in disagreement with her assessment of Jean-Philippe Devereaux, but went on devouring his croissant.

"The Massets…" Emma began. "One of the daughters was culpable in her father's death?"

"Less guilty of her father's death than of the unforgivable trauma Philippe suffered at her hands." Elizabeth shrugged her shoulders and held her cup up for more *café*. "The guilt she bears is more of a punishment than whatever prison time she and her husband receive."

"It appears to me you would be better served by the company of your family on holiday than the seclusion of a lonely steamship." Emma slathered jam on her croissant and poured more *café*. "We would so enjoy having you along."

"I have work to do in America, dear sister," Elizabeth replied yet again. "But perhaps I can live your trip vicariously." She addressed the boy who cleared the remains of her meal. "The *Times* of London, please?"

A warm glow spread over her as she thought of Sigerson, taking his afternoon tea in the parlor while poring over his news sheets. Transported back to those days with him, she felt whisked to another lifetime, finding it difficult to even recall the layout of the parlor before it became Philippe's sickroom. Yet how deep this trivial connection felt, waiting for the papers, knowing how dependent her friend was on the pages that bore weeks-old news to the small village so far from London. She wondered where he was now, and if he, at this moment, sat with the *Times* in his lap, snorting and chortling as he studied its pages. Minutes later, the requested newspaper was laid out on the table before her.

"What horrid bonnets," she said, showing Emma what the English ladies were sporting this fall. They tittered about high fashion having left the European shops for America. A few minutes later, "How could people be allowed to live like this!" was her reaction to the story about a fire that had consumed an entire neighborhood. The newspaper was certainly not for uplifting one's spirits. Perhaps that was the root of Sigerson's grim moods, she thought, chuckling to herself. The man spent entirely too much time in the doldrums, reading about the plight of man. Then, she saw the headline.

"CELEBRATED DETECTIVE RETURNS FROM THE GRAVE TO SOLVE PARKSIDE LANE MURDER"

Parkside Lane. The Parkside Lane Murder. Not so long ago, she had read about this horrific crime. Something about an Australian aristocrat being murdered, and in such an ingenious way as to leave Scotland Yard without any hope of finding the culprit.

Not so long ago was the day Sigerson left Montpellier. As Elizabeth had prepared the cottage for Philippe's release from the hospital, she found an article about the affair. It had been marked by Sigerson and left behind; he had circled a name in the text. Elizabeth scanned the *Times* story as quickly as she could. All-too-familiar names sprung out at her.

> *London has double cause for celebration as the murderer of the Honorable Ronald Adair is brought to justice by a man the world believed to be dead these past three years: Mr. Sherlock Holmes.*

"My goodness!" Elizabeth cried aloud. "Sherlock Holmes! Alive?" Emma and John nodded, acknowledging that they, too, had heard the news.

> *Colonel Sebastian Moran was apprehended attempting to add Mr. Holmes himself to his list of murder victims. The resurrected detective confronted the Colonel with evidence of his responsibility for the Parkside Lane Murder and Inspector Lestrade of Scotland Yard was on hand to obtain a confession.*

> *Although Mr. Holmes had no comment upon his miraculous reappearance, the Times has learned that the revered consulting detective spent the years he was thought to be dead evading the murderous Colonel Moran by traveling throughout Europe and the East (this, according to his friend and biographer, Dr. John Watson) in an attempt to elude the man who would kill him.*

> *Throwing caution to the wind, Sherlock Holmes returned to London from somewhere in the south of France upon learning of the Ronald Adair murder, knowing that Colonel Moran had finally taken the misstep Holmes had awaited. With his return, we have the evil Moran behind bars and the eminent detective back in our midst.*

Elizabeth sat frozen, staring unseeingly before her, digesting what she had just read. The world around her continued as before—the warm sun, the bustling waiter, the sightseers drifting by—but she saw none of it. She was back in Montpellier, the day Sigerson left, remembering all he had said to her, as she had many times since. The less she knew about him, the safer she would be. A cold calculating machine. That he loved her.

Sigerson...Sherlock Holmes?

In her mind, Elizabeth saw herself tidying up the cottage, reading the article he'd left behind, then heading upstairs to the bedroom. The image of his souvenir to her appeared, left on his bed to be found after he was gone. It was the black case containing the cocaine and syringe. A note was tucked inside: "My Dearest Elizabeth—You have forever replaced the need." It was signed "SH."

At the time, the signature made Elizabeth think perhaps Sigerson was, after all, his given name. Now she thought differently. A smile came to her lips. Sherlock Holmes! She recalled that Yvette had given her a magazine once that included a story about the famous detective. Elizabeth had thought the story quite uninspired, but had appreciated her maid's attempt to find something, *anything*, to read in English. Quite an insufferable, pompous bore this Sherlock Holmes had seemed to her. That surely described Sigerson himself, the cold, logical thinker. Then, another thought broke through to the fore.

He wanted her to know.

The marked newspaper article, his real initials. Would one of the cleverest minds in the world have allowed such clues to slip by unintentionally?

Now it was clear to Elizabeth why he would not reveal his identity. Of course it was unwise to tell her about himself.

He was in mortal danger, hiding from a man who had hunted him down for years in a murderous rage. Sigerson… Holmes…would not want her to risk the danger he felt. But he would remember that Elizabeth came to love scanning the newspapers as he did. He knew she would learn of his reappearance and connect the names to those in the article he had left behind. Now that he was safe, he wanted her to know who he was, at least. And now she even knew where.

Cutting through the dervish of thoughts swirling in her head were thoughts of her own mission. If Paris wanted nothing to do with an effort unpopular with the Kaiser, perhaps London might be more willing? Sigerson had admitted he worked as an agent of the "Foreign Office" to ensure the Lilienthal-Devereaux correspondence found its way to America—so Britain had an active interest in the project. Could Holmes help her get the connections and resources to include Lilienthal and his work in the ICAN consortium?

Elizabeth knew she must find out. She looked at her brother and his wife with a childlike twinkle in her eyes. A tingle went up her spine as she spoke.

"I'm wondering if perhaps you are right, after all," she mused aloud. "Company might be best for me now." John and Emma exchanged delighted glances as little Louisa climbed into her lap for a hug. Elizabeth gathered the little girl to her and whispered into her ear.

"Perhaps the breathtaking, dramatic finish promised by the coda is yet to be performed…?"

Acknowledgements

Many thanks to those who inspired my love of words, books, and mysteries; those who stepped in early on to help as I worked to tell my own story; and those who are so precious to me and always in my heart, whatever I do!

- Rose Daly Boyle, my mom, for nurturing my love of books and cheering on my efforts to write my own

- Arthur Conan Doyle, for creating my childhood hero, Sherlock Holmes

- Laurie R. King, for introducing me to a woman who could hang with Holmes, and inspiring me to follow her lead

- Bruce Southworth, BSI, for introducing me to the "real" world of Sherlock Holmes and some of its most amazing inhabitants

- Jill Angel, book coach, editor, proofreader, counselor (www.jillangelbookcoach.com)

- Carla Green, cover/book designer and sherpa to the world of publishing (claritydesignworks.com)

- Pat Walker, my first listener

- Kathleen Brennan, my first reader

- The *Coda* CheerReading Squad, my beta readers, who gave thoughtful, insightful feedback on *Coda's* earliest incarnation:
  - ✧ Genevieve Kirwin Boyle
  - ✧ Katherine Crosson
  - ✧ Bonnie Giunta
  - ✧ Cynthia Ritzler Pulick
  - ✧ Claudia Reinhardt
  - ✧ Joanne Karpinski Sotirhos

- Very special love and thanks to Tyler Murray and Chrissy Murray, my brilliant and patient son and daughter-in-law; the sounding boards who frequently served to clear my often-fuzzy vision of *Coda* and its direction

- And finally, thanks to Lee Murray, the love of my life—with the charm of Philippe and the wisdom of Sigerson—for just about everything…

About the Author

Born a writer, Maryann Boyle Murray's first work appeared during her pre-school years, published in a juicy red marker on the hallway wall outside her bedroom door. Deprived of the critical acclaim she'd expected, she took her fiction writing underground, filling marbled copybooks and yellow legal pads with tales of ongoing adventures through time and space. Later, she kept the literary spark alive through employment as a journalist, marketing consultant, director of non-profit development communications, and in volunteering. Today, unable to find any reason or distraction to prevent her, Maryann has returned to her seemingly doomed fiction-writing career and is thrilled to release the characters she's created into the world and to finally share their adventures.

41427216R00184